KELLIE HAILES declared at the age of five that she was going to write books when she grew up. It took a while for her to get there, with a career as a radio copywriter, freelance copywriter and beauty editor filling the dream-hole, until now. Kellie lives in Auckland, New Zealand with her patient husband and delightful daughter. When the characters in her head aren't dictating their story to her, she can be found taking short walks, eating good cheese and hanging out for her next coffee fix.

You can follow Kellie on Twitter: @KellieHailes

Also by Kellie Hailes

The Little Bakery of Hopes and Dreams

KELLIE HAILES

ONE PLACE. MANY STORIES

HQ
An imprint of HarperCollins*Publishers* Ltd
1 London Bridge Street
London SE1 9GF

This edition 2020

First published in Great Britain by
HQ, an imprint of HarperCollins*Publishers* Ltd 2019

ISBN: 978-0-00-834870-0

MIX
Paper from
responsible sources
FSC
www.fsc.org
FSC˚ C007454

Printed and bound in Great Britain by
CPI Group (UK) Ltd, Croydon, CR0 4YY

For Daisy.
My biggest teacher.
My greatest love.

Chapter 1

The shops either side of the bakery looked like someone had taken in too much festive cheer and then vomited it up. Twinkling golden fairy lights danced around Santa-red tinsel. Snowflakes were spray-painted onto their windows, floating down to sills where they gathered into thick fake drifts.

Josie shuddered. It was all so totally, utterly, over the top. Thankfully Christmas would be done and dusted in a matter of weeks, and then she'd be free of it for another eleven months.

At least the bakery was bare of Christmas decorations. One person's stand against a season that promised so much, but always failed to deliver. At least, it had in more years than Josie cared to remember.

A tendril of hope stirred low in Josie's stomach. Surely the lack of seasonal cheer was a sign she was going to get the position advertised in the bakery's window. She just had to go in there and prove she would do a great job being the front-of-house face of the business.

Squaring her shoulders, she tightened the belt of her lucky tomato-red woollen coat, rubbed her finger across her teeth to make sure her hastily applied lipstick hadn't decided to attach itself, then plastered a smile on her face and opened the door to what she prayed would be the beginning of her new life. Again.

Josie took a tentative step in and glanced around looking for signs of her potential employer. With no one in sight she took a moment to take in the bakery's offerings.

Cupcakes topped with icing in the shape of mistletoe, miniature Santas and itty-bitty Christmas trees were lined up under the counter's glass top, alongside little mince pies. Reindeer-shaped gingerbread lined another tray. On the counter, a cake tray offered up cellophane bags filled with what looked to be spice biscuits, tied with curled green and red ribbons.

Her heart sank. The owner wasn't so anti-Christmas after all. Or maybe they were just pandering to the customers. Meeting demand. Making money while money could be made. That must be the case, she decided, because something wasn't quite right with the treats laid out before her. In fact, something was positively off.

The cupcakes seemed a little . . . flat. Stodgy. With a look of dryness about them that no amount of tea chugged back while munching through a bite of one would fix. And she had a sneaking suspicion the icing decorations on top were store-bought, not made by hand. The mince pies' pastry appeared . . . rock hard. As for the reindeer? Iced by someone with all the skill of an enthusiastic 5-year-old.

For all its apparent jolliness, Josie sensed sadness in the bakery. But why? And where was the owner? You'd have thought they'd have rushed in at the sound of a potential customer.

'Hello?' Josie called out, keeping her tone light, happy. Hoping the desperation that had her stomach stitched up with nerves didn't come through. She waited for the tip-tap of footsteps. None came. 'Hello?' Maybe something had happened to the shop's owner? Perhaps they'd had a fall and couldn't move. Or hit their head and were passed-out cold.

She eyed the door that presumably led to the kitchen. She was going to have to go back there. She couldn't leave without making sure whoever was supposed to be manning the store was okay. It might not be the politest thing to invade someone's work area unannounced, but it was the right thing to do, given the potential circumstances.

Josie summoned up her courage, prepared to deal with the worst, and charged round the counter into the room beyond and smacked into, then rebounded off, something hard, warm and really nice-smelling.

Musky, sweet, with a hint of pine and soap.

'I'm so sorry. Are you all right?' The good smell came with a nice voice. Deep. Strong. But kind. 'Although, I have to ask, what are you doing heading back here?'

Josie scrambled to gather her wits as she looked up into a face that deserved to be on the cover of a high-end men's magazine – certainly not in a small cake shop in the little Cotswolds village of Sunnycombe. Eyes the colour of chocolate icing stared at her with a mix of concern, curiosity and a hint of suspicion. A wrinkle between his brows led to a straight and manly nose.

A nose could be manly? Who knew? But then she had no idea full lips could be masculine on a man either.

He laid his hand on her forearm and crouched a little – okay, a lot – so he was at her height. All five feet four of it. 'Are you okay? Are you lost? Should I call someone?'

Oh great, so now he thought she was in some sort of state. This was not how the interview was meant to go.

Walk in. Appear confident. Ask about the job working front of house. Mention she had experience baking. Charm the owner into saying yes. Tick 'job' off the long list of things she had to do. *Pull yourself together, Josie*, she growled.

'I'm here . . .' The words came out with a waver. Not good. She swallowed, breathed in, breathed out and tried again. 'I'm here to talk to the owner about the job that's advertised in your window. Is she in?'

For a split-second his eyes darkened to the colour of cocoa, a frown line appeared between his brows, disappearing as quickly

3

as it had arrived. He bobbed back up and a slow smile spread across his face, lifting his cheekbones. 'Oh, so you want to see the lady of the house?'

'Yes, please.' Josie nodded, taking a step backwards. Another. Then another. Until she was back in the front of the shop and away from the man who, from the golden band gleaming on his wedding finger, was clearly the husband of the lady of the house, which made him completely out of bounds.

He turned around, cupped his hand to his mouth and called, 'Sweetpea? Can you come down here? There's someone to see you.'

Quick steps crossed the room from the floor above, then clip-clopped down the stairs. Josie sucked in another breath, attempted to smooth the ever-present auburn halo of frizz that refused to be tamed, and returned her customer-ready smile to her face.

'I haven't done anything, I promise. I've been good. I didn't put dolly's head in the toilet again.'

The voice was sweet and soft, and sounded far too young to be the owner of a cake shop.

'Mia, this lady is here to see the lady of the house. And that would be you.'

Mr Out of Bounds leaned down and swooped up the owner of the voice into his arms. She automatically hooked her legs either side of his waist, anchored herself to him and with the same chocolatey-brown almond-shaped eyes that belonged to the man holding her – her father, Josie gathered – stared at Josie with undisguised curiosity.

'I don't know her. Does that make her a stranger? Is she stranger danger? Shall I yell at her to go away?' Blonde curls, a few shades lighter than her father's, bobbed around her heart-shaped face.

'No, she's here for the job. So I don't think yelling at her is going to be the best idea. Besides, we don't yell in this house. Remember?' He tickled Mia's waist, his grin widening as she burst into giggles. 'Giggles only.'

'Giggles only.' Mia nodded. 'And presents. And carols. And

more presents.' Mia turned to Josie. 'Christmas is coming and Santa is coming and Daddy's going to get me a teddy bear and a ballerina jewellery box and a unicorn and a pony and a . . .'

'One present from Santa. One present from me. You know the rules.'

One present from me. Not *us*, Josie noted. Was the wedding ring for show? Was the owner of the cake shop away for Christmas, and he was just filling in? But then who was doing the baking if not the person whose name was swinging from the sign outside? The man before her didn't look the baking type in his perfectly pressed fawn-coloured chinos and olive cable-knit jumper. He looked more like . . . a businessman who was having a day off from the office. So maybe that meant he co-owned the shop with the business partner whose name was on the sign.

'Who does the baking here?' Josie blurted, tired of standing around and trying to piece together what was going on in front of her. Wondering and pondering wasn't going to get her answers any faster. Nor help her acquire the job. 'Is it Abigail? Is it her shop? Her name's on the sign outside. Do I need to speak to her about the job?'

'Mummy isn't here anymore.' Mia's eyes were wide. Serious. Her tone too matter of fact to have come from such a petite person. 'She's gone to a better place. Daddy says it doesn't have unicorns, but I think it does. And clouds made of marshmallows and you can eat them any time you want. Even at breakfast.' She nodded again, sure in her beliefs.

Josie folded her arms across herself, wishing the act could soothe the pain twisting her heart. She knew something of having a mother not be there. The difference was hers had chosen to leave and never come back. Mia, the poor poppet, had had her mother taken from her.

'I'm so sorry,' she whispered, hating how the words sounded so empty. Useless. Unable to soothe, to comfort. To help bring Mia's mother back.

5

'Thank you. And now that you have an idea of what you're potentially getting yourself into, I should introduce myself. I'm Callan. Callan Stewart. I do the baking. Or at least I try to. I'm an accountant by trade, but Abigail taught me a few things. I'm not a patch on her, I'm afraid. In fact, I've yet to meet anyone who can bake as well as she does. I mean . . . did.' The crease between Callan's brows was back, and it didn't look to be disappearing anytime soon.

Josie's heart twisted further. She'd seen that look before. On her father's face, after her mother had left. Bereft. Desolate. The look of a man whose hopes and dreams had been whisked away. Or in Callan's case, stolen.

'And I'm Josie. Short for Josephine. But only my father calls me that. Josie Donnelly.' She thrust her hand out, then realised Callan had his hands full with his daughter. And with life in general. She dropped her hand and offered up a smile. 'It's good to meet you. Now, shall we talk about the job? Is it still available?'

'It is.' Callan grimaced as Mia blew a wet raspberry on his cheek. 'Would you like to take a seat?' Callan jerked his head towards the table setting for two in front of the window. 'I'm not sure conducting an interview standing up is the most comfortable way to do things.' He jiggled Mia on his hip. 'And this one isn't getting any lighter. I swear she eats concrete when I'm not looking.'

Josie nodded and grinned as Mia swatted Callan playfully. She settled herself onto the wooden chair, then smoothed out a wrinkle in the blue-and-white checked tablecloth.

Callan sat down, arranged Mia on his lap, and wrapped his arms around her protectively, like she was the most precious thing in the world to him. Which, of course, Mia was. How could she not be? Children should be a parent's top priority, especially when they were as young as Mia.

Callan dropped a kiss on the top of Mia's head, then relaxed into his chair, and met Josie's gaze across the table. 'So, tell me, Josie, what customer service experience do you have?'

Josie reached into her tote, pulled out her CV and passed it to Callan. 'I've worked in cafés my whole life. Started out as a kitchen hand and waitress when I was a teenager, was trained as a barista, then took a baking course and later a cake decorating course, and since then I've worked where I was needed, when I was needed.'

'Baking? Not chef-ing?' Callan's eyes narrowed, his head tipped to the side. 'I'd have thought chef training would have opened up more doors?'

'It would have. But I like to bake. Have done since I was a young girl. My mother taught me the basics and I liked . . .' *I liked the way she wrapped her arms around me as we held the wooden spoon, beating the mixture together. The way she smelled like vanilla, sugar, and love.* 'I liked the way when people ate the cakes and biscuits and whatever else I whipped up, they smiled. The way my creations made them happy. People enjoy a perfectly cooked steak, but it's a beautifully executed dessert that makes a meal memorable.'

Callan's shoulders rose a tad, his leg, which had seen Mia jiggle up and down on his lap, stilled. Had she said something wrong? Was she going to be marched out? Did he think she wanted to take over? To run the place?

'But, obviously, you've got the cooking part of the business sorted. The job is for front of house, and I'm happy to take that role for as long as you need me.' She gave an affirmative nod and prayed Callan's shoulders would relax, that the jiggle would resume. No job meant nowhere to live, which meant returning to her father's house. And the only thing worse than Christmas was *not* celebrating it with her father. No presents. No carols. No turkey, bread sauce or trifle. No family traditions. Just the constant reminder of the hollowness created by her mother's departure, reinforced by her father's furtive glances at the front door. Hoping the woman who'd left them on Christmas Eve so many years ago would return.

'And how do you feel about life in a small village? Sunnycombe's not exactly a thrilling place to reside. Not much happens. There's the Thursday night pub quiz. The odd band plays on a Friday. Saturday there's a darts competition.'

'Daddy was bestest.' Mia tipped her head up to look at Callan, admiration shining in her eyes. 'He won a gold cup.'

'A trophy.' Callan tickled Mia's side, sending her into another fit of giggles. 'But that was a long time ago. These days the only thing I want to be best at is being your daddy.'

'And you look like you're doing a great job.' Josie clasped her hands under the table. She didn't need to look down to know her knuckles were white. Was he going to offer her the job or not? Was he going to give her the escape route she needed to avoid another fraught family anti-Christmas? 'I can live in a village. I can live anywhere. I've lived in all sorts of places.'

'Does that mean you move a lot? That you're likely to up and leave without giving notice?' Callan's brows drew together. 'Because I can't have that. I don't expect you to stay forever, but I need to have a routine in place. I need to know that you won't just disappear without giving me fair warning. It's important . . . for the business.'

For the business? Or to him? Josie suspected the latter.

'Which leads me to wonder, Josie, what brings you here?'

'My last job was working in a café's kitchen in Chipping Campden. I was filling in for a person on maternity leave. They came back, and now I'm in need of a new job. And I'm not planning on going anywhere anytime soon. I'll stay for as long as you need me.' She caught sight of a dust ball in the far corner of the room and recalled the wonky icing on the cupcakes. He needed her. Whether he knew it or not. Callan might proclaim to know a few things about baking, but Josie could tell, for all his efforts, he was not a baker. Just a man doing his best to keep his wife's legacy alive. Keeping his love for her alive.

'Do you like playing with dolls? And having tea parties? And how old are you?' Mia inquired, her little fingers steepling together in a way Josie bet she'd learned from her father.

'I'm 26, which means I'm kind of a grown-up, but not so grown up that I don't love tea parties. They're my favourite. Especially if real cakes are involved. And I bet I'd be good at playing with dolls too.' She smiled warmly at Mia, her heart lightening as the smile was repaid in kind.

'Babysitting isn't part of the job.' Callan's arms wrapped tighter around his daughter. A barrier.

It made sense. If his wife had passed away, he wouldn't want anyone who might leave to get close to Mia. The small rejection hurt, but Josie understood where it came from. Couldn't blame him for it. Not when she was one for putting barriers up to stop others getting too close. Friendships were kept formal. Relationships of the romantic kind kept loose and easy. Dates only. Rarely more than three before she bowed out. The moment she began to feel cloistered, controlled or claustrophobic in any way, she was gone.

A new town. A new village. A new city. New place to live. New job. New life.

'I'm not a baby.' Mia's face screwed up with disdain. 'I'm 4, remember. That's nearly a grown-up.'

Josie nodded. 'Four is pretty grown up, which means babysitting must be the worst word in the world to describe taking care of such a big girl as you, right?'

Mia nodded so vigorously her head hit the back of her father's chest, causing him to rub the spot, a pained expression on her face.

'But if you're busy baking, I can keep an eye on Mia out here. Perhaps even play tea parties when the shop's quiet. If that sounds good to you, Mia?'

'Sounds great.' Mia reached out to Josie, palm open, ready for a high-five.

They slapped skin and Josie's nerves settled. Whether Callan knew it or not, the job was hers. That high-five was every bit as binding as a handshake.

'Why do I feel like this is a done deal?' Callan shook his head, bemusement lifting his lips. 'Not even 5 and Mia's running rings around her old dad.'

'So that means Josie is staying? Forever?' Mia tipped her head to the side and looked up at her father, her eyes hopeful.

Guilt flooded Josie's stomach. Forever wasn't an option. Forever meant getting comfortable. And getting comfortable meant getting hurt. She wasn't going to give Mia false hope, not when she'd already lost someone she'd loved. Two someones, if you counted the distant relationship she shared with her father.

'I'll stay for as long as your daddy needs me here.' Josie met Callan's gaze. His eyes held approval. And thankfulness. He too knew forever wasn't always an option.

'When can you start?' Callan shifted Mia off his lap and stood. Interview over.

Josie scooted the chair back and pushed herself up onto her feet. 'Soon as you need me.'

'Tomorrow?' Callan's tone was tinged with desperation. 'I haven't hung the Christmas decorations yet, and I really need to. I just can't seem to find the time between the baking, the bakery's book work and serving.'

'Daddy promised we'd have the bestest Christmas ever.' Mia's curls bobbed as she bounced up and down with excitement. 'We're going all out. Whatever that means.'

Josie's heart sank. So much for not having to deal with tinsel and wreaths and fairy lights, and the uncomfortable mix of emotions that stirred whenever she saw them. Still, it was a job, one she needed, and it wasn't like Christmas lasted forever. Just four more weeks and it'd be done for another year.

'I can start tomorrow, but I will have to pop out in the afternoon for thirty minutes or so. I'm staying in one of the rooms above the pub, but I've found a cottage a few minutes away that's for rent. I just need to meet with the landlady so she can vet me.'

10

'That's fine. So, we'll see you tomorrow morning. Eight sharp?' Callan reached out to shake her hand.

Their hands met. Touched. His hand was warm, his palm hard, his hold strong. The handshake of a man who could be trusted to care for his family. To stick around through thick and thin. Who would do his best by the people he loved.

The kind of handshake she could get used to. If she were a sticking around kind of girl. Which, of course, she wasn't. She wouldn't let herself be. Ever.

Chapter 2

'Daaaaddy . . . what shoe goes where?'

Callan looked up from working flour into the fruitcake he was making for the local sewing club's annual Christmas morning tea to see Mia staring at him, her socked foot tapping impatiently as she held up two glittery ballet flats.

'Swap them round.' He went back to stirring, his heart sinking as he took in the stodgy mixture. It wasn't how it looked in the recipe he'd found online. But then, nothing he made looked like the recipes he found online. Not for the first time since Abigail had passed away just over eleven months ago did he find himself wishing she'd kept her recipes inside a book and not in her head. The thought was quickly followed by a sharp twist of guilt in his gut. Abigail hadn't planned on dying. Hadn't asked for the aneurysm that had taken her away from them. He had no right to feel exasperated.

'Daddy, can you put them on for me? I'm tiiiired.'

Callan took a deep, calming breath. Fought the irritation that rose. How his wife had done the baking and looked after Mia without once complaining or raising her voice, he had no idea. Abigail had made it all look so easy, so effortless. Whereas he spent his days feeling like he was fighting an uphill battle. Making the daily quota of food to ensure his regulars had something to eat

12

with their tea or coffee. Keeping the kitchen and shop clean and tidy. Then there was the actual serving of people, all of it done while listening to Mia's constant questions, helping her whenever she asked, ensuring she'd remembered to brush her teeth, put on weather-appropriate clothing, and that the food that inevitably got caught in her curls was brushed out.

What had it been called in the article he'd read on one of the parenting sites he'd been frequenting since Abigail had passed?

Mental load.

A concept that was apparently foreign to the majority of men, but well known among the online mummy community.

All the little things that the person who runs the household has to juggle and keep track of. Things as small as remembering to buy toothpaste before it runs out. Ensuring there's clean under-wear available at all times. Buying Christmas presents. Pulling the Christmas tree out of storage. The last two things he'd not yet done, even though he knew he had to.

There was no way he was letting Mia's first Christmas without her mum be as gloomy and depressing as he felt.

It had to be magical.

Unforgettable.

Infused with all the sparkle and joy that Abigail had brought to the season year after year.

At least now that he'd put aside the pride that had him in 'do it all myself' mode since Abigail's death, and hired Josie, he'd have time to decorate, to get the Christmas tree, to buy the toy ponies or dolls or princess costumes that Mia kept talking about. Two presents? One from Santa, one from him? Who was he kidding? He was going to buy everything on her list and more. He had to if it meant seeing her little face light up. If it helped ease the pain of not having Abigail there.

'Daddy!'

A whine of impatience combined with a soft thump of foot on wooden floor brought Callan back to his senses.

'Mia, sorry. Daddy was in another world.' He abandoned the wooden spoon in the glutinous mixture and squatted down to Mia's level. 'What can I do for you, princess?'

'Shoes. Help me. Put them on me. And you weren't in another world, silly Daddy, you were right here.' Mia collapsed onto the ground and held her shoes up to Callan.

He repressed a sigh. How many times did you have to remind a child to use their manners? An infinite amount of times, it seemed. 'What's the magic word?'

'Pleeeease.' Mia gave him her most winning smile. One that melted his heart when he was sad inside. One that riddled him with guilt on the rare occasion he snapped at her.

'That's the word.' He slipped the pink sparkly shoes onto her feet, then ruffled the top of her head. 'We always use our manners, right?'

'Right.' Mia gave a firm nod then looked up, her serious expression morphing into one of unbridled happiness. 'Josie!'

Callan twisted round to see Josie staring into the cake mixture. Hot embarrassment coursed through his veins, though hopefully not his cheeks. He didn't want Josie to see that he knew he was failing. That he was trying to keep things going, but wasn't quite getting there. He didn't want *anyone* to see it.

'What happened to this?' Josie picked up the spoon and prodded the mixture.

'New recipe I'm trying out. Found it online. I think they may have made a mistake with the quantities. Too much flour. Or not enough eggs, or brandy, or something. I think I'm going to have to start again, with a new recipe . . .' He trailed off, painfully aware that he sounded every bit as uninformed as he felt.

'Hmm, I see.' Josie set the spoon down and reached for the navy-blue apron emblazoned with the shop's logo that was hanging on a hook attached to the wall.

She might have said she understood, but Callan hadn't missed the tightening of her lips, the narrowing of eyes, that told him

14

she saw the problem wasn't with the recipe, but with the person who was making it.

'So, it's a fruitcake you're making?' She efficiently wrapped the ties around her waist then fastened them at the front. 'I know I'm not meant to be cooking, but I have a recipe that never fails. And it uses just three ingredients. I could make it or give the recipe to you if you'd prefer to do it yourself.'

'Daddy, you promised we'd go get some new Christmas decorations.' Mia tugged at his sweater. He looked down to see excitement shining in her eyes. 'Remember? You said now that we had a Josie we could do it. And go see Santa too. I haven't told him what I want.'

'And what do you want from Santa?' Josie picked up the bowl of sludge and scraped it out into the rubbish bin.

'Yesterday I wanted a pony, but today I want a Cinderella dress. And glass slippers.' Mia tapped her chin. 'And a crown. All princesses have crowns, and Daddy says I'm a princess, so I have to have a crown.'

'Well your daddy's quite correct, and I bet Santa will be most happy that you're asking for a costume. Far easier for him to transport. Can you imagine trying to fit a pony in a sleigh?'

Callan nodded a thank-you to Josie over Mia's head. He'd forgotten all about asking what she wanted from Santa. Rookie mistake.

'So, do you want me to whip up that cake?' Josie flicked the kettle on, reached up to the shelf above the stainless-steel bench and fished out four teabags from the box. 'It'd give you the time to go shopping.'

'Would you mind?' Callan lifted Mia into his arms. 'I'm so sorry. I know it's not part of the job, well, I said it wouldn't be. But clearly there's, er, something wrong with this recipe and I've run out of time . . . and if the sewing club don't get their fruitcake . . .'

'Consider it done. You two go visit Santa, buy those decorations. I'll be fine. Just be back by three, if that's okay. I have that meeting with my potential landlady . . .' Josie shooed them away, a smile lighting up her warm hazel eyes.

More green than brown, Callan noticed. And the shooing . . . not dissimilar to how Abigail would hurry him out of the kitchen when she was busy. Never in anger or in frustration, but always in a way that was good-natured, and promised she'd make time for him later.

Not that Callan expected Josie to make time for him. Not that he wanted her to. She was under his employ. Their relationship was purely professional. That, and he wasn't interested in spending time with anyone other than Mia.

An impatient tug on his earlobe brought him back to reality.

'Mia, cut that out.' He jerked his head back and tried to ignore the hurt that flashed through Mia's eyes at being told off. So much for keeping calm . . . He'd apologise to her later. In private. 'Right then. We'd best be off. See you . . . when we see you. Before three.' He waved half-heartedly at Josie but avoided eye contact. The realisation that he'd noticed the colour of her eyes, that he'd noticed something about a woman who wasn't Abigail, saw unease swarming in his stomach. It mixed with the guilt from snapping at Mia and settled dark and heavy. Uncomfortable.

He pressed his nose into Mia's hair and breathed in the pear scent of her shampoo. The familiar fragrance centring him, reminding him of what was important. Of *who* was.

* * *

Josie inhaled the heady, heavenly, sweet and spicy aroma of the fruitcake wafting through the kitchen's air. A smile played about her lips as she recalled the conversation with Callan earlier. The way he'd blamed the recipe for the stodge that was the cake mixture had been too cute. Josie had taken one look at the mixture and seen that the dried fruit hadn't been steeped in the liquid long enough and that too much flour had been added. The mush was now safely in the bin.

It was the opposite of her mixture, where dried fruit was steeped in hot tea, before being combined with self-raising flour and baked for two hours. The result was a gloriously pungent fruitcake, which held an almost malty flavour, and was good by itself, sliced and slathered with butter or served warm with custard.

From the front room came a melodic 'yoo-hoo'.

Josie made a mental note to ask Callan about installing a small bell on the counter along with a sign instructing customers to ring it if the front was unattended.

Smoothing her hair back, she adopted an open smile. The morning hadn't been the busiest she'd experienced in all her years of customer service, but it had been steady.

No doubt people were coming in to see the latest face to arrive in the village. She'd seen that often enough to expect it.

The scent of the stylishly dressed woman reached Josie before she did. White Diamonds. The same perfume her mother had worn. Her heart slammed against her chest, as it always did when for an irrational split-second she believed her mother had sought her out, returned to find the daughter she'd abandoned when Josie was 12 – the age when, with her mind and hormones and body in flux, she'd needed her mother most.

'So, you're the girl I've heard so much about. Welcome, my dear, welcome.' Josie's hand was encased in the woman's tissue-soft palm and pumped twice before being let go. 'My name's Margo. I'm Callan and Mia's neighbour. Owner of the sewing and embroidery shop, among other things.' Margo stopped and sniffed the air. 'That cake's smelling delicious. Every bit as good as Abigail's. My little sewing club is in for a treat. I take it this is your doing?'

Josie shrugged her shoulders. 'It was, not that Callan needed me to do it.' She crossed her fingers behind her back. 'I just had a bit of spare time so thought I may as well help him out.'

'Piffle.' Margo let out a hearty laugh. 'If you can cook as well as his dearly departed wife then you know as well as I do that Callan needs as much help in the kitchen department as he can get. Please tell me he's letting you loose back there?'

'Front of house, mostly.' Josie smiled apologetically. 'He seems to want to do it all himself.'

'That's his problem, you know.' Margo leaned in towards Josie, her demeanour turning conspiratorial. 'Since Abigail passed, he's not allowed any of us to help one iota. I've offered a thousand times, if not two thousand, to take that little angel of his off his hands for a few hours so he can have a break, even if only to go to the pub for a quiet beer, or to bake another batch of his horrifically hard cupcakes without little Mia underfoot. But he won't have it. He's determined to make out like he's okay, but how could he be? He lost the love of his life.'

Josie pressed her lips together and gave a polite nod. Talking about Callan's private life seemed wrong. A crossing of the boundaries between employer and employee, especially with him not being here to defend himself, doubly especially when the woman talking to her was a complete stranger.

'I see that I've put you in an awkward spot.' Margo touched Josie's forearm. 'I apologise. I care deeply for Callan and Mia, and I did for Abigail, too. My family left years ago and they're not ones for visiting, so I began to see those three as my adopted family.'

Shame tugged at Josie's heart. Margo's family had done to her what Josie had done to her father. Not visited. Kept away.

Though why Margo's children stayed away, Josie had no idea. From where she stood, Margo was the opposite of her emotionally distant father. She seemed kind, caring. A person who put others first, who wanted to help. Who wanted to live life, without waiting by windows, staring longingly at the front door, hoping for the past to return, while ignoring the person who was right in front of you, begging you to see them. To love them.

'Oh, look at me feeling all sorry for myself.' Margo waved her hand and let out an exasperated sigh. 'It's not like they hate me. It's my own fault really. I raised two wonderful, successful children. My eldest, Sebastian, lives in Australia and works in IT. He flies over when he can, but he works all hours, and I'm terrified of flying so couldn't even contemplate the flight over that kind of distance. They'd have to give me an elephant-sized amount of sedation.' Margo rolled her eyes towards the ceiling and gave a small, mock-despairing shake of her head.

'And your youngest?' Josie prompted. 'Where are they?'

'Oh, you probably won't believe this to look at me, but Megan's a model. Constantly on the move. New York, Milan, Paris. Wherever her agency sends her. She gets her looks from her father. He was tall, handsome, a good man too. I don't know what I did to deserve him.' Margo's smile disappeared as sadness flashed through her blue eyes for a millisecond before being covered up with a brighter smile, that didn't quite hit her eyes.

'I take it your husband's no longer with us?' It was Josie's turn to comfort, and she did so tentatively, allowing her fingers to lie feather-light on the back of Margo's hand.

Margo's eyes sparkled with unshed tears. 'No. He passed just over a decade ago. I miss him every day. I miss them all. No wonder I keep trying to insert myself in Callan's life. He must think me a nosey old busybody.'

'He wouldn't. He doesn't strike me as the kind of man to think badly of anyone.' Josie straightened up and put her hands on her hips. 'And don't you for a second say your daughter didn't get her looks from you. Women much younger would kill for those cheekbones and eyes of yours. I hope she calls you every single day to thank you for those wonderful attributes you passed on to her.'

Margo let out a light, fragile laugh. 'Maybe not every day, but we aim for a good catch-up phone call or a video chat once a week. She's a good girl is my Megan. As is Sebastian. They may be hundreds of miles away but they're always close.' She tapped her heart.

The shame that had begun to abate returned full force, not just twisting Josie's heart but turning her gut to rock. Her father wasn't that far away. Not compared to Margo's children. Maybe she needed to make more of an effort. To call more. Try harder to connect. But how could you connect with a man who never called first, who kept conversations short, and ended phone calls after two minutes? Who always sounded vaguely surprised to hear from her, like he'd forgotten she even existed?

'So how long are you planning to stay in Sunnycombe?'

Margo, rummaging about in the black leather handbag she had tucked under her arm, missed the flicker of guilt that Josie was sure would've been visible on her face.

'Oh, you know, as long as Callan needs me. I'm not looking to go anywhere anytime soon and the village seems so sweet. The people I've met so far are really nice.'

'And how many people have you met?' Margo looked up and arched an elegant eyebrow.

'I've served a fair few today, but who have I properly met? Just you. Callan. Mia. The owner of the pub where I'm staying.' Josie held up four fingers. 'You're all giving the village an excellent reputation.'

'Well, I'm sure it'll stay that way. The people here are good people. We care for each other. Look out for each other. Even when those we're looking out for don't want us to.'

Josie didn't have to ask to know Margo was referring to Callan and his resolute independence.

'Now, enough of this chin wagging. When will the delicious-smelling cake be ready for pick-up?'

Josie smoothed down her apron, relieved the conversation had returned to work. 'I'll pull it out of the oven in a few minutes, then it'll need to cool down. This afternoon would be fine – although I won't be serving if you plan to pop in around three, I've an appointment . . .'

Margo flapped her hand dismissively. 'Don't worry about the

appointment. The cottage is yours. Treat her with the same care you show your cooking.'

Josie felt her mouth open, then shut. Then open again. 'You're . . .?'

'The landlady. And this chat of ours has given me all the confidence I need that you won't up and leave me without warning. You've got a good way about you, Josie. And I suspect that good way isn't surface-deep.'

Josie nodded. Not trusting herself to speak, lest her voice cracked and she showed Margo who she really was.

A satisfied smile appeared on Margo's lips as she turned and made her way to the door. 'I'll drop the keys in when I pick up the cake. Oh, and Josie?' Margo twisted round and fixed her with serious eyes. 'You won't know this yet. And Callan certainly will refuse to entertain the idea. But he does need you, more than he knows. You'll be good for him.' Margo's gaze roamed around the walls of the bakery. 'You'll be good for this place.'

The door swung shut with a soft *thunk*.

Callan needed her? Josie hoped not. She could cook. She could teach Callan the art of baking, if he let her. But she didn't want anyone to need her. Nothing good could come of that. She'd seen the proof in *that* pudding for herself.

21

Chapter 3

A rustle of bags and the skittering of excited feet greeted Josie as she beat butter, eggs and sugar together, watching the bright orange of the egg yolks morph with the butter into a rich, creamy colour that would lighten until it was the perfect shade of pale pastel yellow and ready for the dry ingredients to be sifted into, then folded through.

'Josie! Josie!' Mia half-ran, half-danced into the kitchen, spinning and skipping, sending the little red bags she was holding flying in all directions. 'Oopsie,' she giggled as she crashed into Josie's legs. 'Sorry, Josie. You should see what we got. We got everything. We got the whole shop. And we're going to decorate the whole shop and upstairs and Daddy bought another tree so we'd have *two* trees and it's going to be the best.'

Josie grinned at Mia's enthusiasm. Sure, Josie was about to descend into what sounded like her idea of hell, but she wasn't going to let her dislike of the season show when the glitter and shine of Christmas was about to bring a little girl who'd lost her mum so much happiness.

She might be a Grinch, but she wasn't a killjoy.

Besides, if she threw herself into her job and convinced Callan to let her help out more in the baking department, then there was the chance she'd get through the season without noticing anything festive at all.

Head down. Bum up. That was the way to handle the oncoming tsunami of tinsel.

'Mia, what did I say about waiting for me?' Callan's disapproving tone didn't match the Santa hat perched jauntily on his head. Or the long ribbon of red and white tinsel that was draped around his neck scarf-style. 'Mia? Are you listening to me at all?' He unwrapped the tinsel scarf and the green and navy-blue tartan scarf hidden beneath it, then shrugged off his long black woollen coat and hung it up on the wooden coat stand that was positioned beside the back door.

Josie tried not to laugh as she took in the jumper he was wearing. Gone was the simple grey knitted jersey he'd left in, replaced by a multi-coloured sweater in red, green and white, featuring a reindeer with bells on its antlers. Underneath it the words 'jingle all the bells' were emblazoned in jaunty script.

'Nice top.' She kept her tone even as she measured the dry ingredients into the sifter, then began jiggling it back and forth, letting the flour and baking powder fall through in a snow-like flurry.

'When 4 year olds attack.'

She could see Callan rolling his eyes out of the corner of her eye.

'Once Mia saw it, I wasn't getting out of the store alive until I forked out the money.'

Picking up a spatula, Josie began to fold the ingredients in with a figure-of-eight motion. 'I think you made the right decision. A Christmas jumper's not worth dying over.' She bit her lip as heat raced over her face and down her neck. *Good one, Josie, way to stick your foot right in your mouth.* 'God, I'm sorry. So sorry. Ignore that last bit. I didn't . . . I wasn't . . . Clearly I need to engage my brain before speaking.'

Callan shrugged her apology off. 'Don't worry about it. I started it with the talk of getting out alive, and I can't have you

23

second-guessing everything you're about to say in case you hurt my feelings. To be honest, there's nothing you can say or do that could. I think my pain quota is filled.'

Josie racked her brain to find something appropriately soothing to say. What did you say to a man who'd lost the love of his life? Nothing had soothed her father's pain, even though the circumstances were entirely different. A devoted mother and loving wife passing away was a million miles away from a wife upping and leaving to go 'find herself' overseas, only to never return.

'So, you managed to get everything you needed?' Josie spooned the smooth batter into a greased and lined cake tin. 'Did Mia leave anything for anyone else to buy?'

Callan stepped forward and inspected Josie's handiwork. 'I don't recall asking you to make another cake. Just the fruitcake.'

There was no reproach in the tone, but Josie had the distinct feeling he was put out. That she was treading on his territory.

'Oh, I had a bit of time on my hands. And I do love making lemon drizzle cake. It doesn't have to be for the shop. I could pay you for the ingredients I used, and you and Mia could take it upstairs and have it for afternoon tea, if you'd like. Consider it a "thanks for hiring me" gift.' She opened the oven and placed the cake on the rack, then shut the door and turned to face Callan. The tenseness had left his eyes but they were still guarded, like a man who was wondering if he were about to fall into a trap, or if by saying 'yes' he'd be agreeing to something else.

Which was ridiculous. She was offering him a cake. To eat. No strings attached.

'If you don't like lemon drizzle cake, I'm sure it would do well in the shop. It was always popular at the cafés and bakeries I've worked in previously.' Josie took the empty mixing bowl to the sink and began filling it with water before the batter stuck to the sides and became an elbow-aching mission to get off.

Callan blinked, hard and fast, then shook his head. 'I'm sure Mia would love a little cake later on for afternoon tea. And there's

24

no need to pay for the ingredients. As a matter of fact, once it's cooked and cooled down, would you join us?'

'Oh, no, I couldn't.' Josie grabbed a fluffy pink hand towel, dried her hands and rehung it neatly over its hook. 'I mean I'll still be on duty, so you should be putting me to good use, not letting me sit around eating cake and drinking tea.'

The corner of Callan's lips lifted a tad. 'Josie, has it been busy today?'

Josie matched his smile. The villagers had got their goggle on that morning, meaning the only person to come in since had been Margo to check on the cake, and check her out. 'No, it's been quiet. Your neighbour, Margo, was the last person I've seen. Hence the cake baking. I'm not good at sitting still. Or standing still. Being still.'

'Or talking still. You're as fast as Mia. No wonder she likes you.' The corners of Callan's lips lifted some more, revealing a sprinkling of wrinkles on either side of his eyes that would have been sexy on any other man. But not on Callan. A father. A widower. A man in mourning. On him they were just . . . a touch charming.

Disquiet squirmed low in Josie's gut. She'd been in the job all of one day and already she was in danger of having people get too close. Worse. It was a 4-year-old who liked her. One who would be happy if Josie hung out with her and ate some cake. It was easy, mostly, to leave towns and cities and the acquaintances she forged there, but to leave a child? To potentially cause a child emotional pain? She'd just have to keep her distance. And that meant no cake.

'Well, I'm not taking no for an answer. You saved my bacon by taking this job, Josie – well, technically, my cake – so I'd like it if you'd enjoy some afternoon tea with us. I'll serve anyone who comes in. When will it be ready?'

So much for no cake. So much for keeping her distance.

Josie grabbed a tea towel and began drying off the bowl. 'It'll be about two hours away by the time it cooks, is drizzled with lemon syrup and cools.'

25

'Perfect, that'll give me time to do the bakery's book work while Mia watches a bit of telly. Chill-out time. I read on the internet that kids need that.' Callan rolled his eyes towards the ceiling and shook his head. 'Chill-out time? What a wonderful thing. I think it should be mandatory for everyone.'

Josie clicked the bowl back into its place on the mixer. 'Oh, to be young again.'

'Indeed. Right. I'll bring Mia down in two hours. Call me if you need a second pair of hands.' Callan stood and made his way up the stairs without waiting for a reply.

Josie slumped forward onto the bench, held her head in her hands and let out a long, slow breath. It was just tea and cake. If she kept conversation light, if she didn't engage too much or too warmly with Mia, she'd be fine. The ties would be easy to untangle. And no hearts would be broken.

* * *

'It's boring here at Christmas time. All my friends go away and don't come back for ages. I have five friends. All girls, 'cause boys are yuck.' Mia stuck out her tongue, then took another bite of her cake, its crumbs catching at either side of her mouth. 'Do you have friends, Josie? Do you have five like me?'

'Not five like you. You must be pretty special to have that many.'

Josie took a sip of tea then set it down on the saucer, with a slight rattle, Callan noticed.

Why would Mia's grilling be making Josie touchy? Or maybe Josie hadn't had lunch so had a case of the lack-of-food shakes. Which would make far more sense. Especially as it looked like she hadn't taken a break since the moment she'd walked in that morning. The floors were swept. The counter gleamed. The dishes were done and packed away. She'd sold a fair bit of his average – below average, if he were honest with himself – baking, and had time to make two cakes.

He'd teased her about not being able to sit still, but from the jiggle of her leg under the table, he may have been on to something.

'Why not five friends?' Mia's interrogation continued. 'It's not like you smell. You don't. You're not stinky.'

Josie's leg stilled as a laugh escaped. The sound filled the space with a light-heartedness he'd not heard in a long time.

'I'm glad I'm not stinky. I appreciate you saying that. I like to shower twice a day to keep myself stink-free.' Josie speared a piece of cake, dipped it in the Greek yoghurt she'd served it with, and popped it in her mouth, her eyes closing for a second as she enjoyed the zesty, sweet flavour, enhanced by the tartness of the yoghurt.

Callan envied her enjoyment. The cake was obviously delicious. Abigail had fed him enough cake for him to know what was good, but since she'd gone, all food – no matter savoury or sweet – tasted like cardboard. Something to be chewed until he could get it down his gullet and into his stomach. Food kept him going, but it didn't give him life.

'Daddy? Can Josie make a cake every day? Hers is better than yours.'

Callan shoved his maudlin moment away. He didn't need food to give him life, he had his life sitting next to him, her little foot nudging his as her leg swung back and forth.

'I think your daddy likes making cake, Mia. And I bet it's just as good as this.' Josie half-smiled at Callan.

'Nope. It's not.' Mia took another mouthful of cake, putting a momentary stop to any further insults.

'She's not lying.' Callan pushed a chunk of the cake, its crumb light but rich with moisture, around the plate. 'This is better than mine.'

'Told ya.' A spray of crumbs flew from Mia's mouth.

'Don't eat with your mouth full.' Callan tapped Mia's hand, then turned his attention to Josie. 'Perhaps I was wrong to keep you out of the kitchen. An old business mentor of mine once said the key to success is to allow people to do what they're good at and not get in their way. And you're good at baking.' He paused. Good? She was great. But so had Abigail been, and putting Josie on par with Abigail felt wrong. Like putting another baker on the same pedestal as Abigail was a betrayal of her memory. 'Really good. Better than I am, hands down.'

'Well, I didn't pay good money to learn how to bake, then spend years bettering myself, for nothing.' Josie shrugged.

'And it would be wrong of me to waste such a talent.' Callan pushed his plate away. 'So if you'd like to take on some of the cooking, then that's fine with me. It would mean an early start but also an early finish.'

'Really?' A smile lit up Josie's eyes. 'Because I'd love to.'

'Really.' Callan confirmed his decision with a nod.

'Yay!' Mia's chubby fists pumped up and down above her head. 'And can we have afternoon tea every day as well?'

Callan shook his head. 'You've got your mum's sweet tooth.'

'And Josie's.' Mia pointed to Josie's empty plate.

A pretty pink flush lit up Josie's cheeks. Pretty? Callan gave himself a mental shake. It was just a flush, there was nothing pretty about it.

Just as there was nothing sweet about the way Mia had evacuated her chair and was now sliding onto Josie's lap. Josie held her hands aloft, her eyes wide, looking for Callan's advice, or permission, to let Mia snuggle in.

He went to reprimand Mia, to pull her away from Josie, but stopped himself. Her small body had cushioned into Josie's, her cheek was settled upon Josie's chest. Her thumb had found its way into her mouth.

All at once his heart restricted in pain, while filling with love. How many times had he seen Mia snuggle into Abigail in the same way? Seeking comfort from not just the warmth of her body, but the warmth of her nature. Her goodness. Her ability to heal a bad day with a few well-thought-out words. To ease a bad day with a hug. To fix an ouchie with a kiss.

He caught the questioning look in Josie's eyes, and gave a nod. Permission to wrap her arms around his daughter. To bring her close. To hold her tight. To treasure her.

'Daddy, can Josie please come upstairs and help us decorate the new tree?' Mia's head tipped up to Josie's. 'Please, Josie? Can you?'

Callan's breath caught in his throat. Regret rolled through him as protectiveness reared its head. Was it right to let Mia become close to Josie? To risk Mia's heart being splintered further should Josie leave.

Sure, Josie said she had no plans to up and go anytime soon, but neither had Abigail. One moment his wife had been smiling and laughing her way through life, lighting up all those she touched with her humour and sweetness, the next he'd found her on the floor. Eyes open. Unseeing. And no amount of saying her name, of pleading or crying, brought her back. Even Mia's tears, dripping on her mother's face, couldn't work their fairy-tale magic and awaken Abigail from her slumberous domain.

Josie looked to Callan for an answer, the shadows in her eyes darkening the longer he took to answer.

The polite thing, and what would make Mia happy, would be to say yes. But being a parent meant setting boundaries and sticking to them. In this case he needed to provide a boundary between Mia and Josie. For Mia's heart's own good.

'I think not, Mia. Sorry, sweetie, but I'm sure Josie's busy doing other things.'

'But I want her to.' Mia's bottom lip pushed out as she tipped her head to look up at Josie. 'Make him say yes, Josie, pleeease?'

'Sorry, lovely, no can do.' Josie took Mia's hand and ran her thumb over the soft, still-dimpled, skin. 'You have to do what your daddy says. He knows best.'

Callan didn't miss the flatness to her tone, but neither did he miss the lightening of her eyes, the forward slump of shoulder that, if he didn't know better, he'd swear was relief.

29

That made two of them.

Gone was the Callan who'd let Abigail soften the stiff upper lip that his emotionless family had instilled in him. Who'd allowed himself to embrace a new community, to become part of it.

Allowing others in, letting them close, no longer seemed like a good idea. It no longer felt safe.

It was better to keep people at arm's length. To keep things professional, detached. Because the moment you cared was the second you opened yourself up to the possibility of pain.

And he had no plans to go through the kind of agony Abigail's death had brought – even a tenth of it – ever again.

Chapter 4

Bye, bed with the back-poking spring.

Bye, curtains that don't quite close.

Josie shut the door to the room she'd rented at the pub and began wheeling her suitcase down the hall, its wheels hitting the old wooden flooring's grooves in a rhythmic *thump-thump*.

Bye, shower that I have to share with Mr Leaves His Hair in the Bathroom Plughole.

She lifted the case and started down the stairs that led to the bar, her stomach squirming with anticipation. The cottage, with its cushion-covered overstuffed sofa and large fireplace, had looked cute and cosy in the photos she'd seen online. She just hoped there was a stock of firewood, as she could feel the cold seeping in from outside, chilling her bones.

'Josie! Get that little bum of yours over here!' The publican's voice boomed, causing those nursing beers and sipping on warming red wine to turn their heads in her direction.

So much for making a quiet, unassuming exit.

'Brendon, hi.' She found a smile and rolled her case in his direction. 'Good to see you've shunned society's illusion of politeness.'

Brendon lightly snorted as he shook his head. 'No time for that palaver. Besides, I was stating the truth, and it wasn't like I was passing judgement on your body. I saw you scuttling out of here and I was worried you were going to leave us without saying a proper goodbye.' Grey eyebrows lifted high on a corrugated forehead. 'Would you like a wine before you go?'

Josie waved her hand, declining the wine glass Brendon held up. 'I'm only moving up the road, and it's not like I won't be back again. Besides, I've seen your pours. I'll end up staggering home. Or having someone push me along, with my passed-out form on top of the suitcase.'

Brendon set the bottle down. 'Well, you won't be a stranger, will you?'

Josie shook her head. 'Of course not. I promise.'

'That's what I like to hear. When you do come by, bring that boss of yours with you, and your landlady, too. I've not seen either of them in here for far too long. Tell Margo she's missed and tell Callan that Old Smithy is getting a bit big for his boots. Thinks he's the champion of the darts world. Needs taking down a peg or two, he does.' Brendon clucked his tongue, then took a sip of his ever-present pint. A smattering of froth decorated his moustache, which he wiped away with the back of his hand.

'I heard Callan was good at darts, though I don't know if I'll be able to get him down. Besides, it'd be weird if I asked, wouldn't it? Being his employee and all.'

Brendon's thick lips curved up in a smile. 'Not weird. Not even a bit. When you live in a village as small as this you end up being more to people than you ever intend. Friends. Enemies. Lovers . . .' Brendon lifted his brows suggestively.

Heat hit Josie's cheeks. The idea of her and Callan being anything more than colleagues was . . . 'Brendon, that is so wrong. He's just lost his wife not that long ago. And more importantly, I'm not interested.' She tightened her grip on the suitcase's handle and glanced towards the window. The sun was dropping towards the horizon, the shadows growing longer, the clouds thicker, heavier.

'Whatever you say, my dear. Time will tell. Speaking of time. Rain's on the way. My gammy hip's telling me so. Best you go before it buckets down. Here . . .' Brendon passed an unopened bottle of merlot to Josie. 'A village-warming gift. Welcome to Sunnycombe.'

'Oh, no, you don't have to . . .' Josie went to wave the kindness away.

The bottle was pressed into her open hand. 'I do have to. It's tradition. How I welcome all new residents.'

Josie accepted the bottle with a nod, tucked it into the crook of her arm and tried to ignore the guilt that sat heavy in her heart. Everyone believed she was here for the long term, trusted her to be there for them. Callan's shop needed her. Margo no doubt relied on the rental money. Even Brendon believed she had a place here, one that would see their old darts champion return.

Two days she'd been there, and somehow Sunnycombe had pulled her in, embraced her, made her one of their own.

And part of her – the abandoned child who had hoped for her mother's return, who dreamed of a day when the closeness she'd once shared with her father would resume – wanted to embrace them back.

She shook the ridiculous thought off. She didn't want to embrace anyone or to be part of anything greater than herself. She was just tired and in need of a good non-poking-spring-in-back night's sleep. 'Right, well, thank you for having me. I'll probably see you later in the week.'

'Don't forget to bring Callan. Or Margo. Both would be good.' Brendon gave her an encouraging nod. 'And don't take no for an answer.'

Josie nodded and managed to lift her lips in the smallest of smiles. It was the least she could do considering how kind Brendon had been since the moment she'd set foot in The Squeaky Wheel.

The light in the pub dimmed as the clouds lowered. Grey, menacing, and threatening to see her a sopping mess if she didn't get home quick.

Home.

She stepped outside and shivered. Not so much because she was leaving the roaring fire and warm atmosphere behind, but because the idea of 'home' left her cold. Frozen to the bone.

Residence. There was a word she could get on board with. A place where she would reside until it was time to move on.

An icy gust of wind whistled past her. She stepped up her pace, tucked her chin down and buried the lower part of her face into her sunshine-yellow scarf. Why hadn't she put her pompom hat on before leaving? Why had she tucked it in the bottom of her suitcase? At this rate her ears would fall off before she arrived at the cottage. Although the bonus of that would be not hearing Brendon's nutty insinuations that she and Callan ought to become an item.

Nutty? More like completely insane.

Her eyes darted to the left and right as she walked. The fronts of the honey-coloured buildings that flanked either side of the street were in darkness, though the flats above glowed as lamps and lights were switched on. Beyond the buildings, she could make out the hillsides that stood sentry on either side of the village, their tops shrouded in cloud.

She followed the road around, leaving the shops behind, and breathed a sigh of relief as she spied Margo's cottage with its thatched roof and twin chimneys poking out almost jauntily from either end, up ahead.

A quiver of anticipation stirred within as she pushed open the front gate, went to the front door and fished about in her pocket for the keys Margo had dropped in when picking up the fruitcake. The lock turned with ease and she crossed the threshold.

Josie set her suitcase to the side of the door and sent a silent 'thank you' to Margo as she spotted the fire cracking softly in the hearth. Judging by the ashes it had been going for some time, which meant Margo had made an effort to keep the fire burning.

A tendril of sadness curled around Josie's heart as she moved to the fire, dropped into a squat and reached her hands towards the fire. Her fingers tingled as warmth melted away the numbness.

What must it feel like to have been brought up by someone who was so caring? So thoughtful? Who put others' needs ahead of their own? Who didn't ignore you, forget you were there or leave you altogether?

She shoved the pity away. It was pointless to dwell on such things.

She couldn't change her parentage. Couldn't go back in time and change her mother's mind or her father's reaction. His grief had turned, briefly, to anger. Harsh and sharp. His anger quickly morphing into never-ending mourning, sprinkled with a melancholic hope that his wife would return. Meanwhile, Josie's hope, along with any dreams of happily ever after, had skulked off as the days, then weeks, months, then years had passed without so much as a call, email or postcard.

Josie stood as three knocks filled the air. She made her way to the door, stopping when it opened and a bright red beret-style woollen hat poked its head through, followed by a soft 'yoo-hoo'.

'Margo. Come in. It's horrid out there.' She ushered her in and shut the door against the frigid air. 'It was so kind of you to start the fire. It was nice to come ho—' Josie stopped herself, remembering the vow she'd made to never think of anywhere as home. To never let herself settle. 'It was nice to arrive to find the place not freezing. It was such a lovely welcome.'

Margo threaded her arm through Josie's without asking permission and walked her towards the door that led to the kitchen. 'Wasn't me, my dear. It was Callan's idea.'

'Callan's?' Josie forced herself not to lean into Margo. To let her nurturing nature infuse her soul. 'Why would he do that?'

'Because he's got a good heart on him. A bit battered these days, but it's still in there.' Margo released her and turned her attention to the kitchen bench. 'Tea?'

'Please. Or there's wine if you'd like?' Josie took a seat at the kitchen table and straightened her tired legs into a deep stretch.

'From Brendon?' Margo's cheeks pinked up as she pulled two mugs down from the cupboard to the right of the sink, then placed tea bags that were kept in a duck-egg-blue tin jar next to the kettle along with identical jars labelled 'coffee' and 'sugar'. 'He's a good man. It's a nice tradition.'

Good man? Josie suspected Margo thought Brendon was a little more than good, if the heightened colour in her cheeks and the way her gaze was focused on the mugs and refusing to meet Josie's, was anything to go by.

'He is nice. Asked me to bring you along to the pub next time I go.'

'Did he now? I suppose it's been a while since I popped in.' Margo's gaze didn't waver as she poured steaming water into the mugs. 'And save the wine for a special occasion. Like inviting Callan over as a thank-you for lighting the fire.'

Josie bit back a grin. She knew a diversion tactic when she saw one.

'Good idea, Margo. I'll keep it in mind. Maybe I should invite you and Brendon around at the same time?'

'Oh, I'm sure he's too busy.' Margo placed the mug in front of her. 'Sugar?'

'No, thank you.' Josie decided to drop the subject. It wasn't her place to get involved. She pushed out the chair opposite and Margo sank into it with a contented sigh.

'I do love this place. I'd forgotten how warm and cosy it gets on a wintry night. My husband and I spent hours snuggled up on that sofa talking about our hopes and dreams. It got a bit cramped once the kids joined us, but I wouldn't trade in those moments for all the cricks in the neck in the world.' She wrapped her fingers around the mug and lifted it to her lips.

Fingers that still wore her wedding rings, Josie noted.

'You still miss him?'

'I do. Every day. I don't know that I ever won't. He was a great, towering, bear of a man with the sweetest, softest heart.

Even after the cancer that saw him leave us took hold, his spark never left him, his humour, his smile. It was all there to the end.'

Margo's eyes had misted over. Putting aside her promise to keep her distance from others, Josie slid off her chair, made her way round to Margo and wrapped her in a hug. Their hearts pressed together in a moment of solidarity.

Two people who had experienced loss, who knew no words could change the past or the way it had transformed them.

Margo released her with a shuddering laugh. 'Look at me welling up after all these years. You must think me a silly old duck.'

Josie slipped back into her chair. 'Not silly. Not old either. Most certainly not a duck. It's not easy being left behind.' She sank her teeth into her cheek and silently reprimanded herself for saying too much. 'At least I imagine it's not easy being left behind.' She managed a half-smile and hoped Margo wouldn't ask questions. Wouldn't push.

She glanced up from her tea to see a speculative look in Margo's eyes. Not suspicious. Not enquiring. Almost worried. Definitely kind.

'It wasn't easy at the start.' Margo pushed the chair back, stood, then picked up her mug and walked to the bench. 'The furthest thing from easy, to be honest. Me and the kids, alone, without the humour John brought. The easygoingness that was so needed on the days when the kids were driving me up the wall with their teenage monosyllabic grunts and almost daily dramas.' She tipped the remaining tea down the sink, then turned around and leaned against the bench, her arms folded over her chest. 'But we muddled along. Found a new rhythm. Developed more patience, more understanding for and of each other. The sadness never left. But it abated. Now it feels more like a sense of peace in here.' She tapped her heart. 'I was lucky to be part of his life while I was. I think he felt he same way about me.'

And yet Margo wouldn't allow herself to entertain her affection for another. Did peace not bring closure? Was Margo happy alone? Or was she not willing to risk that kind of pain a second time round with someone else? If it were the latter, Josie understood all too well.

Relationships, connections, were dangerous things. Why stand in the storm and risk being struck by lightning, when you could take cover and be out of harm's way?

'I'm sure John felt the same about you, Margo. Anyone would. I've known you all of five minutes and I already know I like you.'

So much for not getting close to anyone – but even Josie couldn't deny that Margo made her feel cared for. Something she'd not felt in a long time, and it was hard to resist.

Hard? More like impossible.

'Thank you, my dear.' Margo blew her a kiss then walked into the lounge and looked around. 'You know what this place needs?'

Josie came to stand beside her and tried to see what Margo was seeing. 'No idea. It's perfect as far as I'm concerned.'

'It needs a Christmas tree. One with all the trimmings. Decorations. Lights. Presents underneath.'

Josie was glad Margo was standing beside her so she couldn't see her cringe.

'What? You hate the idea?'

A wave of embarrassment dashed over Josie's face. Hot, tight and uncomfortable. 'You could tell?'

'I've two kids, remember? I don't need to hear your feelings, I can sense them.' Margo smiled kindly. 'So what's so wrong with a Christmas tree?'

Josie shrugged in an attempt to look casual. 'I'm just not a Christmas person. I prefer every other day of the year, if I'm honest.'

Margo's speculative look was back. 'Fair enough. Although, I hate to tell you this, but you've moved to the Cotswolds' most Christmassy village. Possibly England's most Christmassy village.'

'Fairy lights? Decorations? I've seen similar.' Josie moved to the fireplace and threw another log on, not wanting the fire Callan had so carefully set and tended to burn out. 'Nothing I can't handle.'

She turned to face Margo as tinkling laughter filled the room, as bright as the fire was hot. 'Oh, sweets, this is just the beginning. There's an event on every week leading up to the big day. We do Christmas a little differently from other places, you'll see.'

Margo didn't elaborate as she laughed her way to the front door.

'Sleep well, Josie. And welcome. I think Sunnycombe is going to enjoy having you here.'

With a wave Margo was gone, the room gloomier without her presence. Like it missed her.

Josie shook her head. She was being silly. A house could no more miss a person than a mother could miss the daughter she abandoned.

She went to her suitcase, unzipped it, and pulled out the one part of her childhood she couldn't bear to part with, despite knowing better.

A flaxen-haired angel doll. Its arms stretched out in a welcoming manner, and once-glittery wings spread wide. The last Christmas gift she'd ever received from her mother.

She'd tossed the card it came with in a flash of anger years ago, but she'd never forgotten the words that accompanied the gift: *To watch over you.*

And so the angel had, while snuggled in her arms through tears, through rages, through emotional paralysis. The last remnant of a happy, contented childhood.

Josie stroked the angel's now matted hair, sat it on the table next to the front door then made her way to the sofa. She slipped down its arm and let the buttery tan leather envelop her as she pulled down the pink faux-fur throw folded over the sofa's back and tucked it over her legs.

So Sunnycombe was Christmas crazy?

She closed her eyes and shook her head. Only she could find herself living in a place that stood for everything she disliked, everything she didn't want to think about, didn't want to remember.

It was like the universe was plotting, forcing her to face that which she ran from.

If that were the case, the universe was about to be disappointed. She was only staying in Sunnycombe for as long as she had to. In her experience she had six months, tops. Nothing – and no one – could change that.

No matter how hard they tried.

Chapter 5

'Josie, can you give me a hand over here?' Callan twisted round from trying to string fairy lights around the shop's window to see Josie rubbing her temples, her elbows anchored to the counter, her head low and shoulders scrunched up round her ears.

She'd been like that all day. Hunched up. Distant. Like she wasn't one hundred per cent there, and he was starting to wonder if he ought to send her home for the rest of the day.

Josie glanced up and caught his eyes. 'Sorry, Callan. Bit of a sore head.'

Before he could stop her, she came to stand beside him, dragged a chair to the opposite side of the window, climbed on top of it and indicated for him to pass her the string of lights dangling from his hand.

Callan hesitated. 'Are you sure you should be up there? With a headache and all? I don't want you passing out and hurting yourself. Should you be at home? In bed getting some rest?'

'No, I'm fine, honest.' Josie waved her hand like it was nothing. The pain in her eyes said otherwise.

Reluctantly he passed the lights to her and she hung them over the hook that a heavily pregnant Abigail had screwed in for the shop's first Christmas. He'd begged her to let him do it,

41

worried that she'd fall over and hurt herself and their baby, but she'd laughingly shushed him, then flapped him away.

He shut his eyes as a wave of grief surged through him. How was he going to get through Christmas without her? How was he going to get through life?

'Callan? It's my turn to ask . . . are you all right?'

Josie's concern brought him back to the here and now. He took a silent breath in and slowly blew it out, opening his eyes and fixing a smile on his face as he did so. He focused on the carollers who were practising out in the street, their voices jaunty as they sang 'Deck the Halls'.

''Tis the season to be jolly.'

Except jolly was the last thing he was feeling. 'Jaded' he could get on board with.

'I'm fine.'

Josie eyed him. Her expression remained unconvinced. He waited for her to further interrogate him, but no questions came. For that he was grateful. He didn't know how to explain the grief. The intensity. The pain. The way it surged and settled but was always there. He didn't know how to talk about it, and didn't want to. Not to a therapist. Or Josie. Or Margo. Not to anyone. Ever.

Falalalalaaaaa . . . lala . . . la . . . laaaaaa.

'How long are they going to go on for?' Josie sounded as flat as Callan felt.

'Not helping the pain in your head?' Callan stepped down from his chair then offered his hand to Josie.

She hesitated, her eyes narrowing, like she didn't trust him to get her down safely. Just as he were about to drop it, embarrassed for overstepping a mark he didn't know existed, she placed her hand in his.

He was surprised at how soft it was, considering she worked with her hands. Warm, too. And it fit so perfectly. Like it belonged there.

Josie stepped down, tugged her hand out of his and folded

her arms. 'To be honest I'm not a huge fan of carols. They're so . . . so . . .' Her nose screwed up in thought.

'Joyful?' Callan shoved his hands into his trouser pockets and tried to ignore the heat imprinted on the hand that had held Josie's a few seconds ago, like a part of her had been left with him.

He pushed the thought away. Nothing had been imprinted. And hands weren't like jigsaw puzzles, they didn't just 'fit' together. He was being silly. The stress of the season had clearly gotten to him.

The choir launched into a solemn rendition of 'Silent Night', and Callan had to bite his tongue to stop laughter from spilling out as Josie visibly shuddered.

'So joyful. Even songs like that one. It's a peaceful song but it's joyful as well. Uplifting.' Josie's nose wrinkled further. 'The worst bit is you can't escape them. They're everywhere. On the telly, radio, in shops. I clicked onto my favourite baking website this morning and was greeted with a pop-up ad that had packets of baking ingredients singing and dancing to "Jingle Bells". I now have to avoid that site for nearly a whole month. It's a tragedy.'

Callan's lips quirked to the left, disobeying his direct order not to show their amusement. He'd never met a person who disliked carols so much they could rant about it. Never met anyone who had a distinct aversion to Christmas. He'd thought he was the only one. His family Christmases had been staid affairs. Formal. Boring. Midnight mass on Christmas Eve, followed by gifts in the morning, a family lunch at dinner where the conversation was so polite it bordered on painful. After lunch they'd settle round the television to watch the Queen's Christmas Message, then leftovers were had for dinner and they'd retire to bed not long after that.

There was no dancing while cooking. No silly hats or crazy jumpers. No surprise gifts brought out throughout the day. No magic. No fun.

Abigail had transformed his attitude to Christmas with her own traditions. Ones she'd created after a childhood where money was scarce and Christmas was even more depressing than his. She'd embraced the season that could have – should have – made her sad, and she'd made her life richer for it.

With Abigail gone, so had *his* reason for the season.

Irritation jolted him back to reality. This wasn't about him. He was not alone in his grief. He had Mia to think about. Which meant Christmas couldn't be a miserable affair. He wouldn't allow it. Wouldn't let Mia down. Wouldn't allow her to feel as humdrum about the festive season as he once had. As he threatened to feel now that Abigail wasn't there to inject joy into it.

But that didn't mean he couldn't admit his lack of love for the season to a fellow Grinch.

'My least favourite carol is "The First Noel". We'd sing it at church growing up and I sounded like a strangled duck warbling out the words. All the other kids would have a great laugh at my expense.' Callan finished stringing the lights and plugged them in. A warm glow bathed the window, and Josie's face – highlighting her cheekbones and revealing strands of copper in her hair that he'd not noticed.

Not that he should notice them. Or had any reason to.

Annoyed and embarrassed with himself, he set to unravelling another set of fairy lights.

'Do you still go to church?' Josie poked around in a box of Christmas decorations that he'd dragged down from the loft.

She hadn't noticed him noticing her? Good. Callan breathed a sigh of relief. He didn't want her getting the wrong idea. It was bad enough that for a fleeting moment he'd found her attractive.

Not that he hadn't noticed that she was pleasant on the eye. He had in a general manner. As you do when someone good-looking passes by. Just now was different though, because he'd noticed details. The kind of details you only see in someone special, or someone you hope will become special.

He didn't want anyone to become that person. The only person who was special to him was the little girl who was sitting at the

44

table out back watching grown-ups in bright outfits dance to silly songs on the tablet.

'No, we don't go to church. I was never all that much of a church-goer.' He reached up and hung the lights on the hook. 'Only went because my parents did.'

'Do you spend much time with them now? Have they helped out much since . . .?'

'Since Abigail passed away?' Callan jumped in before Josie had the chance to feel awkward. 'No. My parents didn't approve of Abigail. She wasn't from the same social class as the one I was born into. My falling in love with her, giving up a promising career in an accounting firm and moving to the middle of nowhere to do the accounts of people who earn in a year what my father made in a week . . . Well, if there's a black sheep in every family, then I'm it.'

'Wow.' Josie twisted a gold bauble round in her fingers.

Callan waited for her to elaborate, but nothing more came.

'Really? "Wow?" That's all you've got?' He grinned to show her he wasn't offended.

'Well, yeah.' Josie hung the bauble off her finger and spun it round. 'Where should this go?'

'There's a series of hooks under the counter.'

'Great, thanks.' Josie hoisted the box up, walked to the counter, sank down onto the ground cross-legged and began hanging the baubles in their place. 'It's just – and please don't take this the wrong way – you seem so . . . straight. Black sheep of fancy families are meant to . . . I don't know, have tattoos everywhere and piercings in places the majority of us don't get to see. You wear clothing that could be on the cover of a men's fashion magazine. You use your manners. You run a business. And you're a great father. Not what I'd call black-sheep material.'

Callan shrugged. Same way he'd spent years shrugging off the lack of phone calls and visits. The stiff upper lip his family had cultivated came in handy in the face of his parents' reticence to connect with their granddaughter, let alone their son. 'That's my family for you. I don't regret what I did though. Marrying Abigail. Moving here. The seven years we were together brought me more happiness than all the years I spent at home.'

Josie took hold of the counter with both hands and heaved herself up with a quiet 'oof'. 'I can understand that. What's next?'

The simultaneous sounds of something being dragged across a wooden floor and puffing exertion interrupted their conversation.

'Tree next, Daddy. And I know Josie can help decorate this one because it's downstairs, not upstairs.' Mia dragged the rectangular cardboard box that contained the fake Christmas tree into the shop, around the counter, and released it with a dramatic swipe of her brow. 'It's heavy. I need a treat to get my energy back.'

'Lucky your dad owns a cake shop.' Josie plucked a miniature chocolate cupcake, replete with chocolate ganache and red, white and green Christmas tree-shaped sprinkles, out of the cabinet and passed it to Mia who quickly stuffed it in her mouth.

'Thankshoo, Joshie.' The words came out as mushed as her smile was wide.

Callan stopped himself from reprimanding Josie for giving Mia treats without checking with him first. She didn't mean any harm, and it had made Mia happy. He'd have a chat about it later, when Mia was out of earshot and there was no danger of destroying the cheerful ambience.

'Probably should have asked you if that was okay, right?' Contrition was written all over Josie's face.

'Probably. There's always next time. Especially, like you said, when your father owns a cake shop. It's hard to resist temptation when it's right in front of you all day long.' Callan squatted down and began pulling out the pieces of fake tree, hoping Josie wouldn't notice the hot spots burning high on his cheeks. His talk of temptation had sounded way too much like flirtation for his own liking. Not that it was, or that he'd meant it that way. Yet, if he really hadn't meant it to sound like that, would he have thought it sounded like that?

46

He inserted the trunk of the tree into the base, then righted it, faking concentration as he gave himself a stern talking-to.

He was being silly. Overthinking an innocent statement. He wasn't being flirtatious. Just nice. Allowing Josie to feel okay about jumping the gun with the cupcake rather than have the easy atmosphere between them disappear.

'What's with the fake tree?'

Callan gripped the tree's plastic trunk as the closeness of the words took him by surprise, nearly causing him to lose his balance. He glanced over to see Josie hunkered down next to him, her inquisitive eyes just a few inches away. He caught her scent – a sweet, comforting mix of sugar, butter and vanilla. He shuffled away from the inviting aroma, grabbed the final part of the tree, stood and slotted it into the lower half, then began fluffing out the spiky, green fronds.

'We made the mistake of getting a real tree for the shop for the first Christmas. Thought it would add to the festiveness. We may have also been bemused by the rest of the shops' use of fake trees and wanted to one up them.' The memory tugged at his lips and erased his previous unease. 'We found a tree in the woods about ten minutes out of the village, and chopped her down in the middle of the night.'

'Daddy, that's stealing.'

Callan sucked his lips into his mouth at Mia's outrage and forced himself not to laugh. 'You're right, Mia. It was. And I just need to talk to Josie about something grown up, so I'm going to mute your ears for a second, okay?' Mia nodded her agreement, and he placed his hands over her ears. 'Mia's right, of course. It was stealing, but we were just starting out and figured what was one less tree in a populated forest if it meant spreading cheer to the rest of the village. Except what we spread were ants. All through the food.'

'I thought ants nested underground and hibernated in winter?'

Callan shrugged. 'So did we. Turns out Sunnycombe has many

47

quirks, one being that these ants nest and hibernate in trees, and the warmth of the bakery woke them up. We were in catch-and-release mode for weeks, since Abigail refused to harm a hair on their heads. Not that ants have hair on their heads. Although, maybe they do in these parts. Who knows? It wouldn't surprise me.'

Josie's hands went over her mouth to hide her grin, but her amusement was evident in the silent shaking of her shoulders. Her chest rose and fell in a deep breath as she composed herself, then she dropped her hands to her hips, a serious look on her face.

Callan removed his hands from Mia's ears.

'That was very naughty of you, Callan. Did you get a gift from Santa that year?'

'No. Absolutely not. But I was sure to be most well behaved and buy a fake tree the next year so that it would never happen again.' He ruffled Mia's hair. 'So how about we decorate this?'

Mia jumped up and down and clapped her hands with excitement. 'Yay! Can I put the angel at the top, pretty please?'

'Of course you can. It's only right that you, my wee angel, should place the angel on top.' Callan took the bag of decorations that were stored in the tree's box and placed them on the table.

Josie peered in and scanned the contents. 'Pink and purple colour scheme? I love it.'

Before he could say anything, an ornament was in each hand and she was placing them on the tree alongside Mia, who was chatting happily about everything and nothing, as she was wont to do.

Callan picked up his own ornament. A pink and purple tiered cake that he'd bought Abigail that first Christmas. 'You know you don't have to help us. I'm sure you've other things you could do, if you want.' Callan placed the cake on the tree, tweaking it so it was safe, secure.

'I know, but I . . .' A slow smile spread across Josie's face. 'I'm actually enjoying myself. And it's too late in the day to whip anything up for tomorrow and have it done before it's time for me to sign off.'

Outside the carollers rolled from 'We Three Kings of Orient Are' to 'The Twelve Days of Christmas'.

'Want me to tell them to pipe down?' Callan jerked his head in their direction.

Josie shook her head. 'No. They're actually not as bad as I thought.'

She ducked down and placed a glittering pink star at the base of the tree.

Her lips were kicked up, fine lines radiated from her eyes, and for the first time in months Callan felt the ache in his heart lift. He was surprised, and relieved, to discover that the lightening didn't leave him riddled with guilt.

'I agree.' He hung the ornament on the tree. 'They're not as bad as I thought either. In fact, I might actually be beginning to like them.'

Chapter 6

'Oh, my. She's a thing of beauty. You've outdone yourselves this year.'

Josie pushed herself up from behind the counter where she'd been clearing away the trays of leftover food, the sound of Margo's voice bringing an instant smile to her face.

'Margo, it's the same tree we put up every year.' Callan picked up his mug of tea and took a sip. 'Nothing's changed.'

'Really?' Margo crossed her arms over her chest, her head angling to the left, as her eyes narrowed in silent appraisal. 'No. Something's different. It's got a bit more sparkle than usual.'

'Josie helped. Maybe Josie made it sparkle?' Mia turned around from her cross-legged seated position in front of the tree.

She'd been that way for the past hour. Admiring their work, and every now and then pulling down a couple of ornaments for some make-believe play, before placing them carefully back in their spots.

'Maybe Josie did, indeed.' Margo beamed at Mia. 'How are you, poppet? Have you had a wonderful day?'

Mia pushed herself up and spun around in a circle, ending the move with a dramatic flair of her arms, complete with dancing jazz hands. 'Yes! We decorated the tree. And Josie gave me a chocolate cupcake. And I think Daddy and Josie are falling in love with each other and are going to get married and live happily ever after just like the princes and princesses in my books.' She clasped her hands to her little chest and sighed.

'Oh, Lord.' Callan dropped his head into his hands. 'Mia, that's fairy-tale talk. Josie and I work together. We get along. That's what grown-ups do, okay?'

Mia pouted and turned her attention back to the tree with a muttered 'whatever' and an exaggerated eye roll.

'So much attitude in one so little. I'm doomed.' Callan pushed the mug of tea away. 'What can I do for you, Margo?'

'More like what can I do for you!' She turned to Josie with a definite gleam in her eye. 'And you too, Josie. I've decided it's time you had a night off this parenting lark, Callan. You and Josie should go to the pub and have a night out.'

'No.'

Callan's response was short, sharp and so to the point that Josie flinched.

It wasn't that she wanted to go to the pub with Callan. Despite telling Brendon she'd try and get him down, she'd not really considered it, preferring to give Callan his space. To keep her distance. But the way he'd been so quick to not even consider it? Like the idea was completely repulsive?

The little girl in her, the part she'd long ago locked away, wrapped her arms tighter around herself at the rejection, hoping the simple act would protect her from yet another person not finding her good enough or fun enough or wonderful enough to spend time with.

'No? Just like that? Callan, it's been nearly a year since you went anywhere that wasn't to the shops for food or to get something for Mia.' Margo's tone was firm, but kind. 'If I'm wrong, please enlighten me.' She dipped her chin and raised her brows, awaiting his response.

51

Callan huffed out a breath so forceful Josie was sure she saw steam blooming in the air.

'I haven't needed to go to the pub. Haven't had time. You know that.' His words were measured. Too measured.

Josie's heart seized as a thought occurred. Was Mia going to end up experiencing a similar childhood to Josie? Was Callan's grief going to send him down the same path as her father?

He was doing his best, trying to be present, but she'd seen the strain in his eyes. Would doing everything on his own, one day, become too much? Cause him to further withdraw from those who cared for him? Mia included?

Would Mia one day do as Josie had done and beg her father to see reason? To try to get him to understand that putting their lives on hold was holding them back from growing, from healing. That he was better focusing on the future than miserably dwelling on the past. Words her father had chosen to ignore. Words that had caused the emotional fissure that separated them to further expand.

Margo took a step towards Callan and laid a gentle hand on his forearm. 'I understand. I do. You've taken a lot on in the last year. Putting a hold on your own business in order to run the bakery. Being the sole carer for Mia. But now you've Josie on board and she can help. She already is. Josie, tell me dear, are there enough cakes and slices and whatnot out back to open the bakery with tomorrow morning?'

Callan widened his eyes at Josie, silently asking her to back him up. To give him an excuse to sit at home with Mia, but very much alone.

For a split-second Josie saw a different man. One with hair that had begun to grey prematurely. One with deep lines bracketing his mouth, running the length between his brows and across his forehead. Furtive eyes that flicked to the door like he was waiting for someone to knock . . . or return home.

She couldn't let Callan become her father. She could understand

52

him mourning his wife's passing, but putting his life on hold? He might think it was a good idea, but Josie knew it wasn't. Mia was young now, but she'd soon grow up and realise something was amiss. Begin to feel she wasn't enough for her father. That she couldn't make him happy.

Mia deserved more. As did Callan.

She tore her gaze from Callan's penetrating pleading. 'Plenty, Margo. And I'm happy to start even earlier if Callan's concerned we'll run out.'

'Bu—'

Josie wasn't going to let Callan back out of this. He needed to break out of his routine. Needed to remember his life hadn't died with his wife. 'Besides, it would be nice to get to know some of the locals properly. I didn't spend too much time chatting to them when I was staying at the pub. Kept myself to myself in case I didn't get this job. But now that I'm here to stay . . .' Josie forgave herself the fib. Why let a white lie get in the way of saving a man from himself? 'I should get to know them. And, Callan, with you by my side it'll make the whole process easier. Oh, and Brendon misses you.'

'Misses me?' Callan's eyebrows arrowed together.

'Terrible choice of words. I made it sound like he's been pining after you.' Josie flapped Callan's consternation away. 'All he said is that he's not seen you around and that it would be good to see you. The opportunity to do so is being handed to us on a plate, so we could hardly let him down, could we?'

'Exactly.' Margo pulled out the chair opposite Mia's and picked up one of the crayons scattered on the table, twisting and twirling it between her fingers. 'What do you think, Mia? Should your daddy and Josie go out and have some fun.'

'Margo.'

The steel with which Callan stated Margo's name set Josie on edge. Had they pushed things too far? Cornered him into doing something he truly didn't want to do?

'Daddy.'

The edge was there, but the voice was sweeter, and every bit as determined.

'It's funny how very much like us they can sound at times, isn't it?' Margo winked at Mia, who enthusiastically nodded.

'When I'm about to be in big trouble that's how Daddy says my name.' Mia shrugged before returning her attention to her colouring in.

Callan rubbed the back of his neck and sighed. 'If I go out can we make it quick? Just one. Then home again. It's a big de—'

'I understand.' Margo set the crayon down and sat back in her chair. 'Trust me. But hiding away isn't doing anyone any favours. It took me an age to get out and about, but it was the best thing I could do.'

Josie picked up the stack of trays. 'Just one drink. I promise. We'll be back before Mia's bedtime.'

'And if you're not, that's fine, too. Mia and I will have a great time together. Won't we, poppet?' Margo reached over and patted Mia's forearm. 'Besides, you're doing me a favour. If I'm lucky I'll be a grandmother one day and this is excellent practice.'

'You have two kids, remember?' Callan sunk down to Mia's level. 'You hardly need practice at taking care of one.'

'Motherhood and grandmotherhood are two very different things, I'll have you know. Being a mother means being firm and fair. Being a grandmother means getting to spoil the heck out of a little one without dealing with the consequences.' Margo winked at Mia, who returned the wink with a butter-wouldn't-melt grin.

'She's already had a cupcake, so keep treats to a minimum.' Callan shoved his hands into the pockets of his tan chinos and huffed out a deep breath. 'Well then, I guess I'll go upstairs and grab my wallet . . .'

He paused, like he was waiting for a fairy godmother to swoop in and save him from having to socialise.

'Right you should. Now, scoot.' Margo waved her hand in the direction of the door with mock impatience.

Josie bit the inside of her cheek to stop the laugh that was caught in her throat from escaping. If Callan was after an anti-fun fairy godmother, he was out of luck. The one life had sent his way was determined he was to enjoy himself, whether he wanted to or not.

'Stop looking so pleased with yourself.'

Josie picked up the pile of trays and turned to Margo, whose pretend glare was still in place. 'Who? Me? Pleased with myself? Not at all. More like pleased with you.'

Margo widened her eyes and angled her head in Mia's direction. 'Shall we have a chat out back?'

Before Josie could answer, Margo had her by the elbow and was guiding her into the kitchen towards the kitchen sink.

'Dump the trays. Turn the tap on. We need to mask our conversation.'

Margo's tone was low, serious. Like she meant business. Once again, Josie had to bite back a giggle. Anyone would think they were planning a kidnapping. Which, in some ways, they kind of were.

She dumped the trays into the kitchen sink, turned on the hot water, squirted them with a blob of dishwashing liquid, picked up the scrubber and began to clean them vigorously, hoping the scratching of nylon on plastic would help keep their conversation under wraps.

'Our work here is not done.' Margo picked up a tea towel. 'I've done my part. Got him out the door. Now it's up to you to make sure he doesn't down a pint and leave in ten minutes. Get him talking. Make him engage with others. Help him remember there's life outside of these four walls. Bonus points if you can get him playing darts.'

Josie passed her a soapy tray. 'If I can get him to stay for more than twenty minutes I'll already deserve bonus points. He looked like he'd rather be dropped into a vat of hot oil than go to the pub with me.'

Margo patted Josie's forearm and clucked her tongue. 'Don't take it personally. He's been rebuffing me for months. I started trying to get him out and about six months ago. Lucky I've got tough skin or I'd have given up long ago.'

Josie watched the soap bubbles burst and hoped they weren't a sign of the night to come. If this was as big a step as Margo said it was then she had to make it a success. If she could walk away from the village knowing she'd made a difference to Callan, knowing she'd helped him heal in a way her father never had, that Mia's father wasn't going to ignore her in favour of wallowing in the past the way Josie's had, then her time in Sunnycombe would've been worthwhile.

'I'll do my best to keep him out, Margo. Promise. I won't let your persistence be wasted.'

'Thank you, Josie.'

Margo pulled her into a side hug, one that was floral-scented and soft, homely. Josie was tempted to melt into it but she knew better. She was already walking a fine enough line becoming involved in Callan and Mia's life. In conspiring with Margo. She had to keep some barriers up, even if for one brief moment in time she really didn't want to.

'You two look cosy over there. Planning to railroad me into doing something else?'

Josie passed the last tray to Margo to dry and twisted round to see Callan filling the doorway that led up to his flat. With his wavy hair freshly combed and parted to one side, a hint of stubble and his ridiculously sharp jawline, emphasised by the upturned collar of his navy pea coat, he looked like an old-school Hollywood matinée idol.

Definitely chat-up worthy. If he were anyone other than Callan Stewart. Recent widower. Father of one. Employer.

Utterly handsome. Totally untouchable.

A subtle dig to the ribs from Margo's direction brought Josie to her senses. Perving on the boss was a no-go, even if it was just a general, non-lusty appreciation.

'No, no plans to railroad you into anything else. We were just chatting about the upcoming Christmas festivities. Isn't that right, Josie?'

Josie nodded and mentally added Christmas festivities and what that involved to her list of pub conversation topics to keep Callan occupied. A list that was so short, that was the only thing on it. She unhooked her black puffer jacket from the coat stand and jammed her arms into it, pulled her yellow and white polka dot hat down over her ears, then wrapped the matching woollen scarf around her neck and up over her chin.

Josie glanced up at Callan ready to give him the nod of 'let's go', glanced away and then looked back again. Was she seeing what she thought she was seeing? Callan wearing a bright pink pompom hat, shot through with glittery silver strands?

'You can laugh. I won't be offended.' He tugged the slightly-too-small hat down further, then gave it one final yank, so that it just covered the top of his ears.

'Not going to laugh. I'm too busy thinking I'm having a turn. Are you really wearing that to the pub?' Josie resisted the temptation to reach up and flick the pompom. 'Are you hoping to be laughed out before you even get to order a beer? Is that your plan to get out of this?'

Callan's nose straightened in a prim and proper manner. 'I'll have you know that real men can wear whatever they want, and not be afraid of what others might think or say.'

'Aha.' Josie looped her turquoise cross-body bag over her shoulders. 'Sure they can. But I'll bet a round of drinks that you're going to take it off just before we head indoors.'

'I'm going to enjoy my free beer.' Callan's lips kicked up in a

57

smug smile. 'Shall we go? The sooner we leave, the sooner I'm back.'

'We shall.' Josie made her way to the front of the bakery, with Margo in tow.

Seeing Callan walk into the pub wearing a pink pompom hat was totally worth a round of drinks. Two even. Not only had it lightened the mood between them, it would be a talking point at the pub.

'Right then.' Margo clapped her hands together authoritatively. 'You two have a good time. And don't forget, if you choose to stay out later that's fine. I can put Mia to bed.'

Callan raised two fingers to his forehead in a salute. 'Roger that. But don't hold your breath.'

With a kiss from Callan to Mia and a wave, they stepped out into the lightly drizzling night. The precipitation so fine it looked like tiny diamonds in the lamp light, giving the village a magical quality.

Like if you wished for something it could come true.

And what would you wish for? What do you dream of?

The answer rose unbidden in Josie's mind. Unbidden and uncomfortable.

A proper family? Really? After all these years, was that what she truly wanted?

Not likely. It would take a miracle to change her mind. Not that she believed in miracles. Besides, it was never going to happen anyway. Not if she kept up her nomadic ways, which she had to if she wanted to avoid the heart-wrenching ache of being left or pushed away by those she loved most.

Still, if a wish could be made that might come true, Josie was going to put it out to the universe.

She closed her eyes and let the wishful words fill her mind.

Not for her. But for the man beside her. The little girl back at the bakery. For a small family who deserved a second chance at happiness.

She opened her eyes and focused on the glow emanating from the pub. Wishes didn't always come true overnight, some took their time. And the time to start this wish in motion, to make her hopes and dreams for Mia and Callan come true, was now.

Chapter 7

Callan paused at The Squeaky Wheel's entrance, unsure what to do, what to say, whether or not going into the pub after shunning it for so long was a good idea. He reached for the pompom hat and cursed himself for not buying a new hat while he and Mia were out shopping the other day, to replace the one that had gone missing the previous week.

Grabbing Abigail's hat had been a last resort, but it was either that or risk frostbitten ears.

'Planning to take that off, are you? I can taste that free mulled wine already . . .' Josie's teasing was emphasised by the tip of her tongue poking between her white, even teeth and her far-too-blue-too-be-good-for-her lips.

He dropped his hand. 'And I can taste my free beer.'

Josie reached up on tiptoes and tweaked the pompom on his hat. 'Worth it.' She shot him a cheeky grin and shouldered the pub's heavy door open.

'About blimmin' time, my old friend.' Brendon's voice boomed over the bustling crowd. Punters' conversations stopped as they craned their necks to see who'd been so warmly welcomed. 'Nice hat by the way.'

Callan cringed as his cheeks fired up in embarrassment. He

pulled the hat off and pushed it into his coat pocket, all the while wishing he'd not let himself be pushed into coming. He wasn't ready for this. Didn't want the attention. Didn't need it. The pitying stares and kind words that had been piled upon him after Abigail's death had all but turned him into a recluse. An avalanche of benevolence that he'd neither asked for nor wanted. Each nicety adding to the pain in his heart, causing him to keep the people he'd once spent hours with at a distance, using the bakery as a shield. The bakery was a place where he could be polite, but remote when they came in to see how he was, to support him in the one way they could, that he had no control over – by buying his terribly average food and keeping the bakery afloat.

He kept his head dipped and through half-lowered lids scanned the faces before him, searching for signs of sympathy. The panic that had skittered through his veins, threatening to send him bolting back into the night, subsided as he registered genuine warmth from those who knew him. No sign of compassion or condolence in sight, just happiness at seeing a good acquaintance, an old friend.

He lifted his head and met the smiles that greeted him. His heartrate settled into its regular rhythm.

He slid onto a stool at the bar and pulled the one beside him out for Josie, who took it with a nod of thanks.

'It's been too long, Callan.' Brendon reached his hand over the bar and vigorously pumped Callan's hand in greeting. 'First beer is on me. Second too.'

'We're just staying for one.' Callan released the buttons on his coat, shrugged it off and placed it over one of the hooks that ran under the length of the bar. 'I've got to get back to Mia.'

'What Callan's trying to say, Brendon, is that he'd love a beer. It's very generous of you. And I'll have a mulled wine.' Josie fished her bank card from her pocket and held it out to Brendon. 'And don't worry about it being on the house, it's my shout.'

Brendon's gaze moved between the two of them, a smirk appearing on his lips. He said nothing, but his expression showed exactly what he was thinking.

Callan lowered his brows into a glare and briefly shook his head, silently sending the message to Brendon that whatever he thought was going on, was in fact not going on at all. This wasn't a date. Furthest thing from it.

'Margo's forced Josie and I to go out tonight.' He inwardly cringed. Good one. How to make a not-date sound exactly like a date. 'It's her reckoning that Josie here needs to meet some people, and that I'm the one to help her do it.'

'I see.' Brendon's smirk showed no signs of disappearing. 'Pity she wasn't the one to pop in. I have a lot of time for that Margo, I do.'

'And she does you.' Josie pushed in her bank card and entered her pin. 'She mentioned in passing that you were one of life's good men.'

'Did she now?' Brendon passed Josie her wine, then began to pull Callan's beer.

Was it Callan's imagination or had Brendon's chest puffed up a little? And was that a blush blooming on his cheeks? The man looked like a chuffed schoolboy who'd just found out his crush felt the same way.

'We'll have to bring her in for lunch one day.' Josie fingered the stem of the glass of wine Brendon had set in front of her. 'Bring Mia as well. Do you have a kids' menu?'

'I can make one if it means seeing this one come in a bit more.' Brendon nodded in Callan's direction, then passed him the beer. 'There's not much here for kids to play with, but you're more than welcome to bring some toys or colouring-in books. Wouldn't want her getting bored and dragging you all home too soon.'

Callan took a long sip of his beer and used the time to get his thoughts in order. Brendon had a thing for Margo?

And Margo potentially felt the same? And why was tonight feeling like a giant ambush? From one quick drink at the pub, to lunch with Mia, Margo and Josie? It was like the universe wasn't trying to inch him out of hiding so much as drag him, kicking and screaming.

Except he wasn't kicking or screaming. If anything, for the first time in a good while, his shoulders had loosened. He didn't feel like he was holding his breath waiting for something to go wrong. If he didn't know better, he'd say he was almost relaxed.

'Can we take that silence as a yes?' Josie nudged him with her elbow, her eyes shining with what looked like delight, but was probably just a combination of a few sips of wine and the pub's golden-toned lighting.

Callan set his pint glass down. 'I think you can.'

'Excellent.' Josie clapped her hands with enthusiasm, then swung around on her seat so she was facing the crowd. 'So, now that we're here, what do we do?'

Drink the beer and go home. Sooner rather than later. The words were on the tip of Callan's tongue, but he swallowed them. Maybe staying a little longer wouldn't be a bad thing. He eyed the currently unused dart board. Could he still play after all this time? Or would it be an exercise in embarrassment? The old pub champion falling flat on his face as darts landed anywhere but on the board?

'The dart board's free . . .' Josie turned to him, her eyebrows raised in challenge. 'Feel like a game?'

'Do you know how to play?' Callan picked up his pint and got off the stool, his body making the decision before his brain could make its mind up.

Josie grabbed her wine and followed suit. 'Nope. Never played. You'll have to teach me.' She weaved her way through the crowded tables and chairs, then glanced over her shoulder, a cheeky smile on her face. 'Though, really, how hard could it be?'

63

Callan pinched the bridge of his nose and shook his head. What had he gotten himself into?

He set his glass down on a table and made his way to the board, more pockmarked than not after years of use. He plucked the darts down from their stands. The weight of them in his hands familiar yet foreign after not playing for so long.

He turned to see Josie warming up at the line, stretching her arms above her head, while jogging boxer-style on the spot.

'What?' She shot him a quizzical look, her brows drawing together, as she hooked one arm under the other and pulled it across her body. 'I want to be limber. Don't want to seize up.'

'We're playing a friendly game of darts, not running a marathon.' Callan offered up the darts. 'Which colour? Red or green?'

Josie's lips slackened into a mock-pout. 'What? No rainbow ones?'

'If you win, I'll buy you a set for Christmas.'

'You're on. Green, please.'

Callan passed the darts over, then turned to face the board. A competitive surge he'd all but forgotten raced through him, simultaneously centring and energising.

'You know the rules of 501?'

'First to get to 501 wins?' Josie flashed him the thumbs-up.

'Er. No. The opposite. First to get to zero wins, and the last dart must land in the middle on the bullseye, or on a double.'

'A double?' Josie ceased bouncing on the spot and focused her attention on the board. 'What's the double?'

The competitive edge fell away as he realised playing against Josie would be like shooting fish in a barrel. Too easy, and far too cruel.

'The double is the outside ring, but I'm thinking we should start with an easier game, like Around the Clock.' He turned to face the dartboard. 'It's really simple. When it's your turn you get three goes to hit the board. You start at one then, once you've

64

hit it, you move onto the next number, then the next. The first to hit twenty–five and the bullseye wins.'

'I can do that. Easy.'

Callan smiled at the determination in Josie's voice, which was matched by a set jaw and a narrowed gaze.

'Right then, in that case, ladies first.' He stepped out of the way, leaving the line free for Josie.

Squaring her shoulders, she lifted a dart up, pulled her arm back like she was about to throw a baseball, and flung the dart at the board. Her triumphant grin disappeared as it went wide and hit the wood panelling a good half a metre away.

'Nice start.' Callan forced a serious look to his face to hide the smile that threatened. He didn't want Josie to think he was laughing at her. He'd seen enough enthusiastic beginners give up too quickly because people had taken the mickey out of them for not getting the hang of throwing a dart quickly. 'Might I suggest a quick lesson in how to throw a dart?'

'You mean there's another way to throw it? One that doesn't involve chucking it at the board with all your might?' Josie grinned.

'Something like that.' Callan released the smile he'd held back as he positioned himself behind Josie, then paused as he realised he was going to have to touch her. Again. For the second time that day.

Apart from the initial hugs of condolence, he'd not been in close contact of any kind with another woman since Abigail had passed away. Even being careful when passing over change or cakes at the shop to ensure fingertips didn't brush. Logically he knew it was stupid to be so overly zealous, yet part of him felt that closeness of any kind with another woman was a betrayal of Abigail, of the love they shared.

Callan sucked in a reassuring breath. This was not a big deal. He was just showing a colleague how to throw a dart. The only part of them that needed to touch was their fingers as he showed her the correct positioning. Finger touching in the name of sport was not a betrayal. It was just being helpful.

'Right. So . . .' Callan forced himself to move closer to Josie. He caught her warm, inviting, sweet vanilla scent, and resolved to hold his breath as much as possible during the lesson. 'First things first, you don't want to be so tense. Keep things firm, but relaxed.'

'Firm and relaxed.' Josie bounced up and down, shaking out her arms and hands, then stilled. Her attention fixed on the board. 'Pass me a dart. I'm ready.'

He offered the dart to her and she took it. Her fingers pressed so tightly around the barrel as she held it up, her hand was vibrating.

'Hold it as you would a pen.' With tentative hands, he reached up and reorganised Josie's grip, trying to ignore how soft her skin was. How it emanated warmth. How the smallest touch sent a tingling sensation through his own fingers. An unexpected, gentle kind of chemistry.

He shook his head at himself. He was being daft. There was no chemistry, just a strange mix of nerves, beer and concentration.

Josie followed his directions, the joints in her fingers blooming white.

'Still too tight. Relax.' He squeezed her fingers in an awkward massage until the colour returned to her joints. 'Good. Now that you've got your hand positioning sorted, you want to think about your stance. Right foot forward, and put your weight mostly on your front foot, but not too much.'

'Like this?' Josie lined herself up and practised aiming the dart at the board.

'Great, except if you lean any more forward, you're going to find yourself unbalancing and kissing the oak floor.'

Josie's nose shrivelled as she eyed the floor. 'I don't think there'd be enough hot showers or antibacterial creams to make that okay.'

A laugh erupted from Callan, taking them both by surprise.

'No, I think you're right on that.' He touched Josie's forearm and ushered her out of the way. 'Look, it's easy once you get the hang of it. Keep both feet on the floor with your right foot forward. Hold the dart like I showed you. Lean in a little, but not so much that you and the floor become intimate. Aim, keeping it relaxed but firm. Then, release.' The dart flew from his fingers, sailed through the air, and hit the bullseye.

'Wow.' Josie's shoulders slumped. 'I'm not playing with you. You're too good.'

'I just got lucky.' Callan strolled to the board and plucked the dart from it. 'Probably muscle memory. Besides, we're not being serious. It's just for fun. The way I see it, if we stop playing then the only thing to do is finish off our drinks and head home to an annoyed Margo. You're meant to be keeping me out as late as possible, right?' Callan raised an eyebrow, amusement bubbling up as Josie suddenly became fascinated with the floor.

'I figured that would be the case, and I'm not angry about it. In case you were wondering.' Callan picked up the darts and held them out to Josie.

She took the darts then met his gaze. Her eyes filled with a mix of remorse and defiance. 'Were we that obvious?'

Callan placed his hands upon Josie's shoulders and lined her up in front of the board. 'Ridiculously obvious. That and Margo's been trying to get me out of the house for months now.'

Josie brought the dart up, one eye closing as she zeroed in on her target. 'It's only because she cares. It's not good for a person to hide away for too long.'

Embarrassment gripped Callan's heart as he realised he was still touching Josie. He released her shoulders and took a step back.

Josie brought the dart back, ready to throw. 'At least, I don't imagine it would be.'

Callan's ears pricked up at the change in Josie's tone. For one moment she'd sounded like she knew about loss, about grieving. Then she'd shrugged it off, like it was pure speculation rather than experience. But that didn't explain why her knuckles had bloomed white with tension, something he suspected had nothing to do with beginner's nerves.

'Josie, breathe.' The words were slow, low and did their job. 'Keep it firm but relaxed, remember? Then when you're ready, throw.'

Her shoulders hitched up and sank down as her arm pulled back, then pushed forward, releasing the dart in one fluid movement.

He followed its trajectory. Solid. Strong. It flew towards the board. Landed. And held.

'I did it!'

Josie's squeal of delight caught the attention of the crowd, who turned to watch her fist-pumping the air while she jumped up and down, repeating 'I did it' over and over again.

Before Callan knew what was happening Josie had grabbed his hands and swept him into her on-the-spot leaping exuberance.

'You did great.' He gave her hands a squeeze, then made to extract himself, only to find a tangle of arms around his neck, and a soft body pressed against his.

'I did great because of you. That was so fun. What a rush.'

Josie's words were hot against his neck and tickled his skin. The combination stirred something deep down that he'd long forgotten. Wanting. Need. Desire.

Feelings he shouldn't be feeling and had no intention of experiencing again.

He took hold of Josie's forearms and gently put space between them. Then as quickly as he'd taken hold of her, he dropped his hands and folded his arms across his chest. A barrier to further excitable advances.

Josie's mouth formed an 'o' as her cheeks flushed a deep shade of pink.

'That was inappropriate of me. I'm so sorry.' The words

68

tumbled from her mouth as she picked up her jacket that was draped over a stool, grabbed her hat from its pocket and shoved it on top of her head. 'I had no place hugging you like that. I was excited. That's all. It meant nothing. I promise. And, well, we should probably go, before my actions start the village rumour mill going.'

Callan went to take her hand before she ran for the front door, but he stopped himself. Touching her was a very bad idea. Not only would it make Josie more uncomfortable, he feared it could reignite the confusing emotions that had flooded through him.

'Josie, take your hat off and look at the board.' He twisted around to the bemused audience. 'And you lot get back to whatever you were doing. There's nothing to see here.'

When he returned his attention to Josie, he saw her mouth had relaxed. The colour in her face was no longer so vibrant.

'The dart fell out.' She shook her head and face-palmed herself. 'All that hubbub for nothing.'

'Not for nothing. You hit the board. That's a big deal. Especially on your second go. Maybe give it a little more oomph next time.' Callan plucked the hat from Josie's head and put it back on the stool. 'We've a game to finish. Well, technically, begin. Which means one of us has to get things started.'

* * *

Josie sipped her water and thanked herself for remembering to switch out the wine after the third glass. Baking and serving and being perky for a whole day after a night on the drink? Never a fun time. Satisfaction warmed her heart as she took in the table of people who'd joined her and Callan after their game of darts. If you could call it a game. A trouncing would've been a better description. It had become increasingly clear that darts was not her thing. She'd managed to get to two on the 'clock', whereas

Callan had sped around the board. Nailing every number like a pro. *Nearly* every number. She had the distinct feeling his couple of misses had been purposeful. A small kindness she was grateful for.

She'd been saved going again by an acquaintance of Callan's stepping up and challenging him to a proper game. He'd been nice enough to turn him down, saying he didn't want to abandon Josie, but she'd quickly told him she was fine and that she'd be happy enough at the bar talking to Brendon.

Before long a group of men had surrounded the dart board, with Callan winning each of the games with ease. Friendships were renewed, more beer was served, and next thing she knew she'd been pulled down to a table filled with locals, a glass of ruby liquid in front of her, and conversation flying across the table ranging from family news to sports to the weather, and everything in between.

'Will you be entering the Christmas Cake-off competition, then?' Lauren, the wife of Will, one of Callan's friends, propped her chin in her hand and drummed her fingers on her cheek. 'It's a big deal, you know. Fiercely competitive. We had twenty entries last year. Probably will have more this year now that—'

Lauren halted mid-sentence, her happy demeanour morphing into that of a woman who looked like she might be sick at any moment.

The table fell silent, and Josie got the feeling some line had been crossed.

She turned her attention to Callan. His gaze was fixed on the foamy head of his beer, his shoulders bunched around his ears.

Click. Callan's wife, Abigail, had been the local baker. There was every chance she would have been the reigning champ. But now she was gone, leaving space for someone new to take the crown.

Josie shot Lauren a sympathetic smile. She seemed like a good person, and Josie didn't believe the conversation came from a place of malice. There was no reason why her faux pas should put a stop to what had been a fun evening so far.

'A cake baking competition, you say? I guess I could take a shot. What kind of cakes are they looking for? Are there rules? Am I allowed to enter as an outsider?'

The tension surrounding the table eased, though didn't wholly disappear.

'If you live around these parts you can enter.' Callan looked up from his beer, his shoulders inched down. 'The kind of cake you make is up to you, but it has to be Christmas-themed.'

'Of course it does.' Josie rolled her eyes at Callan.

The corners of his lips lifted in a small smile and a twinkle appeared in his eye.

'Sorry. Those are the rules.' He shrugged in a 'what can you do?' manner.

An idea bubbled up in Josie's mind. A way to completely erase the strain that still hovered around the table. 'Has anyone ever done a roast turkey cake before?'

'A cake made with turkey? Sounds revolting.' Will blew out his cheeks like he was about to vomit.

'Not an actual meat cake.' Josie grinned, glad to see the conversation topic had the desired effect. 'But a cake that's made to look like another thing. You know, kind of like how on those cooking shows on television they'll have a challenge where you bake something that looks nothing like baking. So a hamburger cake. Or a burrito cake.'

Will continued to fake-sick up, while Lauren laughed, and the rest of the table looked confused.

'You could try it, I guess. Maybe add some cake roast potatoes around the edge, and chocolate icing as gravy.' Lauren grimaced as she shook her head. 'Can't see the judges going for it, though. They're pretty traditional.'

'Some traditions were made to be broken.' Josie raised her brows.

71

Lauren shook her head in return. 'Not this one.'

'Yeah,' Josie sighed. 'Not this one. I'll just have to get my thinking cap on and figure out something amazing to bake. Speaking of . . .' She covered her mouth as a yawn escaped. 'I have a job to do and I'd hate to be late tomorrow. The boss would be all sorts of grumpy.'

Callan tutted, then scraped his chair back and stood. 'Wouldn't want a grumpy boss. I heard he's a tyrant.' He turned his attention to the group sitting around the table. 'It was good to catch up. Thanks.'

'Don't leave it so long next time.' Will raised his pint. 'In fact, I expect to see you here next week. If not before. We need our best player back. We've been on a losing streak since you've been away.'

Callan wrapped his scarf around his neck, then reached out and shook Will's hand. 'You're on.'

Josie tamped down the excitement that rushed through her at seeing Callan commit to playing darts once more. If he saw how happy she was about him coming out of his self-imposed shell, he could well scuttle back in there again. Holding her joy in wasn't an option, so she settled for the next best thing and pulled her mobile from her pocket.

Job done.

She hit send, and the phone vibrated seconds later with a message from Margo.

Job just beginning.

Of course it was. One small step didn't make an entire journey.

Josie had seen her father take cautious steps, at her insistence, towards embracing their new life after her mother left, only to retreat time and time again. Not only backing away from his friends, the things he loved doing, but withdrawing from her, becoming an emotionless guardian rather than a loving, engaged father. Their weekly trip to the cinema lost to sudden 'headaches'. Plans to go on holiday put on hold due to 'urgent work'. Josie had believed his excuses at first, but the older she got the more obvious the truth became. Her father wanted nothing to do with her, with anyone. He just wanted his wife back. His old life back. Nothing else, no one else, would ever be good enough. Including her.

Josie shoved the mobile back into her pocket and waved to the group, then to Brendon, before following Callan out into the frigid night air. She focused on her feet as they traipsed up the road, not wanting Callan to see the emotion that had surfaced, that blurred her vision. She swallowed hard, pushed away the pain.

'Never. Gets. Easier.' Callan puffed the words out in time to his steps as they tackled the lane's incline.

'Well, that's life, isn't it?' Josie exhaled extra hard as she realised he was talking about the slope, not pain, or grief, or life. 'I mean, if you don't exercise or push yourself a little harder every time you walk up this road, then it's never going to get easier, is it?' She gritted her teeth into a smile and met Callan's narrowed gaze.

No way did he believe she was talking about walking up the slope. And no way was she opening up to a man she barely knew. It was one thing to be honest about her feelings surrounding Christmas, but it was another to explain the family dynamics that had led her to those feelings. That had led her to keeping people at an arm's length. Friendly, polite, even warm at times – but never so close that she could hurt anyone when she left. That she could be hurt if they left.

'If that's your way of trying to get me to join an exercise class or a social jogging group, you're out of luck. You and Margo can conspire all you like to make me more active in the community, but running after a 4-year-old is exercise enough. I'll stick to darts at the pub.'

He was letting her off the hook. Keeping things easy. If she hadn't already hugged him once that night, Josie would have done it again.

73

Except she wouldn't. Couldn't.

Not when microscopic butterflies had soared through her veins the moment their bodies had pressed together back at the pub, invading her heart with tiny wings that beat a billion times a second.

An unexpected reaction from her body, and not an unpleasant one. But one she knew she had to ignore.

'Well, here's home.' Callan stopped outside the bakery and pulled out his keys. 'Better get inside before I turn into a pumpkin.' He went to insert the key in the lock, then paused, the key hovering in the air. 'I should probably walk you home. Sorry, so rude of me. It's been a long time since I've done this.'

Josie shrugged, and tried not to think about how he'd just made it sound like they'd gone out on a date, which they most certainly hadn't. Falling for the boss? Bad idea. Falling for someone you'd only end up leaving? Worse idea.

'You're fine. You go in. Relieve Margo from her babysitting duties. I can look after myself, which means I can walk myself home. I get the feeling it's pretty safe around these parts.'

Callan's eyes glittered, every bit as bright as the stars above. 'Are you sure? If anything happened to you I'd feel terrible.'

'Nothing will. Thank you for a good night.'

'No, thank you. I had fun. The most I've had in a long time.'

Callan moved forward, his hand reaching towards her hip, his head angling as if he were about to kiss her goodnight on the cheek, then jerked back, shaking his head and blinking.

'Right, well, night.' He turned his back on her and in seconds was gone. The only proof he'd been standing so close was the lingering scent of his musky, warm aftershave.

Josie sighed and began the trek to her cottage, torn between wondering what a kiss on the cheek from Callan would have felt like, and grateful he'd had second thoughts. That he must have realised any touch, no matter how innocent, would be a bad idea.

For both of them.

Callan was out of bounds. Josie had her own boundaries. And no amount of curiosity was worth risking what could happen if those lines were crossed.

Chapter 8

'Too. Much. Wine.' Lauren lowered her head onto the table and moaned. 'Why didn't you stop me, Josie? We're meant to be friends.'

Josie laughed as she placed a pot of tea and a cup and saucer in front of a groaning Lauren. 'We've known each other for all of five days. That hardly puts me in a position where I can tell you when you've had enough.'

Lauren pressed her hands together in a plea. 'Then promise me next time we're at the pub together that you'll make me drink water, and that when I think another glass of wine along with a shot of tequila is a great idea, you'll remind me that I hate having my head feel like someone is sawing their way through my soft matter with the world's tiniest and bluntest knife.'

Josie thrust her tongue out at the description. 'Gross. But okay. I promise I'll try to stop you, but if you don't listen it's not my fault.'

'You're on.' Lauren poured her tea, then shovelled three spoonfuls of sugar into it. 'It was good to see Callan down at the pub again. Twice in one week. You must be really good for him.'

'Good for him?' Josie crossed her arms over her chest, as discomfort squirmed in her stomach.

'Yeah, you two seem to really like each other, and it's great to see Callan smile again. It had been too long. Will and I had begun to wonder if he ever would again.'

Is that what the word was down at the pub? That she and Callan were potentially an item? The discomfort in her gut made its way into her heart, hitting the accelerate pedal en route.

'You've got it wrong.' Josie had to shut the gossip down. Now. If Callan got wind of it, he'd never leave the house again. 'We do like each other, I guess. But only as friends. That's all. Not even that, really. He's just been spending time with me at Margo's insistence.'

'Do I hear my name being taken in vain?'

Josie spun round to see Margo at the entrance to the shop with a pleased smile on her face and a sprig of mistletoe tied with string in one hand.

'Margo. You scared the heck out of me. We really need to put a bell or a chime of some sort on that door.' Josie shook her head. 'I'm lucky hearts can't burst out of chests, because if they did mine would be on the floor right now.'

Lauren shuddered. 'Who's being gross now? Can we not be so visual when my stomach is in full lurch mode?'

'Too much fun at the pub last night?' Margo raised a manicured brow.

'Way too much. 'Tis the season, and all that.' Lauren pulled a seat out for her. 'I was just telling Josie here how much we're enjoying seeing her and Callan at the pub. How good she is for him.'

Margo slipped into the offered seat and presented the mistletoe to Josie. 'There you go, dear. If you could hang that from the ceiling you'll be saving me a job. Then after you've done that, I'd love a slice of that carrot cake, and a pot of tea, too.' She leaned forward and addressed Lauren in a conspiratorial manner. 'Have you tried Josie's carrot cake? Divine. So moist. And I'm not sure what she does with her cream cheese icing, but it's unlike any I've tried before. I've half-convinced myself it's healthy.'

Josie set the mistletoe on the counter. 'You can have the cake,

77

but there's no way I'm hanging this up. Seeing random people being forced to kiss? Not my cup of tea.'

'Oh, but you've no choice, Josie.' Lauren gave a little snort. 'It's tradition. All the shops do it. You wouldn't believe how many couples have formed because of it. Mum reckons I would never have existed if it weren't for the mistletoe. She kissed Dad in the tinned fruit and veg aisle at the shop, and the rest is history.'

'Is it how you and Will got together?' Josie grabbed a chair and dragged it to the spot under the ceiling where a random hook was screwed in. 'And I guess I know why this is here. I've been wondering.'

'It was one of Abigail's favourite traditions. Although I don't think there was a Christmas tradition she didn't like. This was her favourite time of the year.' A fond smile tilted Margo's lips. 'And yes, that's why the hook's there. Pop her up, and watch the magic happen.'

'I can't believe I'm doing this,' muttered Josie as she gave the chair a shake to make sure it was steady before climbing up. 'Please tell me that's the last of the traditions. This. The cake-making competition. That's it.'

'Hardly. The lighting of the Christmas tree is tomorrow tonight, which you must come to. I insist. It's a huge village event. Everyone will be there.'

Josie went to beg off going but was interrupted by an excitable Mia.

'Josie! Josie! Josie!'

Josie struggled to keep her balance as little arms wrapped around her legs in a vice-like cuddle, sending her askew. She pinwheeled her arms and leaned forward in an attempt to regain balance.

'Mia, let go of Josie before she falls over.'

Callan's curt tone as he rushed towards the pair sent Mia running from the room, her eyes wide and brimming with tears.

Too late. The words raced through Josie's mind as she felt the chair skitter out from beneath her as one leg fell back, the other flying up. *This is going to hurt.*

She braced herself, ready for the pain. Ready to brush it off like it was no big deal. Ready to give Mia a cuddle, to assure her that she wasn't angry and that she loved getting Mia cuddles.

Except no hard floor rushed to meet her bum. No elbows drove into timber. No bolts of pain raced through her body. Instead she found herself hanging in mid-air, two strong arms, that most definitely did not belong to her, holding her tight – one hooked under her knees, the other curved around her back.

'It's all right. I've got you.' Callan's voice was low and calm, the opposite of her racing heart.

Racing due to being oh-so-close to a painful accident, or because she was pressed up against a firm chest that smelled deliciously manly? A mix of both, Josie decided.

'Look at you being a regular knight in shining armour.' Margo clapped her hands. 'I'm impressed. Those are some excellent reflexes you've got, Callan.'

'Just got lucky.' Callan's cheeks pinked up as he set her down. 'You okay? You look a little dazed.'

Josie scrambled for an answer that didn't involve telling Callan how good he smelled . . . and felt. 'Just a touch shocked, to be honest. I thought I'd come a cropper, was waiting for a world of pain, and then . . . there was none. Thank you.'

Callan shrugged. 'It's no big deal. I'm sure you'd have done the same for me.'

'Had I tried, we'd both have ended up on the floor.' Josie became aware that his arm was still around her, the palm of his hand resting on the curve of her waist. 'So, yeah. I'll get back to it, shall I?'

She made to move away but was stopped by a hail of 'no, you don't', 'uh-uh', 'stay right there', from Margo and Lauren.

Josie twisted around to give them her most growly 'what are you on?' glare, but stopped as Callan's head tipped back and an exasperated groan left his lips.

'You have got to be joking me.' His eyes closed for a long few seconds, then opened in a glare that zeroed in on the two women who were barely able to contain their laughter. 'I'm the owner of this establishment and this is not going to happen.'

'Rules are rules, Callan.' Margo wagged a finger at him. 'You know that. And they won't be broken.'

Josie looked up to see what Callan was seeing. Her stomach plummeted. No wonder he was looking more than a little murderous. In saving her he'd ended up under the mistletoe. With her. Holding her. And now he was going to have to . . .

Callan's head was moving back and forth so furiously it was in danger of becoming unhinged and flying off. 'I can't kiss an employee. It would be highly unprofessional.'

'Only if it meant something,' Margo slung back. 'If it doesn't mean anything, what's there to be concerned about?'

An unimpressed 'ugh' came from Callan. 'If I could go back in time and convince whoever it was that this tradition was a very bad idea, I would. I'm so sorry, Josie.'

Until this moment Josie had believed that the concept of knees knocking together was just that – a concept. Yet here hers were, shaking like two saplings in a storm. Not because she wanted to kiss Callan. Not because she was nervous. But because it was just so . . . *wrong*. Kissing a recently widowed father of one who also happened to be her boss, and a hot one at that?

All of it was totally, utterly, embarrassingly, ridiculously, all the adverbs in the world, unacceptable.

'Do we have to? I mean, what's a broken tradition?' She gritted her teeth and hoped for a reprieve.

'Bad luck.' Lauren's tone turned serious. 'That's what happens if you don't follow the tradition. The last person who chose not to kiss under the mistletoe never found love. Ever. Do you want that to happen to you, Josie? Spend the rest of your life alone, miserable, without someone to keep you warm at night?'

'Sounds pretty much how I spend my life now.' Josie forced

a laugh, hoping it would release the tightness in her stomach. 'Minus the miserable bit, of course.'

'Well, imagine the life you live with an added dose of miserableness, because that's what's going to happen if you don't kiss. So . . .' Lauren leaned forward in her chair and flapped her hands in their direction, egging Callan and Josie on. 'Sooner it's done, sooner you don't have to think about it.'

Josie turned to Callan. 'Let's just get it over and done with, hey?'

'Let's. So, um, on the count of three?'

'Mature way to do it.' Josie rolled her eyes, then nodded. 'On three. Lauren? Can you count us in?'

Lauren flashed her a thumbs-up. 'One.'

Callan craned his neck forward.

Josie stood on tiptoes in order to meet Callan halfway and found herself staring at his lips.

Full on top, but not too full. A little pouty in the middle of the bottom lip. And there wasn't a whisker around them. Just how she preferred a man's upper lip and chin to look.

'Two.'

Was it her imagination or was Lauren spending far too much time between numbers. Her throat, constricting more and more with every passing second, was in danger of cutting off air to her brain, especially with those nice lips of Callan's now puckering out as far as they could go.

Josie did the same, hoping the less lip area that connected the less odd things would be between them post-kiss. She closed her eyes and forced herself not to screech 'hurry up' at Lauren.

'Three.'

She bounced up on her toes a little more as Callan's lips crashed down upon hers.

'Ow!' She took a step back, her hand cupping her lips. She ran her tongue over her teeth to make sure they were still in the right place.

'Josie? Are you all right? I'm so sorry.' Callan took a step towards her, his hand reaching for her. Concern was etched upon his face.

She waved him away. 'I'm fine. Really. Probably shouldn't have closed my eyes at the end there. Or tried to take the lead, or meet you in the middle, or . . . whatever it was we just tried to do.' She clapped her hand more firmly over her mouth, as much to stop herself chattering away as to put pressure on her throbbing lips.

She whirled around to see Margo and Lauren staring at them, mouths gaping and brows quirked.

'Are you happy now? We've kissed. Avoided bad luck. If you don't count our lips ramming into each other hard enough to hurt our teeth. Or my teeth. Callan, how are your teeth?'

'My teeth are fine. Lips still in shock. Humiliation levels are high.' He reached up and plucked a berry from the heavily laden mistletoe. 'One kiss down. Could you have found a bunch with a few less berries, Margo?'

Margo's cheeks flushed pink. 'The more the merrier.'

'Well, not for me. I'll be avoiding that spot for the rest of the month.' Callan picked up the chair that Josie had sent flying earlier and pushed it up against a table.

'That makes two of us.' Josie crossed her arms and wilted against the counter. The adrenaline that had her blood racing, her heart pumping and every sense on high alert, had abated, leaving her nothing but tired. And strangely relieved.

She'd been far too aware of Callan's touches. What few they'd shared. The way his hand had felt strong and sure while helping her learn to play darts. The tingling thrill that had rushed through her when they'd hugged. How she'd hated the way he'd dropped his arm that had caught her just now.

For a split-second she'd dared to wonder if she was falling for her boss, just a little. Post-mistletoe-kiss she knew she had nothing to worry about. There was no spark, no chemistry, no anything. Anything she thought she'd felt before had been imagined, simple as that.

Speaking of no anything . . . 'Where's Mia?' Josie hadn't seen her since her hug had sent her flying off the stool and Mia running from her father's sharp words. 'Mia?'

She rounded the door that led to the kitchen and caught sight of two small feet – shod in bright pink and baby blue canvas shoes with cartoon princesses printed on the sides – poking out from beneath the spare aprons that hung from a hook on the wall.

Poor thing must've thought she was in trouble. Josie's heart squeezed tight for the wee girl. She had the feeling Callan wasn't one to use sharp tones on her that often, so to hear them would have given her a huge fright.

'Oh, no. There's no Mia here.' Josie projected her voice so it would penetrate the thick material surrounding Mia's ears. 'I was so hoping she'd be here. I need help decorating some cupcakes and I really need her thoughts on the matter. Do I add sprinkles or silver balls? Top them with a sweet? But if so, what kind? Jelly babies or pear drops? Wine gums or chocolate buttons? And what colour should I make the icing? I was thinking blue might be good. Better than silly old pink . . .'

A muffled giggle erupted from behind the pinnies.

'Did I just hear a Mia? Surely not?' Josie took a step towards the giggles. 'I can't see her . . .' Another step. 'Has she become invisible? Does she have a superpower?' She crouched down so she was at Mia's height. 'Which leads to the very important question . . . Does a super-powered invisible girl feel tickles?'

She reached around the aprons and, with wiggling fingers, tickled Mia's waist, until she folded forward and emerged from her cotton-cave, her eyes glistening with unshed happy tears, her cheeks red from laughing so much.

'Stop, Josie. Stop.' Each word punctuated with another breathless, high-pitched giggle.

Josie dropped her hands from Mia's waist then opened her arms out for a hug. 'I'm sorry you were scared before. I'm fine. You didn't hurt me. And I love that you wanted to give me a cuddle. You made me feel very special.'

Mia took a cautious step towards her, then another, then flew into her arms and snuggled close, burying her face in Josie's shoulder.

Josie stroked Mia's hair and rocked her back and forth, soothing any remnants of upset. A silent promise that she meant what she said. And she did. She wasn't angry. She did love that Mia wanted to cuddle her. And Mia had made her feel very, very special. For the first time in far too long.

She closed her eyes as a memory rose from a time long ago. A time when laughter had rung through the house, where tinsel had been hung from every bough of a Christmas tree. Where carols were sung. Hands were held. Love was abundant.

Her family of three might have been small, but to her, they'd been perfect.

Until they weren't.

She held Mia a little tighter. The wee poppet had been through so much, and yet she was still so full of fun, delight, laughter and love. Josie hoped she'd stay that way, that nothing more would happen that could threaten to stamp out Mia's light.

And it wouldn't. Not on Josie's watch. Josie wouldn't let Callan retreat into himself. Would encourage him to see the good things in life. To want to be part of his community once again. No backwards steps. No anger from being left behind that morphed into never-ending sadness. No becoming like her father.

'No blue icing.'

The words were hot and insistent against Josie's ear.

Josie released Mia, folded her arms and tapped her chin. 'Not blue? Are you sure?'

Mia shook her head, her eyes serious. 'Pink.'

'What about pink and white swirled, like a candy cane? Maybe with crushed candy canes sprinkled on top?'

A furious bobbing of head followed, and Josie had her answer.

'Sounds fancy. Are they for the shop?'

Josie twisted around and looked up to see a no longer red-faced

84

Callan leaning against the doorway, hands in pockets, one ankle hooked over the other.

Definitely handsome. And she was most definitely not interested. The awkward mistletoe kiss had proven that, well and truly, once and for all. The fizzy feeling that bubbled up in her body on seeing him was just . . . appreciation of an excellent combination of genetics. That was it. At least, that was what she was going to tell herself. On repeat.

'They are, although . . .' The cogs in Josie's brain turned as another way of infusing Callan and the bakery back into the community began to form. 'Margo has insisted I go to the lighting of the Christmas tree, so maybe instead of selling them in the shop I could give them out to the villagers during the event? A bit of promotion for the shop, and a nice gesture of seasonal goodwill. But only if you think it's a good idea.'

'I think it's a wonderful idea. It'd be nice to give back to the community after the support they've given us. Given me. Thanks, Josie.' Callan squatted down as Mia came towards him. 'Sorry about before, my sweetness. Daddy got a fright.'

Mia shoehorned herself between Callan's thighs, threw one arm around his neck and held her other hand up index finger pointed straight at Callan. 'I didn't like it, Daddy. I was just being nice to Josie.'

'You were.' He kissed her forehead and looked up at Josie. 'Will you need a hand with the cupcakes? We could help you give them out?'

'Does that mean Josie's going to come with us?'

'Of course, if she wants to, that is.'

Mia turned a pair of large, pleading eyes to Josie.

How could she say no? The answer was simple. She couldn't.

'It sounds like an excellent plan. But first, we need to decorate the cupcakes. Mia? You in?'

Mia abandoned her father like he was yesterday's news and ran to Josie, her hand raised, palm facing forward.

They high-fived, then Josie pulled a stool over to the bench for Mia, grabbed an apron, and tucked it up and tied it so Mia wouldn't get in a tangle and trip over. She lifted Mia onto the stool and began measuring out the icing sugar for the vanilla buttercream icing.

A warm arm wrapped around her neck, before a soft kiss pressed against her cheek.

'You're my best friend, Josie.'

Could a heart simultaneously grow and break?

Josie had a feeling she was in danger of finding out.

Chapter 9

Callan kept an eye on Mia as she stood at the edge of the crowd watching the choir sing, while a duo of fire artists twirling flaming batons performed on either side. He'd cautioned her against getting too close, but every time the flames went within ten metres of her his heart leaped into his throat.

'She's going to be fine.' Josie nudged him as she rearranged the selection of Christmas cupcakes she'd created.

The peppermint swirl cupcakes had ended up sparking a small selection of bite-sized Christmassy treats. The Grinch cupcakes, complete with Smarties eyes, liquorice eyebrows and a jaunty red and white icing Santa hat had been swooped up by the local children, while the adults had feasted on vanilla cupcakes topped with an eggnog buttercream, gingerbread cupcakes complete with a miniature gingerbread man on top, and chocolate Christmas tree cupcakes heavily laden with 'Christmas lights', also known as colourful sprinkles, thanks to Mia's enthusiastic hand.

'What makes you so sure?' He turned to Josie, who was in the middle of handing a cupcake to a harried-looking mother. Her smile was genuine, her eyes luminous, in part due to the fairy lights that were strung around town, but mostly because she was radiating happiness. Joy, even.

For someone who wasn't huge on Christmas, she sure seemed to enjoy the Sunnycombe festive season. He'd even caught her humming along to 'We Wish You a Merry Christmas'.

Josie pointed towards the crowd. 'Look who's behind her.'

Surely enough Margo was to the left of Mia, one hand hovering over Mia's shoulder, ready to grab her should she bound forward.

Callan shook his head, embarrassed at his overprotectiveness. 'Will I ever stop worrying about her? Is that just what fathers do? Is that how your father is with you?'

Josie glanced down, but not before he noticed a shadow darkening her expression. A fleeting sadness that haunted her eyes, then was gone in a blink.

'I'm sorry, Josie. I didn't mean to pry.' He grabbed an eggnog cupcake and held it out to her. 'Cupcake? I hear they're delicious. Much better than I could make.'

Josie took it from him, a hint of a smile tugging at the corners of her lips. 'People have been actually saying that? To your face?'

'Actually. Truly. Honestly. My ego is not dealing well with the news.'

'Poor ego.' Josie bit into the cupcake, then set it down on the trestle table. 'I'm sure it'll survive.'

'I'm sure it will.' Callan grinned as he noted the blob of icing on the tip of her nose. 'You've got . . .' He thumbed his own nose.

'Do I? Messy eater.' She rolled her eyes.

Before he knew what he was doing, before he could stop himself, Callan reached out and ran his finger over the blob, ridding it from her nose, then popped his finger in his mouth and licked off the icing.

He closed his eyes and thanked the organisers of the event for insisting on lighting the village's Christmas tree in the evening, because the dimness of the night hid the heat rushing to his cheeks. Here he was, glad that yesterday's forced kiss hadn't made things awkward between them. That they'd gotten on with things afterwards like it was no big deal. And now he'd just re-fanned the awkward flames by behaving in the most ridiculous manner.

'Did you just lick my nose icing?' A fine line appeared between Josie's eyebrows as her head angled to the right. Amusement was written all over her face. 'Cat got your tongue? Or has the icing stuck your tongue to the roof of your mouth?'

Josie's gentle teasing, combined with the cute way the tip of her tongue peeked between her soft pink lips, something he'd not been able to get out of his mind since their kiss-fail, saw any attempts to formulate a reply fail.

How could he explain away doing something so extraordinarily stupid in a way that didn't make you look even more daft than you already felt?

He turned his attention to the last of the cupcakes on the stands before them, hoping they'd provide the answer his brain was refusing to give.

A blurry, white blob entered his field of vision. Something cool, wet and sticky smushed into his nose. Before he could give a 'hey' of surprise, a finger swiped his nose and the blob was gone.

'Delicious. No wonder you were tempted.'

He gaped at Josie who was licking her finger clean, her eyes half-closed in appreciation.

'I can't believe you did that.' Callan didn't know where to look. What to do. He'd never met a person so fearless. Or kind. Because that was what Josie was. *Who* she was.

Kind.

She could have left Mia to hide behind the aprons. Instead, she'd not only helped her feel better, she'd included both of them in her plans to show customers their appreciation. And just now she could have let him wallow in his embarrassment, instead she'd swooped in and saved him.

When Josie had walked into the shop she'd just been another person, someone to help him out while he dealt with the Christmas rush. Now? It was too soon to say it, but deep down he knew it . . . Josie was becoming special to him. Not yet a friend, but somehow more than a friend. He didn't want to put a name on his feelings for her. Wasn't ready to. But he was grateful she'd entered their lives.

'What?' Josie's eyes widened. 'You started it. What else was I meant to do?'

Callan shrugged. 'Call me a weirdo and send me marching?'

Josie laughed. 'Not likely. Besides my father taught me nothing good came from name-calling.'

Her father. Not her mother? Surprising. The general rules of politeness had always been enforced by Abigail, with him as back-up if needed. Did that mean Josie's mother hadn't been around? Was that why she was so good to Mia? She felt for her because she knew what it was like to grow up without a mother?

Callan handed out the last cupcake. 'Teaching manners. It's something I never really thought about doing until after Abigail. From what I've gathered from the online parenting forums, it's usually the mum's job. Whether they like it or not.' He kept his tone neutral, not wanting to sound like he was prying.

Josie shrugged as she set the cake stands to one side, pulled the tablecloth off and began to fold it into a neat square. 'You're doing a really good job. You can only do your best, and I like to think that's what my dad did right after Mum left. His best.' She mustered a smile that didn't even begin to touch her eyes. 'Right, so now that we've been cleaned out, shall we join Mia? It must be nearly time to light the tree?'

Callan pulled out his mobile and checked the time. 'Twenty more minutes. That means twenty more minutes of warbling from the carollers. Do you think you can handle it? If you want to escape you can use putting the trays and tablecloth back in the shop as an excuse to leave. I won't hold it against you.'

As if to prove his point, the carollers broke into a rousing, and slightly off-key, rendition of 'The Twelve Days of Christmas'.

'I'm not leaving you out here to deal with this all alone. Moral support. That's what we anti-Christmas types need to provide for each other if we're going to get through it.' Josie offered her arm to Callan. 'You with me?'

Callan slipped his arm through hers, amused by her old-fashioned gesture. Touched that she took his rediscovered aversion to the season so seriously. Surprised at how glad he was that Josie didn't take him up on his offer to bow out.

'I'm with you.'

* * *

Josie led Callan through the crowd, amazed at the sights before her. Santa hats topped heads, tinsel was used as scarves and she'd never seen so many ugly Christmas sweaters in her life.

She didn't hate it.

And that confused her.

Was her dislike of Christmas truly hers? Or was she holding on to it because her father had declared it a no-go zone. A harsh reminder of the woman who'd left them. Who'd made the day so very special. So unique. Creating traditions that no other family had. Weaving her effervescence through the season, which made the day and the weeks leading up to it so stark, so hollow when she left.

'Ho ho ho!' A gent wheeling by on a unicycle tapped his reindeer-eared hat at them. 'Merry Christmas.'

'Merry Christmas,' she called to his disappearing back before turning her attention back to Callan. 'This place is mad. I think it's getting to me. In a good way.'

'It really is mad. And I absolutely understand how it gets under your skin.' Callan slipped his arm out from hers as Mia and Margo came into view.

Was he embarrassed to be seen being friendly with her? Josie ignored the thought. Refused to entertain the hint of hurt that had risen. Callan probably didn't want to confuse Mia, or have to explain that you could link arms with a friend and that it didn't mean you were about to get married.

91

'Mia! Have you got a hot chocolate?' Josie abandoned Callan's side and ran the last few steps to Mia, kneeling down to check out her drink. 'Wow, how many marshmallows are in there? One? Two? Three? Four? Four marshmallows! Aren't you lucky?'

'Very lucky.' Mia took a long sip then looked up with a grin, a foamy moustache on her upper lip. 'Yummy.' She smacked her lips for emphasis.

'You are.' Josie reached out and tickled Mia.

'Not too much.' Margo admonished her. 'She's had so many treats, too much tickling's likely to bring them all up.'

'And who's to blame for giving her all the treats?' Callan dropped down beside Mia and wiped her milk-moustache away with his handkerchief.

Margo made a show of checking her wristwatch. 'Would you look at the time? Must dash. This tree isn't going to light itself.'

In a blink Margo was gone. Josie stood and followed her movements as she weaved her way towards the main stage in the small village square, beside which a massive tree towered above those who'd come to celebrate.

'Margo's the village's Christmas Spirit.' Callan hoisted Mia up so she could get a better view. 'She's in charge of the festivities, which means she has to ensure the village Christmas traditions are adhered to. She even takes it upon herself to deliver gifts and spend time with those who don't have anyone else on Christmas Day.'

Josie suspected Margo threw herself into the season as much as she did because she was lonely without her own family around her. She made a mental note to buy Margo a Christmas gift and to invite her around on Christmas Day for dinner, once Margo had finished her visiting. It was the least she could do for the woman who hadn't just accepted her arrival in Sunnycombe, but embraced it. Embraced her.

An uneasy mix of happiness and discomfort battled for supremacy. What was she doing spending time with the locals? Allowing them into her life? And just now, when she'd revealed

92

to Callan that her mother had left her and her father? That was a first. Just as buying a Christmas gift and inviting someone round to celebrate the day was.

This was dangerous territory, and the sensible side of her was begging her to back off, to back away. But for the first time ever, she was tempted to navigate this new path. To see where it led.

A light tapping of finger on microphone echoed over the crowd, silencing them.

Margo stood on the stage wearing a Santa hat covered in red sequins that glinted and gleamed in the fairy lights. A tumble of tinsel was draped over her shoulders and round her neck, and she'd donned a pair of glittery silver wings that shimmered with every movement she made. She was every inch the Christmas Spirit, and Josie promised herself she wouldn't run from her plans to invite Margo to Christmas dinner.

Margo's smile broadened as she looked over those who'd gathered. 'Welcome all to the annual Sunnycombe Lighting of the Christmas Tree. Have you all had a good night?'

The crowd whooped and hollered their approval.

'Are you ready to get your cheer on?'

The crowd roared again.

'In that case . . . hit it!' Margo pointed a finger at the band who struck up a jazzy performance of 'O Christmas Tree'.

To Josie's left a couple began to dance, spinning and whirling, which set off other couples around her. Meanwhile those who chose not to dance began to sing, bellowing out the words to the song.

'I'll say it again . . . This is madness.' *Wonderful, beautiful madness.*

She turned to Callan to see him standing still and ignoring an excitable Mia, who was shaking his hand, encouraging him to dance.

She flashed back to a similar scene. A girl, older than Mia, but still in love with Christmas, begging her father to sing along with carollers who'd come to their door. Her heart breaking when he shut the door in their faces, abandoning her in favour of watching something boring on the television.

History would not be repeated.

She took hold of one of Mia's hands and began swishing it back and forth in time with the music. Callan made to back away. Josie caught his hand before he could and drew him into their circle.

'Uh-uh. We're sticking together, remember?' She raised her brows and threw him a look of mock-disapproval.

With a laugh, he slipped his hand into Mia's outstretched one and the three began spinning around faster and faster until the world around them was a blur.

She should have broken her hold right then and there. Begged off with some excuse. Headache. Tiredness. An unsettled tummy from sampling too much of her baking that day. Left the two of them to make a beautiful memory together. Instead she followed Callan's example and tipped her head back to the shining stars and let the music envelop her, lead her, weave its cheery magic.

With great gusto, Margo bellowed the final line into the microphone, joined by the rest of the people in the square, and the song finished.

Josie waited for Callan to drop her hand. Instead he held fast as they puffed and panted and tried to get their breath back. He didn't let go even when the Christmas tree's lights were switched on and the rest of the town broke out into a raucous round of applause that had them stamping their feet and clapping their hands above their head.

Callan's eyes locked on Josie. A mixture of emotions she couldn't put her finger on raced through his eyes in those seconds. Surprise. Confusion. Happiness. And what looked like desire, but surely was not.

Except maybe it was, because in that moment as they stared at each other, unable to break away, her senses went into high alert, sending a ripple of goose bumps all over her body. Her heart raced in a way that had nothing to do with the dancing. And her soul brightened, like for the first time ever the world made sense.

She was where she was meant to be. There was no need to leave. She'd found her home.

All she had to do was the one thing she'd never been able to do her entire adult life.

Stay.

Chapter 10

Callan ran through his shopping list one more time:

Sparkly unicorn soft toy.

Pony with blue body and rainbow hair.

Slime. That must be pink. And glittery.

Strange plastic animal that attaches to your finger and responds to touch and voice commands.

And a Cinderella dress with shoes and a crown as Mia's gift from Santa.

He glanced over at Josie who had offered to drive them to Broadway so they could get their Christmas shopping done. Her hands were relaxed on the wheel, a small smile lifted her cheekbones high, and every now and then she hummed the final line of 'We Wish You a Merry Christmas'.

'I do believe, Miss Donnelly, that the Christmas spirit may have done a number on you.'

Josie glanced over at him, her eyes twinkling. 'I know. I can't believe it. I'm in shock. There's a chance I might actually become a Christmas person.' She paused, pressing her lips together. 'Will you think less of me if I do?'

Callan snorted. Couldn't help himself. As if he could dislike someone who had in the space of a fortnight filled his life with more laughter and happiness than he'd felt in all the months since Abigail had passed.

What surprised him more was that he didn't feel guilty about it. Even after experiencing what he could only call 'a moment' with Josie the night of the Christmas tree lighting.

Specifically, the moment when the final song had ended and the three of them had continued to hold hands as he and Josie had faced each other, her eyes as bright and alive as he felt, and . . . connected.

That was the only word for it.

Something unspoken – something he couldn't quite get a handle on – had passed between them. And it didn't scare him or make him feel like he was betraying Abigail's memory.

Since that night, Callan had wrestled with his feelings towards Josie for hours, trying to make sense of them.

With Josie there was none of the heart-racing anticipation he'd experienced when he'd met Abigail. With Abigail he'd had to force himself to not text her, or call her, or email her constantly. When he and Abigail had gone on dates it had been pure hurricane-force attraction. The possibilities that their relationship could bring, the chance of a life so different from what he'd grown up in, fuelling his desire. His life with her had been so new, so fresh, exciting and vibrant. He'd fallen hard and fast, and by the end of their first date he'd known that she was the one.

The only.

Which meant . . . despite the warmth, the happiness she brought him, Josie could only be a friend. Even if he did find her attractive. Enjoyed her company. Didn't hate holding hands or linking arms with her.

Even if, in that moment as they'd held each other's gaze, the heaviness in his heart had lifted, and pure joy had raced through him, filling him with a *joie de vivre* he'd thought well and truly gone.

'Really? You're seriously considering hating me for warming to this season your village has inflicted upon me?' Josie shook her head slowly back and forth, her mouth opened as long as her eyes were wide in shock. 'Consider me stunned.'

Callan shook himself free of his ponderings and brought himself back to the present. 'Sorry, Josie. I was away with the fairies for a second there. Of course I'm not considering holding this newfound enjoyment of Christmas against you. In fact, I'm considering joining you. The other night was fun, wasn't it? I never thought it could be again.'

Josie tapped the brake, slowing the car down as the shops drew near. Her eyes darted back and forth as she searched for a parking space. 'It really was. I haven't laughed or danced like that in years. At least, not while one hundred per cent sober.'

Other than being curious about her family situation, Callan hadn't thought about Josie's life pre-Sunnycombe. What it had looked like. Where she'd lived. Truth be told, he'd not had any reason to. Now? He wanted to know. Needed to.

'Did you go out a lot? Before moving to Sunnycombe?' He indicated to her left. 'There's a space just up there.'

'Fab. Thanks.' Josie pulled over and parallel parked in one fluid move. 'A little bit. I wasn't a huge party girl or anything like that. But I'd go out with workmates on occasion. Mostly kept myself to myself, to be honest.' She released the seatbelt and stepped out of the car.

Callan shut the car door behind him and waited for Josie to make her way to the pavement. 'And why would you do that? You're young. Fun. I'd have thought you'd be out socialising most nights? Going on dates, and things like that . . .'

Josie fiddled with the strap of her tote bag. 'You make it sound like you're a hundred years old and I'm a youngster in comparison. You can't be much older than me?'

'Just gone 31.' Callan had a feeling Josie was about to steer the subject away from herself. 'And before you switch the subject around to me and my lack of socialising, I'll have you know I used to be very social. It was only after Abigail passed that I began to stay home. I wanted to be there for Mia. Wanted to make sure she felt secure, happy, safe in the knowledge that she wasn't going to be left by me.'

'I know I said it the other night, but I want you to know I mean it. You're a really good dad. Mia's lucky to have you.'

Josie's voice was quieter than usual, like she was holding something back. An emotion she didn't want to acknowledge. Or feel.

'It must've been hard having your mother leave. Were you very young?'

Josie nodded. 'I was 12. So not super young, but young enough.' Her jaw tightened. Her chest rose and held.

Callan instinctively knew to tread carefully if he wanted to know more. 'So your father brought you up?'

'He did. By himself. Like you, there wasn't family around to help out.'

Muffled chatter and the warm glow of a well-lit café caught Callan's attention. A hot drink in a cosy place might be a good way to get Josie to open up. To share her past with him. To relieve the tension that had her shoulders all but touching her earlobes.

'Do you want to pop in there? Have a cup of tea or coffee?'

Josie shook her head. 'No, I'd rather keep walking and get the shopping done, if that's all right with you.'

He wasn't surprised she'd declined, but he was surprised at how his heart stuttered a little at the rejection. Even though he knew it wasn't directed at him, it was just Josie's way of not having to reveal more about herself.

Still, it stung. And not in a 'friend said no' way, either. More in a 'woman I'm interested in doesn't want to spend time with me' way.

Callan shoved his hands in his coat pocket. What was going on with him? Was this part of the healing process? Part of moving on? He made a mental note to look it up on the internet later that night.

'How did your dad handle your mum leaving?'

99

Josie shrugged. 'As you'd expect. Not well.'

It was like getting blood out of a stone, but Josie could stonewall him all she wanted, Callan wasn't giving up.

'He must've been hurt. Angry.' He pointed out the toy store. A spacious shop filled to the brim with toys for all ages and stages, it was where he and Abigail had come to buy the toys that would furnish Mia's nursery, and returned every birthday and Christmas since.

'Yeah, well. When your wife walks out without a word on Christmas Eve, you're going to feel some feelings, aren't you?' Josie pushed the door open and walked in without making eye contact.

She didn't want to show Callan the hurt, the pain she felt after all these years? Fair enough. He could understand that. As much as he'd stayed home the past year for Mia's sake, he'd also done it for himself. Wanting to avoid looks of pity and well-meaning meaningless advice.

What could he say to a woman who'd been abandoned by her mother, at what was meant to be the happiest time of year, that she hadn't already heard before?

Nothing. Not a thing.

Except maybe share his experience and hope that by doing so Josie would realise she wasn't alone. That he was there for her.

Callan followed Josie inside and found her browsing the soft toy section.

'I've come to think, to believe, that when someone you love leaves you, not only at Christmas, but at any time of year, the pain never goes away.' He picked up a smiling emoji cushion, turned it over in his hands, then set it back down again. 'I'm proof of that. And I suspect you might be, too.'

Josie picked out a rainbow-coloured kitten with glittering eyes. It purred as she hugged it to herself. 'I don't know what you're talking about.'

Except the way her thumb was stroking the kitten's head, while she continued to avoid eye contact told him she did.

100

Callan resisted the urge to bundle her into his arms, to hold her close, to circle her back with the palm of his hand. To ease the pain she kept so close while she treated her mother's abandonment like it was nothing.

'You're too flippant about it not to care.' If he couldn't soothe her with touch, perhaps words would help. 'You tossed the circumstances of your mother's leaving out there like it meant nothing, which, to my mind, means it meant a lot.'

'Mia would love this.' Josie thrust the kitten in his direction. 'I saw that unicorn she wanted on a shelf just round the way.'

Callan followed Josie's stalking form, determined not to let her change the subject or avoid it altogether.

'If you and Margo can have secret plans to get me out of the house, to pull me from the doldrums, then I think it's only fair you let me have my say. That you let me talk you through whatever it is you're holding so tight. Caring isn't just one-sided. It's reciprocal. And I care about you, Josie. Especially when I see how much hurt you hide.'

Josie spun round. Her face blanched as her eyes narrowed. Her hands fisted at her sides.

Callan took a step back and raised his hands. He didn't want her exploding in the shop. He hated the idea of Josie despising him for pushing her too far. 'Look, I don't want to argue with you. Truly. Or make you angry. I just want to . . .'

'To what?' Her breath was ragged, harsh, as she pushed the words out. 'To try and make it better? To get me to move on? I've moved on. I'm always moving on. It's what I do best.' Josie sucked her lips into her mouth, like she didn't want the words to tumble out, or like she'd said too much.

'Ignoring your feelings isn't the same as moving on.' Callan fought the urge to tuck his fingertips under Josie's chin, to bring her lowered gaze up to his so she could see the sincerity of his words in his eyes. 'I never ignored my feelings after Abigail passed away. If anything I paid too much attention to them. Lost myself in my grief. Until you came along to snap me out of it. To make me realise that there was life after Abigail, one that didn't revolve around being the perfect father, while doing everything to keep Abigail's memory alive. Even making the worst baked goods the villagers of Sunnycombe have ever tasted.'

Josie blew out a long shuddering breath. 'They really were diabolical. I'm surprised you didn't go out of business.'

'Sunnycombe's full of kind people. They'll bend over backwards for you, if you let them.' Callan rolled his eyes. 'Or in my case, even if you won't let them.'

'Margo is a force to be reckoned with.' Josie bent over, picked out a jewellery box and opened it to reveal a plastic ballerina taking centre stage. She twisted the knob at the back once. Tinkly music filled the space between them. 'I'll get this for Mia. I think she'll like it.'

'She'll love it.' Callan felt his shoulders relax as the tension between him and Josie simmered down. 'You don't have to do that, though.'

A small frown line appeared between Josie's brows as she looked up at him with serious eyes. 'But I want to. Just like I want to say sorry for getting so worked up just now. You're right, I am flippant about my mother leaving. It's the easiest way to cope. And I'm not used to people pushing me to talk about it. Not used to them caring . . .'

'Well, get used to it, because I care.' Callan plucked the unicorn off the shelf and tucked it under his arm. 'And when you care about someone you don't let them flail. You don't let them fall. And if they do you make sure you're there to catch them, to save them. Margo taught me that. You did, too. So feel free to tell me to bugger off, but shall we pay for these toys, pick up our gifts for Margo, then go get a hot drink and . . . I don't know . . . talk about it? Get in touch with all those horrid feelings?'

Josie's furrowed brow deepened. She shivered, like a ghost had walked over her grave. And maybe it had. One that she'd once called 'Mum'.

102

Josie's brow smoothed as her chin tilted in a defiant manner. An action that made Callan sure he was about to hear a 'no'.

'You know what, Callan? I think you're right. I've kept myself to myself for too long. And while I don't think I'll ever get over my mother leaving me, I do think I probably need to talk about it. But promise me something.'

'Anything.'

'Don't let my story change how you see me. No pity. No feeling sorry for me. And no pats of "you poor dear" on my hand. Deal?' She narrowed her eyes and waited for his answer.

'I don't do pity. I've seen enough. So it's an easy deal to make.'

'Good.'

Without another word, Josie made her way to the counter and paid for the toy, while chatting amiably with the girl serving. She turned around, bag in hand, and flashed him a brave smile.

Callan's stomach clenched. His heart skipped. And somewhere, buried deep in the back of his mind, he remembered the last time he met a woman who'd made his stomach tighten, and his heart race.

It was time to admit the truth: he could friend-zone Josie all he wanted in his head, but his heart knew better.

He waited for the guilt to hit hard and fast.

Prepared himself for the self-loathing.

There was no guilt. No self-loathing.

There was just hope that spread through him as he realised perhaps there was life after Abigail.

Life, and maybe even a second chance at happiness.

Chapter 11

Josie placed her bags under the table, pulled out the chair opposite Callan, settled into it, and tried not to talk herself out of
sharing her past with Callan for the hundredth time in the past
few minutes.

She still couldn't believe she'd agreed to open up. To let him
in on her family history. But when he'd pulled out the far-too-
good-for-her-own-good point that she had been the one to get
involved in his life without his permission first, she knew she had
to relent. She was no hypocrite, and knew if she saw fit to poke
her nose into his life, then she couldn't complain when he did
the same to her. Especially when his interest came from a good
place. All these years of hiding her pain and Callan saw through
it so easily. Wanted to see her heal, to move forward with her life.
In a way that didn't mean physically running away.

And who knew? Maybe if she opened up about her past, she
could change her future. Stop running. Start staying. Settle in
Sunnycombe.

'Menu?' Callan offered her a folded piece of cream card that
had the café's name, 'Home', emblazoned on it in gold script.

She shook her head. 'I'm fine. A latte's all I'm after. Here.' She
reached into her bag to grab her wallet.

'Oh, no, you don't.' He waved her offer away. 'It's on me. You saved me much head-scratching over what to get Margo. That scarf you picked out for her is perfect. I'd have probably bought her a three-pack of handkerchiefs if left to my own devices.'

'She'd have loved them.' Josie dropped her wallet back into her bag and sat back in her chair. 'You could give her anything and she'd love it. She adores you and Mia. Thinks the world of you.'

'And we her. After, well . . .' Callan paused. His lips pursed – like he was self-censoring himself – then released. 'After what happened, she got her Mother Hen on and took such good care of us. Dropping off meals. Giving Mia loads of hugs. Offering to help wherever she thought she could. And she was never offended when all the help she offered was met with a no. Even when I was ruder to her than I should have been.'

'Grief makes you behave in ways you otherwise wouldn't.' Josie settled her chin into her cupped palm. 'When my mother left, when I realised she was never coming back, when things changed at home, well, it's safe to say I wasn't the model daughter.'

'Is that your way of saying you went off the rails? I can't imagine you acting out.' Callan's chin met his own palm, mirroring Josie's pose.

A shadow darkened their table as the waitress came to take their order.

'Latte for the lady, a long black for me, please.' He tipped his head back and eyed the cabinet, which was filled with sweet and savoury scones, crumbly pastries, sandwiches stuffed full of meats and salads, and an array of brownies, cupcakes and slices. 'A cheese scone too, please. Warmed and buttered?'

The waitress noted down their order and left without a word.

'She's a chatty one,' Callan observed, his lips quirking to the side.

'Maybe she was forced to get a job by her parents. It's what my father did to me when he decided I'd gone too far with my behaviour.' A hot flush rippled over Josie as she recalled some of her less than wonderful moments. Being found drunk as a skunk outside their house while trying to crawl undetected up the stoop. Sitting in the local stationer's backroom while a phone call was made to her father explaining that if his daughter was caught stealing pens and highlighters again the next phone call would be to the police.

'It must've been bad. You've gone red.' Callan nodded his thanks to the waitress as the coffees were plonked unceremoniously on the table along with the scone.

Unheated and unbuttered, Josie noted.

'I can't help but feel humiliated about the things I got up to when I was in my mid-teens.' Josie squeezed her eyes shut. 'Drinking too much, when I shouldn't have been drinking at all. A bit of shoplifting . . . of stationery, of all things. Going out till all hours and never letting my father know where I was.'

'He must've been worried sick.' Callan's brow furrowed and not, Josie suspected, because he'd just picked up his stone-cold scone and noticed its lack of dairy spread.

'Not so much. But then, that's why I did it. I wanted him to take notice. To pay attention. But he was too wrapped up in his own sadness, in his own misery, he didn't care.'

'Until he was forced to.'

Josie nodded and grimaced at the memory. 'Exactly.' She took a sip of her latte and relished the creaminess of the steamed milk and earthiness of the coffee. 'It was the shoplifting that did it. He was called down to the shop, and . . . I don't know . . . I guess it pulled him back into reality. For a few hours, anyway. It was the first time he'd ever properly told me off. There was finger-wagging, pacing back and forth, and a whole lot of "what were you thinking" shouting. Soon as he calmed down, he marched me down to our local café, a CV I'd been forced to write in hand, and asked about a job. Next thing you know I was doing dishes, then working on the counter, and the rest – as they say – is history.'

Josie eyed Callan picking apart the scone, but not putting even a morsel of it in his mouth.

'You could take it back, you know?'

Callan shook his head, then placed a hunk in his mouth, and chewed. Chewed some more. After what felt like forever, he forced it down in a large swallow.

He pushed the plate away. 'Didn't seem worth it. Complaining over a scone. Getting someone in trouble when, as you said, they probably don't want to be here.'

'Sometimes we need a bit of a push to sort ourselves out. Realise what's important. Kind of like what you're trying to do with me right now.' Josie caught the waitress' eye and waved her over. 'Let's give her a second chance and see what happens.'

The girl slunk over, her expression devoid of contrition.

'Yeah?' She popped a hip out, her hand settling upon it.

'Hi, thanks for coming over.' Josie offered up her warmest smile. 'My friend here asked for his scone to be warmed and buttered, but it's cold and there's no butter. Could you take it back and sort it, please?'

'Really?' The girl picked up the plate and eyed the scone. 'Oh my . . .' She pressed her palm to her head. Her eyes squeezed shut. 'I'm sorry.'

She looked up. Her wide, blue eyes swam with apology, and maybe even – when Josie looked closer – pain.

'So sorry. It's just my head's aching. So's my stomach. That time of the . . .' She cut herself off. Stopped herself from over-sharing. 'I'll get you a fresh one, warmed and buttered.' She made to turn away, before turning back around. 'Would you mind not mentioning this to the lady behind the counter? I can squirrel away a fresh scone on the sly, but if she knows I've messed up she might lay me off – this is my third mistake today and I've only been on since eleven. And if she fires me I won't be able to buy my family presents this Christmas.'

'Your secret's safe with us. We promise.' Josie laid her hand over her heart and nodded.

The girl smiled gratefully, then took the plate away, dumping

107

the scone surreptitiously in the bin as the manager took another customer's order, before returning with a warmed and buttered scone that was served complete with a smile and a 'thank you'.

Josie's tummy grumbled as she took in the golden butter melting on the fluffy scone. 'See. She just needed a chance to prove herself.'

'Is that your way of telling me that you were right?' Callan bit into the scone and breathed out an appreciative 'mmm'.

'My subtlety knows no bounds.' Josie's stomach rumbled again. Loudly.

Callan grinned and pushed the plate towards her. 'Here, take this half. I can't have my resident criminal starving to death. Worse. I can't see you get hangry. Lord knows what you might do – what acts of violence or thievery you might commit.'

Josie groaned. 'I should never have told you about my rebellious past.' She took a bite of her scone and wished she'd had something to stuff in her mouth before the story of her teenage past had tumbled out. Callan might think it amusing now, but after he'd had a while to digest what she'd told him? He'd never look at her the same way, even though he'd promised not to judge her.

'I'm glad you told me. It makes you more . . .' Callan paused. His gaze went to the ceiling, as if its cream paint might give him the answer he was looking for.

Josie's hand fell upon her chest. She gulped loudly for effect. 'It makes me easier to fire?' Despite her dramatics, her words held no fear. She knew her place at Abigail's was secure, and for the first time in all her working career, the knowledge that her job was safe – that she had a place to stay, if she chose to – didn't set a jitter of nerves alight in her gut.

Callan met her gaze. 'It makes you more real.'

Josie held her hand out. 'Here. Prod it. I'm real.'

Callan shook his head. 'Not like that.'

'I know.' Josie grinned and pulled her hand back. 'But I still don't understand what you're getting at. You didn't think I was real?'

108

Callan circled his coffee round in its saucer, his eyes on the beige foam that lined the half-full cup. 'You just seemed too good to be true. Happy, bright, great with the customers. You've integrated yourself into the community like you've been here forever. Pushed me out of my comfort zone.'

'With Margo's help,' Josie interjected. Heat washed over her cheeks and spread down her chest. Callan made her sound like a saint, when she was anything but. What he was seeing was the result of many moves, much change, and the need to morph from situation to situation with ease. There was nothing perfect about her life, her decisions. *Her*.

'Margo's been trying to force me into the great wide world for months. It would never have happened without you. It's more than that. Mia likes you. You've brought . . . joy back into the store.'

'That's just my baking. Not me.' Josie shook her head in protest, then registered the set line of Callan's jaw. A hint of impatience. She pushed her palm into her forehead. Here he was being kind to her and she was throwing it back in his face. 'God, I'm so sorry. I'm an idiot. A rude one. What I should be saying is thank you. It's not every day that a girl is called perfect.'

'Almost perfect.' Callan's clenched jaw relaxed. 'I know about your delinquent past now, remember?'

Josie's palm slid down her face to cup her chin. 'I'm never living that down, am I?'

'Never.' Callan shook his head, the amusement in his eyes replaced by seriousness. 'Josie, why did your mum leave?'

Josie shrugged. She didn't know what to say. Even after all these years she had no real answers to that question. The usual squall of anger, sadness, hurt and confusion eddied in her stomach. Threatened to rise. To consume.

'Honestly? I don't know. I mean, I have my suspicions, but that's all they are. Suspicions. Maybe she was bored of the drudgery of being a mum, a wife. Maybe her feelings for Dad had changed, and she didn't know how to face him. Both my grandparents, her parents, had passed away within a year of each other. Maybe that triggered something. Maybe she was going through something and escape seemed the only option?'

Callan leaned forward in his chair, his forearms rested on the table. His attention was one hundred per cent hers.

'What I do know is that she picked quite possibly the worst day to leave. Christmas Eve. And her leaving came out of nowhere.' Josie picked up her teaspoon and turned it over and over, watching her blurred reflection appear then disappear as she flipped the spoon. 'Dad had taken me to the cinema to give Mum a chance to do all those last-minute Christmas things, like wrap up the presents, make sure we had all we needed for Christmas Day. We had a nice time. Stuffing our faces with sweets and popcorn, then going out for a sneaky burger afterwards. Promising each other we'd eat dinner so that Mum wouldn't know that we'd ruined our appetites.' Josie set the spoon down and folded her arms across her chest, afraid if she let her walls down much more, her pain would spill out. Cause a scene. Embarrass both of them. 'We arrived home and the house was quiet. In the weirdest of ways. Not the usual stillness of a house that was empty, but it felt . . . hollow. Like something was missing.'

Josie closed her eyes, seeing the kitchen's gleaming benches, the lack of dust balls in the corners of the sitting room and hallway. The lemony, chemical scent of surface spray filled the air. And the hook on the coat rack that would usually sport her mother's ankle-length sunshine-orange woollen coat and yellow scarf was bare. Empty.

'We went through the house, roamed from room to room, calling her name. Eventually, we figured she'd popped out to the shops and that she'd be back in her own good time. As the day wore on and became night, Dad became more concerned. He hovered at the window, checking the street every five minutes. Then he went to the neighbours, who knew nothing. It was when I started to complain that I was hungry that he found the note.

In the fridge of all places. You can't say my mother didn't have a sense of humour. Leaving us in the cold, and letting us know about it by putting her goodbye note in the fridge.' Josie's harsh bark of laughter filled the space between them, and she hated how bitter she sounded. How bitter she felt. Even after all these years. 'We tried to do Christmas that year. Dad doggedly followed through with his annual Christmas present treasure hunt because he knew how much it meant to me. He muddled through as best he could, trying to cook the turkey – which ended up burnt on the outside, raw in the middle. He grilled it instead of baked it. Dessert was ice cream from the freezer. Had the situation been different it would have been comical.'

'Except there was nothing funny about the situation.'

'Not one darn thing.' Josie searched for signs of pity in Callan's eyes but saw only empathy. Understanding. And was grateful for it. Any latent concerns she had about revealing her past disappeared. 'Initially he went through these bouts of anger over the silliest things, like his T-shirts being inside out and his shoes not lined up straight. Over time he became a shrivelled version of himself as his sadness consumed him. Birthdays were acknowledged, but never celebrated. His parents – while they were still alive – would send a gift. But that stopped after my grandmother passed. And Christmas . . . Well, while every other family on our block celebrated, we commiserated, at worst. Pretended it was just any other day at best.'

'Did your grandparents not realise what was happening? Did they not . . . shake your father out of it? Tell him to pull his socks up and pay attention to what was important? To those who were still there, who loved him? Needed him?'

Josie took in Callan's stricken face. He was such a good man. Such a good father. Not that her father wasn't. They were just . . . different. Reacted differently to a similar situation, as people do. Callan dug in. Stuck around. Went over and above to make sure Mia's life was as good as it could be after her mother died.

Josie's father became distant, a ghost of his self. Did what had to be done, but no more.

'My grandparents never suspected a thing. When they visited we put our best faces on. Didn't show them we were struggling. Besides, not everyone's like you, Callan. People react in their own way. Do what they can to protect themselves. For some – like my father – that means keeping their distance, emotionally or physically. For others – like you – it means holding those they love tighter than ever.'

'And which category do you fall into?' Callan's lips pursed.

Guilt formed a knotted ball in Josie's gut. 'It's always been easier for me to go from job to job. Village to village. City to city. Town to town. Keep things light and easy. Keep things simple, uncomplicated. The less ties you have the less you can lose, if you know what I mean?'

'Does that mean you plan on leaving us?' Callan finished the dregs of his coffee and set the cup down hard enough that the people at the next table turned to see what was causing the commotion. 'What I mean is . . . will you be leaving Sunnycombe sooner rather than later?'

Would she move on and start fresh once more? Or could she stay and experience a new kind of life? One where friendships flourished. Where stability brought happiness.

She thought back to all the wonderful moments she'd experienced in the past few weeks . . . A small hand holding hers. A joke shared over a flour-dusted bench. Strong arms holding her tight, stopping her from falling, from hurting.

Memories that warmed her. Gave her hope. Made her believe her life could be different. Be rich, and full. Like it had been once upon a time. Many years ago.

Josie met Callan's penetrating gaze. Her decision was made. Her answer would be a promise. To Callan. To Mia. To herself.

'I do believe I'd like to stick around. At least until you all get sick of me.'

112

Callan nodded. Short. Sharp. 'Good, because I was going to ask if you'd like to join Mia and I – and probably most of the village – to watch the sunset tomorrow. Assuming there is a sunset. Weather being what it is at this time of year . . .' He paused and his cheeks flushed an embarrassed shade of pink.

'But you didn't want to invite me if I was going to leave? Didn't want Mia to become too attached? To be hurt when I left?' Josie filled out the rest of his sentence, saving him from having to spell out the obvious and potentially hurt her feelings.

'Yes. That.'

'I understand. And I promise you have nothing to worry about. In all the places I've lived nowhere has sucked me in quite as much as Sunnycombe.'

'"Sucked me in"?' Callan grinned. 'Charming.'

'Well "entranced me" sounded a bit heavy-handed.' Josie matched his grin.

'So you'll come?'

'Absolutely. I can't wait. And thank you for inviting me.'

'Thank Mia. It was her idea.'

Disappointment hit Josie, hard, right in the solar plexus.

Had she *wanted* Callan to be the one to invite her? Did some ridiculous part of her see him as more than just her boss? Her friend? See him as . . . dating material? More than that? *Boyfriend* material?

Had her simmering attraction to him, kept at bay because of his situation, grown more than she'd realised?

She surreptitiously glanced at Callan as he smiled up at the young waitress when she slid a plate with a piece of caramel slice, cut in half, onto their table. His eyes crinkled at the edges. His lips were slightly parted, and looked . . . far too kissable for Josie's liking.

Get a grip, she cautioned herself. Callan was not interested in dating anyone, let alone her. And if he should step into the dating fray, she was the last person she'd recommend he get involved with.

At least, she was, up until very recently. Now? Maybe she was dating material, after all.

'A small thank you.' The waitress pressed her finger to her lips in the universal 'keep it on the down low' sign, then hurried to an empty table and began piling up the plates and cups.

Callan picked up his half of the slice and held it up to Josie. 'To being forced to change . . . for the better.'

Josie lifted her square of slice and clinked it against his, her heart warming as Callan smiled at her. 'To second chances.'

Chapter 12

Callan opened the picnic basket, for what felt like the hundredth time, and checked over the feast he'd put together. Raggedly cut ham and cheese sandwiches – Mia's handiwork – were placed next to a couple of oranges and apples that he'd thrown in as an attempt to make it look like he fed Mia fruit. Which he tried to, repeatedly, but short of hiding it in his rock-hard muffins as suggested by many a mum on the internet – muffins she refused to eat anyway – he'd yet to convince her of the benefits of fruit. He'd popped in a couple of leftover white chocolate peppermint cupcakes from the day – Josie's latest experiment as she prepared for the Christmas Cake-off – knowing that Mia would eat those if nothing else. At the last minute, he'd also bought a bottle of merlot, should Josie want a glass.

Even if she didn't, he was certainly keen – anything to settle the skitter-skatter of nerves that had risen on and off throughout the day whenever Josie had come to mind.

Seeing her vulnerable, seeing her wear her heart on her sleeve, and how unharmed it was, considering her childhood experiences, had made her more than just an attractive face. It had only emphasised the qualities he'd seen in her. Her kindness, her self-assurance, the quiet strength that saw her get on with things.

It had been a strange thing to admit to himself, but he *liked* her. Could imagine chatting with her, the way they had at the café, on a regular basis. He'd enjoyed spending time with her. Getting to know her.

And that frightened him.

As irrational as it was, part of him felt being attracted to another woman was akin to cheating on Abigail. Something he'd never done, never even contemplated doing, when she was alive. He'd loved her so much. He still did.

The front door opened with a bang as the frame hit the door-stop, and a cheery 'yoo-hoo' filled the shop.

Margo. Of course.

She always had a way of knowing to pop in when he needed someone most, but had no intention of asking for help, or advice.

Except maybe, just this once, he needed to put himself out there. To ask for help. To seek her advice.

'There you are.' Margo appeared in the doorway, a warm smile on her face.

Without waiting for an invitation to come into the kitchen, she made her way to the bench and pawed through the picnic basket.

'A bottle of wine?' She looked up, a twinkle in her eye. 'Is this just for you? Or do you plan on sharing it with someone special?'

'Just with Josie. If she wants some. She might not. I wasn't sure. Maybe I should have got that pink wine. Women like that, right? At least the mummy bloggers I follow on the internet seem to. I should bring a bottle of water, too. Do you think she'd prefer fizzy water or still?' Callan, aware he was rambling, squeezed his eyes shut as he noted Margo's lips quirking to the side. The twinkle in her eye turning into a proper sparkle.

'There's nothing "just" about our Josie. At least not from the way you're talking.'

Warm hands enveloped his, and Callan forced himself to open his eyes. To not hide from the emotional turmoil that surged through him.

116

'And there's nothing wrong with having feelings for someone, Callan.' Margo jerked her head out to the shopfront. 'Shall we take a seat and have a wee heart to heart?'

Callan blew out a long breath and nodded. 'I think I might need one.'

He followed Margo out, took a seat, shoved his hands in his pockets and took in the view outside. The sky was a sea of blue ombre, as the sun began its meandering descent. Not a cloud marred its perfection.

Callan half-wondered if the weather was in cahoots with Cupid. Compelling him to take Josie out – even if he had used Mia as the excuse. That had been something of a fabrication. It had been he who'd asked Mia if she thought it was a good idea to invite Josie to watch the sunset. Not the other way round, as he'd led Josie to believe. He hadn't wanted to admit it was him doing the asking. He wasn't ready to put his heart on his sleeve.

Margo stood beside him, her finger raised, a thoughtful expression on her face. 'A talk like this needs cake.'

She made her way behind the counter and pulled out a piece of hummingbird cake. She placed it on a plate, grabbed two forks from the tray beneath the counter and brought the plate back to the table and set it down between them.

Callan took the fork offered to him, but didn't dig in. He was afraid that eating the cake Josie had made earlier that day would somehow emphasise his feelings. Grow them. Again, irrational. But then whoever said emotions were rational things?

Margo speared the slice and pulled away a chunk of the moist, pineapple-rich, cake, brought it up to her lips and paused. Her gaze grew distant, like she were travelling to another time, another place.

'When John passed away I couldn't imagine ever being attracted to anyone again. Let alone loving someone. It felt like if I were to develop any kind of feelings for another man it would be a betrayal of the love that John and I shared.' Margo placed the cake

117

in her mouth, closed her eyes as she chewed, then swallowed. 'A woman could get used to eating cake like this. It's divine. Dig in, please, before I scoff it all.'

'Well, with a recommendation like that, it'd be rude not to at least have a little.' Callan pushed his reservations aside and dug his fork in, marvelling at how the tines slid through it like it was softened butter. 'So is that why you never met anyone else? Why you've kept your own company all these years?'

Margo laughed. 'Such a polite way to put it. What you're really asking is if that's why I never dated anyone? Hooked up, as the youngsters call it?'

Heat hit Callan's cheeks as Margo's laughter grew.

'I may be in my fifties, darling Callan, but I'm not ancient. And not oblivious to the rest of the world, either. There's still a part of me that feels like an 18-year-old. She's just hidden away by a bit of face-creasing and age-appropriate clothing.'

Callan forked the cake into his mouth to stop any chance of his second foot making its way in there.

'The answer to your question is . . . it's complicated. A bit of yes. A bit of no. Initially I was like you. I went into my shell. Hunkered down. Spent time with the kids. Tried to make up for them not having a father by going over and above what I'd done in the past. Ice cream for breakfast. Trips to the cinema. Little gifts just because.'

Callan swallowed his mouthful and nodded. He knew exactly what Margo was talking about. He had done, was still doing, that exact same thing. 'Mia's collection of dolls and teddy bears has exploded.'

'It can't be helped. It's natural to want to smooth over their pain. To fill in the sinkholes of hurt.'

'It's a pity that ice cream and dolls can't do the same for us adults.'

'You're right, ice cream and sweets and saying yes when you should say no might help the little ones, but the only thing that

118

can help us deal with our grief is connection. Love can be . . . cloistering. In the best way. But when that love is taken from us we need to reach out, find new connections, foster friendships. Not ignore the opportunity of new love, should it present itself.'

Callan caught a note of sadness in Margo's tone. Sadness, regret, maybe even a touch of remorse.

'Is this coming from someone who passed up a chance of falling in love again? And feel free to stab me with your fork if I'm crossing boundaries by asking that.'

'I'll spare you this one time.' Margo set the fork down and propped her elbows on the table, then settled her chin into her open palms. 'About eighteen months after John died there was interest from another gentleman. He would pop by to see how I was going. Offer to fix anything in the cottage that might have deteriorated. We'd have cups of tea together, which progressed to going for walks along the river. The odd lunch out. It was the gentlest courtship one could imagine.' A bittersweet smile tugged at her lips. 'Nothing like the heady rush of first love, where you spend your time counting the minutes until you'll see your beloved again, where you'll do anything and everything to keep them happy. And they you. The second time around love looks different. There's not as much of the heart racing or the stomach twirling or the itchiness you get when you've not seen or heard from them in a while. The pace is slower, gentler. There's not the rush to fall headlong into the affair.' Margo pushed the plate towards Callan. 'The rest is yours. Talking about my mistakes does nothing for my appetite.'

'I take it things didn't work out? Did he want too much too fast? More than you were able to give?'

'No, he was wonderful. So patient. Thoughtful. A good man. It was I that pushed him away.' Margo rubbed her eyes with the back of her hand. Kept it there. Hiding her feelings from him. 'I got scared. The moment I knew it might be more than just friendship, the moment I felt a hint of the affection for him that I

119

felt for John, I called it off. Explained that I appreciated him, but that I wasn't ready for anything more than friendship.' Margo's hand fell from her eyes, revealing a world of regret. 'Then I made a point of avoiding him completely. Well, as much as is possible when you live in a village. Horrible person that I am.'

Callan reached for Margo's hand and held it in his own, gave it a reassuring squeeze. 'Not horrible. Human.'

'Kind of you to say, Callan, but it was gutless of me to avoid him. Then and now.'

'Is that why you won't go to the pub?' Callan raised his brows, and waited to see if his suspicions, which had been growing as the conversation went on, were correct.

'Poor Brendon,' sighed Margo. 'He really is a good man. And part of me – a rather large part – wishes I'd handled things differently. Been brave. Willing to take a chance on him, rather than keep myself secluded away.' Margo laughed, a short, hard, derisive bark. 'I convinced myself initially it was the best thing for the kids. That I didn't want to bring change into their life when they'd already experienced so much. Then they grew up and made their way into the world, leaving me to rattle around in the cottage. At least until I bought the place next to yours and told myself that a cosy, simple life with just my shop and myself to care for was enough.'

Callan picked up the last bit of cake and pondered Margo's predicament, and how it related to him. Was he looking at his own future? Would he end up alone, and *not* okay with it? Because Margo clearly wished she could turn back time.

And if he did one day feel it was time to see someone else, when would be the right time? It hadn't even been a year since Abigail passed, and he still missed her. How would it be fair to another person to spend time with them when his wife still held so much space in his soul?

He forked the cake into his mouth, held it there and tasted its comforting flavours of spice, sweet and a hint of tang. The crumb so fluffy and moist it almost melted on his tongue. Soothing and sweet. Rich, with depth. And entirely moreish. Like he could spend a lifetime enjoying it and never tire of it.

'I told you it was good. Better than good. It's excellent.' Margo sat back in her chair, all hints of moroseness gone. The sparkle in her eye had returned, shining as brightly as ever. 'That Josie is a keeper. I'd have to have a stern word with you if you ever let her go.'

'So you're telling me I should keep her on? As the house baker? For as long as she'll stay?' Callan knew exactly what Margo was getting at, but wasn't willing to fully admit she was right. Or that the reason he'd been so preoccupied with making Josie happy – ensuring the picnic was perfect – wasn't because he wanted to keep his employee happy, but because he wanted to make Josie, the woman, happy. Because he liked her. Very much so. And, as much as it scared him, as much as a voice deep down kept saying 'it's too soon' on repeat, his heart was warmed by Josie. In a way that indicated she was more than just a friend.

'Callan Stewart, I think you know exactly what I'm getting at.' Margo pushed her chair back and stood, then shot him a cheeky wink. 'You have a nice time tonight. She'll love the wine.'

'And you make sure you pop into the pub, sooner rather than later. Brendon keeps asking after you. Time may have passed, but I don't think his feelings for you have.' Callan picked up the plate and forks, stood, and made his way over to Margo. 'Thank you.' He wrapped his arm around her shoulder and brought her in for a half-cuddle. 'You've been so good to our family, to me. For a long time now.'

'And I'll continue to be so for as long as you need me.' Margo returned the hug, her head angling to the side as she heard the pitter patter of feet in the room above. 'And the wee pet, too.'

Callan opened the door for Margo, not really seeing her leave, or hearing the excitable shouts of 'Daddy, Daddy' as Mia thumped down the stairs, ready for the evening's event.

What had Margo told him? Love looks different the second time round.

Did it look like a woman who made cakes so delicious they'd see the toughest man crumble? Whose smile lit up the room even on the gloomiest winter's day? Whose heart was so big even the harshest rejections life could throw at her hadn't soured her good self? A woman who went out of her way, when she didn't have to, to make sure he didn't swallow himself in self-pity and take his daughter down with him?

It would be so easy to listen to his fears, to believe them, to put his life on hold . . . not just 'for now' but for good.

But where would that get him? How would his life have turned out had he listened to that same voice when it had told him to stay in London. To do as his family told. To be who they wanted him to be. Instead he'd ignored it, and his life had opened up, bloomed, into something more wonderful than he'd ever dreamed possible.

They said fortune favoured the bold, and for the first time in nearly a year, Callan was feeling bold.

Chapter 13

Josie tossed her latest brainstorm fails into the faintly glowing embers, watching as the flames flared for a second then died down as the scraps of paper containing good-for-nothing Christmas cake competition ideas, blackened and crumbled.

'Come on brain,' she muttered. 'Now's not the time to be giving out on me.'

She shuddered, despite the warmth of the room, at the thought of not creating the winning, or even place-getting, entry for the Christmas Cake-off. She'd scoured the internet for information on previous years' entries and the bar was set much higher than she'd expected. From simple but beautifully executed one-layer cakes to towering delights decorated to within an inch of their lives, many of the creations wouldn't have been out of place on a television cake baking show.

Pouring pressure upon pressure was that Callan's wife had won every single year that she'd entered. Deservedly so. Her entries were works of art. Featuring everything from iced mistletoe that was so intricate it looked like the real deal, through to a sweet-festooned gingerbread house set upon a cake surrounded by gingerbread Christmas trees. And then there was the five-tier cake – each tier a Christmas present, the wrapping made from icing, the bows from fondant. The tiers were stacked upon each other in a way that was so precarious, Josie was amazed one of the 'gifts' hadn't toppled over and fallen to the ground with a resounding splat.

Not that she was in competition with Abigail, she reminded herself for the thousandth time. She just didn't want to let Callan down. It was important to her that she created something that lived up to the bakery's once stellar reputation.

A series of beeps from her phone snapped her out of her lip-gnawing musings.

Hot date with the hot boss still on for tonight?

Josie rolled her eyes at Lauren's text, and silently chastised herself for letting a couple of things slip after a few wines the night before: a) that she thought Callan was good-looking and b) that they were going to watch the sunset that evening.

It's not a date. And it's still happening.

She tapped 'send' on the message.

A reply flashed up seconds later.

You didn't reject the hot bit . . .

That's because I'm not a liar. And you'd better not have told Will I said that I thought Callan was easy on the eye or I'll cut off your cake supply.

Josie grimaced at the phone.

Your lusty crush is safe with me. Don't do anything I wouldn't do.

A winking emoji followed by a heart-eye emoji flashed up underneath the latest message.

See you on the hill!

Josie tucked her phone away, relief settling her swirling stomach. She shrugged on her coat, pulled her beanie low over her ears, wound her scarf round her neck, then shoved her gloves in her coat pocket for good measure.

Callan was due any second now and she didn't want to be late for the big event that the villagers had been buzzing about all day. Why they were so excited about watching a sunset, she had no idea – the most she'd got out of them was 'you'll see' and 'if it's you, you'll know', whatever they meant – but their enthusiasm was contagious, and she was strangely keen to see the spectacle of a sun setting, despite having seen many sunsets before.

She made her way to the front door, opened it and ricocheted off something scratchy-woolled and heavenly scented.

'Josie, are you okay? Sorry. I didn't realise we were meeting you out the front. Though why we'd do that I've no idea. It's already ridiculously cold out here. You've got gloves right? And please tell me you're wearing some sort of woollen tights underneath those jeans? Can't have my girl catching a cold.'

My girl? A spark of warmth ignited low in Josie's stomach at the term of endearment. Was that how Callan saw her? As more than just the bakery's baker? As someone he felt protective over . . . maybe even affectionate towards?

Despite the cottage casting a shadow over his face, she could see he'd turned a violent shade of beetroot.

Callan squeezed his eyes shut and pinched the bridge of his nose. 'I can't believe I just said "my girl". That's so condescending of me. Totally patriarchal. I do apologise.'

Patriarchal? Josie kept her lips as straight as she could, despite their twitching to lift into a grin. Anyone would've thought Callan had swapped parenting boards for feminist forums. Which, if he had, only made him more endearing.

'Sorry. I'm tired. Not thinking straight. I had an old client of mine contact me the other day about doing his accounting again, and I agreed to it. Now that you're here, it's time I got back into what I'm actually good at. The problem though is that his tax is now late as he was waiting for me to "come right", as he so charmingly put it, and didn't want to use anyone else. So I was up far too late last night looking over his bits and bobs. And they seriously are bits and bobs. He brings in shoeboxes filled with receipts. They need sorting. Arranging. Then there's figuring out his bank statements. I should really ask him to organise it himself, but he's going on 80, refuses to retire, and well . . .' Callan shrugged. 'He's been doing his taxes that way forever. And I've let him. Who am I to suddenly impose new rules upon him?'

Mia, who'd been holding Callan's hand the whole time while staring up at her father, a look of confusion on her little face, tugged his arm. 'Daddy, you're blavering.'

Callan turned his attention to Mia. 'Blavering?'

'You're talking too much. Like the man on the telly that you called a blavering idiot.'

Callan's flush, which had shown signs of disappearing, renewed itself, even brighter than before. 'I have got to remember to watch my language around you. And the word's blathering.'

'That's what I said.' Mia's brows drew together. 'Blavering.'

Callan dropped into a squat and kissed Mia's temple. 'You're right, I was. And if I don't stop blavering and get moving soon, we'll miss the big event.'

'In that case, let's get a wriggle on.' Josie locked the door and waited for Callan to point them in the right direction. 'I don't suppose you can fill me in on why this is such a big deal? Everyone I've spoken to keeps saying the event is held every year but that "this never happens", and I've yet to figure out what this great "this" they're talking about is.'

The three began walking down the lane. Mia's hand finding its way into Josie's.

'It's an old Sunnycombe legend. Probably ridiculous, but those that've been here forever swear it's true.'

'You're being as obscure as the rest of them, you know that?'

'What's obscure?'

Josie tightened her hand around Mia's, loving the away her petite gloved fingers followed suit. 'It means annoying and difficult.'

'Stop being annoying and difficult, Daddy,' Mia instructed.

The same serious frown she'd had on her face earlier had returned.

Josie couldn't help but notice how it matched the frown she'd seen on Callan's face. The same said frown that Callan was currently sporting.

'It means Josie thinks I'm not being as clear as she'd like.'

'Is Josie being impotent, Daddy?'

Josie clapped her free hand over her mouth to stop the laughter that threatened.

'You mean impatient, and yes, just a little.'

'Are you two going to be grumpy at each other? Like you and Mummy would be sometimes?'

Callan's frown softened as he shook his head. 'No, my princess. We're not going to be grumpy at each other.'

'I didn't like it when you and Mummy were cross.' Mia's bottom lip protruded, and trembled a little, as her small chest rose and fell.

Josie crossed the area over her heart. 'Promise we're not being grumpy, but I am being impatient. I'm sorry. Shall I work on my patience, do you think?'

Mia nodded, and a smile found its way back to her lips.

'Wonderful. Now's a good a time as any.' Josie looked over at Callan. 'So, tell me this tale. And take as long as you like.'

They crossed the lane and began the journey over the sodden field, their wellington boots squelching into mud with each step. The hill above was patchworked with blankets and dotted with villagers. Their chatter and laughter rolled down the hill to greet them.

'Many moons ago, at this exact time of year, not long before Christmas – or so the story goes – a shepherd around these parts was searching for a sheep that had escaped its winter lodgings.'

Josie grinned at the solemn tone Callan had taken. Like the tale wasn't just a made-up story, but a piece of Sunnycombe history, told around fires and passed from generation to generation.

'He wandered for hours, not seeing a hint of its cream wool, not hearing a single bleat. The sun was coming down. The wind was whipping around his prematurely bald, hatless head, leaving him freezing and foul-tempered. He'd all but given up hope, when he looked up and spotted the sheep on the hill before us. He trudged towards it as fast as his feet would carry him, puffing and panting, and swearing black and blue that if the sheep ran off it would be destined for the dinner table.'

'Daddy means the sheep would die and become dinner.' Mia joined the dots for Josie in a matter-of-fact tone that had Josie stemming another laugh, so as not to insult the wee poppet.

'Lucky for the sheep, it stayed where it was, and the shepherd reached it without further hassle. It was then, just as he was about to take hold of the sheep and lead it home, that he saw the sun. Slowly sinking between the "V" where the two hills appear to meet on the horizon at the very end of the village. He watched the sun dip between the hills, struck by its perfect symmetry, and then, thinking nothing more of it, he took the sheep home and went about his usual routine.'

Callan paused. His chest rising and falling as he took in great breaths as the incline steepened.

'That's it?' Josie couldn't believe what she was hearing. 'He caught the sheep, watched a sunset, and we're here celebrating that in the freezing cold?'

Callan's eyebrows lifted. 'What did I say about patience?'

'I need to have some?'

'That's right. Now if you don't mind . . .'

'Tell her the rest, Daddy. The rest is the best.' Mia swung both their arms with excitement and they found themselves 'one-two-threeing' her up the hill. Her giggly squeals as they swung her high in the air on three caught the attention of the locals who waved and began to chant 'one-two-three' along with them.

Finally they reached a spot that wasn't as steep as other areas, and was relatively free of the rocks that jutted from the ground.

'This'll do.' Callan set his picnic basket down and pulled out a blue and green striped, plastic-backed picnic blanket and spread it out on the hill in one flourish.

'You are wonderful.' Josie settled herself on the blanket. 'I was worried my bum would catch cold from sitting on the damp grass.'

'Well, your bum is safe. Would you like a glass of wine?' He wiggled the bottle back and forth. 'I've got water, if you'd prefer.'

'Wine would be lovely. Though I thought you prefer beer? I noticed it's what you drink when we're at the pub.' Josie ducked her head as an embarrassed flush hit.

'Hey, you three! Got space for us?'

Josie glanced up to see Lauren and Will making a beeline for them, their reddened cheeks puffing out great white plumes with each step. She said a silent thanks, grateful for their appearance, and hoped it would stop Callan extrapolating her interest in his drinking habits and flippant-but-true 'wonderful' comment into realising that she might have feelings for him. Feelings that, even if she did have, she knew she shouldn't have – there was no way he would ever return those feelings, therefore it was better to ignore said feelings completely.

'I can't believe it's going to happen.' Lauren spread the blanket out, and plopped down, then opened the basket she'd been carrying and pulled out a little bottle of gin and tonic. 'After all these years. Finally.'

Josie slapped her palm on her forehead and let out an over-exaggerated groan. 'Not you too? Honestly it's easier to make the perfect meringue than it is to get this story out of you lot.'

'She doesn't know?' Will ducked back and caught Callan's eye. 'You've not told her?'

'I was telling her, but I got distracted.' He poured himself a glass of wine. 'Happy to continue though, assuming you haven't lost interest?'

Josie shook her head, zipped her lips, and gave him the silent nod to go ahead.

'So, the story goes . . . the next morning the shepherd woke up and the strangest thing happened. He rubbed his hand over his bald head and discovered . . .'

Josie leaned in as Callan's voice dropped lower with each word. 'Bristles.'

Josie sprung into a straight-backed position. 'Bristles? You're kidding me, right? You're having a laugh. Pulling my leg. I've heard of ridiculous folk tales, but that's just . . . I'm sorry to say, it's absurd. I'd sooner believe a genie could come out of a lamp than a man could grow a head of hair overnight.'

Callan fixed her with an eyebrow raised stare. 'Patience? Remember that? We talked about it not that long ago?'

Josie dropped her head into her hands and shook her head back and forth. 'Fine. Patience mode engaged. Continue.'

'So, he woke to find hair that he'd not previously had but wished he'd had. A hope. A dream come true. The first of three.'

Josie lifted her head at Callan's serious tone, at the sombre atmosphere that had thickened around the small group.

'The shepherd went about his business that day. Checked on his flock. Did whatever else shepherds do.'

'City boy.' Will laughed, his guffaw ending as quickly as it started, like he didn't want to miss a word of the story.

'Then he went to the local pub for an ale, the same pub that stands today, and the publican, who was notoriously tight-fisted, decided that in the spirit of Christmas he would shout those who'd braved the thundering rain to come to the pub. Not just one drink, mind. But for the rest of the night.'

'Can you imagine Brendon doing that?' Lauren elbowed Will. 'He'll give the odd freebie, even a bottle of wine to newcomers, if he likes them enough. But a whole night of free drinks? Never in a million years.'

130

Callan brought his finger to his lips, silencing Lauren, who mouthed 'sorry'.

'Earlier that day the farmer had wished he had more money so that he could buy more than one drink. Coincidence? We think not. Then, that night his most closely held hope came true. The shepherd, who had a thing for a local lass, found himself standing under the mistletoe, right at the exact time she did. Tradition being tradition . . .'

Josie held her hand up. 'Was this the same tradition the town's got going now?'

Callan nodded his head by way of an answer. 'Tradition being tradition, they kissed. Not just any kiss, mind. This was the kiss . . . of true love.'

Will and Lauren clapped their hands together, closed their eyes and went into a swoon. 'True love,' they repeated, then collapsed against each other.

Josie searched for a sign that they were mocking the tale, or that it was all a big joke, but when they opened their eyes again they were as serious as Callan's.

'If we see the sunset tonight, Daddy, does that mean I'll find true love?' Mia shuffled into Callan's lap and wrapped his arms around her for extra warmth. 'Will I meet my prince?'

Callan dropped a kiss on her head. 'I hope not, my princess. You're too young to be spirited away by a prince on horseback.'

'Silly, Daddy. He'll have a car, not a horse. It's not the olden days, you know.' Mia rolled her eyes and clucked her tongue, sending the group into a fit of laughter.

Their laughter became a roar when she put her hands on her hips and let out a grumpy 'what?'.

'So what you're saying is that if we see the sun dip below the horizon in the middle of those two hills over there then everyone here is going to get a full head of hair, free drinks at the pub, and then meet their true love?' Josie set her glass down at her side then stretched out on the blanket, her eyes on the

131

horizon, which the sun was minutes away from caressing with the last of its rays.

Lauren shrugged. 'We're not entirely sure. It hasn't happened again in living memory, that we know of. According to the oldest folk in the village, it's always been cloudy or raining on the day that the sun's due to set in the middle of the hills. This is the first time in ninety-seven years, at least, that there's been any real point in traipsing up here.'

Callan brought Mia into a tighter cuddle as a visible shiver rattled through her little body. 'I've heard it's not always the same miracles. Apart from the true love bit. That always happens. Apparently one woman woke up the next day to find an uncle she didn't know she had had left her a great deal of money, then one of her onions won first prize at a fair, then she fell in love.'

'And don't forget that man whose mother-in-law who lived with them, she passed away, then she left the family money, then he and his wife fell in love all over again.' Will stroked his chin thoughtfully. 'Luckiest bugger out of the lot, I reckon.'

Lauren playfully slapped the back of his head. 'Cheeky beggar.'

Will planted a kiss on her cheek. 'Joking. I'm a lucky man. Your mother makes the best roast. That, and she made the most beautiful woman in the world.'

'Forgiven.' Lauren returned his kiss. 'I guess that means you don't care if the setting sun doesn't grant you the three things you hope for most?'

'Nope. I'm not interested. I'm here for the spectacle, not the reward.'

'Good. Hopefully the great "they" are listening and your desire to not be part of this has narrowed the field by one.' Lauren turned her attention back to the sun. 'What would you want to have happen, Josie?'

Josie pondered the question. What did she want? What did she need? Oodles of money would have been the obvious answer, but

132

she wasn't driven by material things. As long as she had enough to eat, a roof over her head, and enough money to treat herself once in a while, she was happy.

The only thing she'd long hoped for, dreamed of, was a close-knit family, and that was never going to happen. She'd learned that the hard way by wishing for her mother to return night after night, for months, and then years. Her wish remained unfulfilled, replaced by the belief that it was better to keep to yourself than to hope for others to bring you wholeness, happiness, or love.

'You know, I'm good.' Josie forced a smile. 'I'm fine. Which I guess means the field of those who could have lady luck bestowed upon them just narrowed again.'

Lauren pressed her hands together and rubbed them back and forth. 'The odds are getting better with every second.'

A hush fell upon the crowd as the sun hit the horizon, and began to drop lower and lower, until there was nothing but a faint glow along the edges of the valley as the top curve of the sun touched the place where the two hillsides appeared to end in a v–shape, before disappearing out of sight for another day.

Lights flickered over the hillside as mobile phones and torches were turned on, and the chatter returned, though not quite so loud. The air of expectation, of hope, filled the air.

'Anyone feel any different?' Josie turned to Callan, Will and Lauren.

'Nope.' Will shook his head.

Lauren shrugged. 'Same as usual, unfortunately.'

Callan scratched his bare chin. 'I'm itchy here. Must be about to sprout a full beard.'

'Idiot.' Will reached round and gave him a small shove. 'You're the only man I know who can grow a full beard within a week.'

'In that case, I'm the same as usual. No miracles here.'

Lauren pushed herself up with a groan and rubbed her backside. 'All that sitting on uncomfortable ground for what?

133

Nothing. Will? Time to head home before my behind freezes off?'

'Absolutely. We can't have that. I'm far too fond of it.' Will tossed their rubbish into the picnic basket then picked it and the blanket up. 'See you guys at the pub later?'

'I wish I could.' Callan smoothed back a stray piece of Mia's hair. 'But there's this one to think about.'

Josie mentally wired her jaw shut so it wouldn't fall open from the shock of Callan's readiness to go out. When had spontaneity been his thing?

Lauren pulled out her mobile and began to tap. Seconds later her phone beeped a reply. 'Mum can take care of her. Said it would be her pleasure.'

Callan enveloped Mia's cheeks in his hands. 'Would that be okay with you, Mia? Would you mind if Lauren's mum came over to our house to hang out with you?'

'Will she bring treats?' Mia's brows drew together in thought. 'Because I do like treats. Especially sweets and crisps.'

Lauren took Mia's hand and shook it in promise. 'She will bring many. She keeps a stash at home for when I come round, because I'm quite the fan of treats myself.'

One baby-toothed grin and a happy wriggle later, and they had their answer.

They picked their way carefully back down the hill. Josie used the silence to ponder the questions that her mind had thrown up.

Callan had wished to go to the pub, but didn't think he could.

Then just like that, with help from Lauren, his wish had come true.

Did that mean the sunset legend was more than just a fanciful tale, and that Callan was the one being granted wishes?

And if so, what other hopes or dreams did he have hidden away that he'd like to see fulfilled?

A shiver of delight skittled down Josie's spine as a myriad of possibilities arose.

Riches. Happiness. Success.

All things Callan deserved after the trauma of the last year. All things she'd be happy to see him receive.

Especially the last part of the legend. Last, but never least, and apparently guaranteed . . .

Love.

Chapter 14

A wave of heat hit Callan as he pushed open the door to the pub and held it open for Lauren, Will and Josie. The place was heaving, and combined with the roaring fire that Brendon started first thing in the morning, The Squeaky Wheel was a furnace. A quick glance inside saw as much bare flesh being flashed around as you'd see at a beach in summer.

Josie fanned herself as she walked past. 'Thank God for layers.'

He followed her in, watching as she divested herself of her coat, scarf, hat, gloves and jumper before they'd made it to the bar, revealing a basic grey T-shirt tucked into belted skinny jeans. Basic . . . but somehow attractive, bordering on alluring in its simplicity.

Standing on tiptoes, Josie surveyed the room. 'There's a table over in the far corner. It'll be a squish, but it's either that or stand and be elbowed in the stomach every five seconds.'

'You guys go grab it. I'll get drinks.' Callan pulled his wallet from his coat pocket.

'Good one, mate. Beer for me, gin for my lady.' Will slapped him on the back, took Lauren by the hand and braved the throng.

'Thank you.' Josie's cheeks were flushed, her eyes sparkling. 'You know what I like.' Josie winked, then set off into the crowd.

Callan followed her progress as she weaved her way through, unsure what to make of the wink. Was it flirtatious? Or just friendly? Was he reading too much into her 'you know what I like' comment? Were her flushed cheeks and glittering eyes really caused by heat and happiness, or something else?

And how was it possible to go, in a blink of a second – or a wink of an eye – from being a man in your early thirties to feeling like an awkward teenage boy with a bit of a crush just because a pretty girl was being friendly to you?

He turned around and nodded to a pint-pulling Brendon, who dipped his chin in response, then held up his hand, fingers spread, letting him know that he'd be there in five minutes.

Callan checked the bar for more staff, but the help that Brendon got in for busy days like this was nowhere to be seen. Probably picking up glasses. Getting fresh ones from out back. Or rustling up something salty and greasy for the hungry hordes.

He pulled out his mobile and went to text Lauren's mum, Bridget, to check on Mia. He still couldn't believe that he'd just left her with a near stranger. Not that Bridget was a stranger to him. She was somewhat of a regular at the bakery. She had even kept on coming in a couple of times a week after he took over the baking and began producing his . . . well . . . stodge. But Mia didn't know her all that well. What if she was frightened? Felt abandoned? Was scared?

His phone lit up with a message from Bridget. A picture of the two of them, each enjoying an ice cream with giant grins on their faces, put paid to his concerns.

'She looks like she's having a great time. Should I be worried that I'm no longer flavour of the month?'

Callan glanced up to see Margo standing opposite him, her eyes crinkled in amusement, staring at his phone.

'Margo, you're on the wrong side of the bar.' His heart warmed as he realised the significance of what he was seeing.

'Or, should I simply be saying . . . Margo, it's good to see you in the bar.'

Margo spun round, then tugged on the shoulder straps of her black pinafore. 'Suits me, doesn't it?'

'That it does. But it doesn't explain why you're over there and not on this side.'

'Poor Brendon.' Margo inhaled a deep breath, her eyes filling with sympathy. 'I popped in earlier today to say hello and he was hunched over the bar, head in hands, looking most sorry for himself. Turns out both people he'd had lined up to help tonight had cancelled. He was beside himself with worry, so I did what anyone would do, and offered my services. Beer?' Margo grabbed a pint glass.

'Two, please. And a gin and tonic, and a glass of merlot. Two bags of crisps too, please. Any flavour.'

'Coming right up.'

Margo pulled the pints, then began putting together the rest of his order, leaving Callan to watch in awe – and not just a tiny bit of surprise.

He'd hoped after telling Margo that Brendon still held her in high esteem, despite her pushing him away all those years ago, that there was still a chance for them, should she still be interested – but he'd not expected her to grab that notion with both hands and run with it.

He blinked hard and fast as Brendon made his way down the bar, snaked his arm around Margo's waist, pulled her close and whispered something in her ear that made her cheeks pinken and sent a girlish giggle dancing from her mouth.

'She's a lifesaver, this one.' Brendon addressed Callan. 'I'd have been a ruined man tonight if it weren't for her.'

Margo set the rest of the order on a tray and Callan went to pass her his card.

'On the house.' Brendon waved his card away. 'In fact, whatever you order tonight, it's on me.'

Callan made to protest, but Margo shot him down with a stare that told him in no uncertain terms that he should take the kind offer and not question it.

'Well, er, thank you.' Callan picked up the tray and turned around. Then he turned back. 'Margo . . .' He waved her closer. 'Did either of you happen to see the sunset tonight? Were you up on the hill?'

'Us?' Margo's cheeks flamed bright once more, as her lips quirked. 'Oh, no. Not us. We were far too busy for that.'

Callan didn't wait for her to elaborate, and wasn't about to ask. He had a feeling he knew exactly what was causing Brendon's genial mood. Or *who*. And it had nothing to do with sunsets that brought a person's hopes and dreams to life.

He weaved his way through the revellers and found Lauren, Will and Josie at the table Josie had spotted, which, apparently, only had two chairs. Lauren was settled on Will's lap, which left one chair, which Josie was occupying.

He set the tray on the table and passed the drinks around. 'On the house. As are all our drinks for tonight only, according to Brendon.'

Lauren's mouth formed an 'o' as she clapped her hands together with excitement. 'It's the magic of the sunset. It's happening. To one of us! Or maybe to Brendon?'

'Not to Brendon. He was too busy here to watch the sunset.' Callan didn't go into further details. If Margo and Brendon were making a go of things, the last thing they needed was nosey villagers getting in the way.

'Well, whichever one of us has gotten a night of free drinks bestowed upon us, I salute you.' Will grabbed his beer and raised it high. 'To lady luck. And those who find her.'

Callan hunkered down into a squat, not wanting to hover over the table, and the quartet clinked their glasses, and took long sips.

'Oh my gosh, where are my manners?' Josie set her glass down and sprung out of the seat. 'Here, you take this. You've been running round after Mia all day, and you carried her down the hill, your legs must be buggered.'

'Oh, no. I couldn't. You sit.'

'I insist.' Josie didn't budge.

'I insist more,' Callan shot back.

A groan of impatience came from Lauren. 'And I insist you compromise. Callan, sit on the seat. Josie, sit on his lap. If his lap's too close for comfort, then make use of his knees. Just . . . sit . . . both of you. Or I'll take my free drink and throw it over you. Then I'll take Will's free drink and do the same.'

'Oh, no you won't.' Will tickled Lauren's waist, causing her to nearly spill her drink anyway. 'I like my free drinks in my stomach, not soaking into clothes and carpet.'

Josie folded her arms, her brow crinkled in indecision. 'Wouldn't it be weird?'

Callan wasn't sure if she was asking him or talking to herself. What he did know was that they couldn't just stand about awkwardly for the rest of the night.

'Not weird. Not when we're just making do.' He sat himself on the chair and angled the length of his thighs so there was plenty of clear space for her to sit in whichever way felt most comfortable and least weird.

'Making do,' she murmured, then settled herself gingerly, not quite on his knees, nowhere near his nether regions, more smack bang in the middle. She twisted round to face him. 'You okay? I'm not cutting off the circulation to your legs?'

Callan jiggled her up and down, similar to the way he did Mia when they played horsey. 'You're light as a feather.'

'And you're too kind. Also a bit of a liar.'

The dry reply saw Lauren and Will raise their glasses with a laugh.

'Cheers to you two finally getting it together,' Will rolled his eyes, then downed half his beer in one go. 'So, who's getting the next free round?'

140

Callan held his ribs, laughing long and hard for what must have been the thousandth time that night, as Will demonstrated the Irish dancing he'd learned as a boy. Forced into it by his mother in the hopes it would tire the boisterous lad out, he'd demonstrated quite the talent, and had at one point been offered a job with a dance company that toured the world, only turning it down because he'd met Lauren, and deigned her the true love of his life. Dumping dancing like it was yesterday's news and throwing his excess energy into farming by day and wooing by night.

'Brilliant. Amazing.' Callan gasped. 'I can't believe I'm only seeing this now.'

'Blame the beer.' Lauren giggled as she pulled Will onto her lap and wrapped her arms possessively around him. 'It's the only time he'll do it.'

'I can't believe you could have toured the world doing that.' Josie sipped her glass of water and leaned back into Callan with a tired sigh.

Callan wasn't sure who stiffened first at the unexpected closeness. Or who apologised first.

'Oh, God, I'm so sorry.' Josie bolted upright, her face scarlet.

'No. I am. Sorry. I mean. Very sorry.' Callan raked his hand through his hair and tried to ignore the stiffening of another area of his body that had no place standing to attention. Even if he'd spent the night encouraging said area as he'd admired Josie's sense of humour, her easy way with people, the soft curve of her cheek, the glossiness of her hair, the sweet aroma of sugar and vanilla that emanated from her . . .

'Oh, for Pete's sake.' Lauren rolled her eyes. 'What are you apologising for? Josie, you leaned back because you were feeling at ease, comfortable. Callan, you provided said comfort. It happens. It's not like Josie straddled you and kissed you silly. Now *that*

141

would be worth apologising for.' Lauren waggled an unsteady finger at the two of them. 'And not because there's anything wrong with you two kissing. It's more that we who've been together this side of ever are made to feel inadequate when young lust is thrust in our faces.'

Callan's hand slid from his hair to cover his eyes. He didn't know whether to laugh, cry or give Lauren a stern talking-to about inappropriate topics of conversation that were sure to embarrass the people who the conversation was directed at.

'Will, I think it's time we went home.' Lauren laid her head against Will's back. 'Carry me, sweet man? I think the free drinks have rendered me a touch legless.'

Will stood, then wrapped one arm around her neck, tucked the other underneath her thighs, and heaved her up with a dramatic squinting of eyes and a loud grunt, which earned him an ear flick from Lauren.

'Thanks for the fun night. Sorry about this one. Her tongue gets a touch loose after a few gins.' He clenched his teeth in a grimace.

'Never heard you complain about my loose tongue before,' Lauren mumbled as she snuggled into his chest, her eyelids drooping more and more with every second that passed.

Callan watched them leave, while trying to figure out what to do, what to say next. Should he ask Josie if she wanted another drink? Invite her back to his for a night cap? Before any kind of invitation, should he apologise for Lauren and her straddling and kissing comments?

'Right, well, I've got to get home. Early start tomorrow.'

He twisted round to see Josie rugged up in her outdoor clothing and already moving towards the door.

Questions answered. There'd be no 'one for the road'. No nightcap. No need for an apology either as any hint of redness in Josie's cheeks had subsided and her shoulders were no longer trying to touch the ceiling.

'Wait up. I'll walk you home.'

Callan grabbed his coat and scarf and stepped up his pace to catch up with Josie, waving a quick goodbye to Margo and Brendon who were sitting at the end of the bar, wide smiles on both of their faces as they chatted.

He pushed the closing door open and jogged the few steps until he reached Josie.

'Didn't you hear me say I'd walk you home?'

Josie continued her determined march forward. 'I did. Sorry. I've just been hit with a wave of tiredness, and as you well know I do have work tomorrow, and, well, I just thought it was best if I headed home before . . .' Her top teeth sunk into her lower lip, like she was censoring herself.

Callan shoved his hands in his coat pockets. Not because they were cold, but because he had an urge to take Josie by the hand, to stop her in the lane, to cup her face, and to kiss her . . . just to see what it would be like. To know if her lips were as soft as they looked. If the sweet scent that surrounded her extended to her lips. If the feelings that had been building all night – all night? More like for the last couple of weeks – were real, or just a figment of his imagination.

'Before what, Josie?' He ducked his head so he could see her face more clearly.

The hint of tension in the air thickened. The puffs of mist that had escaped Josie's lips with each breath, stilled. Her eyes went to her feet, denying him any chance of seeing what was going through her mind.

He could make a joke, say something light-hearted, let the moment pass. That would be the safe thing to do. Yet he couldn't. His tongue refused to leave the roof of his mouth.

This was not the time for words.

He reached out and tucked his fingertips under Josie's chin, sensed the taut muscle of her jaw tighten further, as she lifted her gaze to meet his.

143

'Before what?' he whispered.

'I didn't want the villagers to get the wrong end of the stick. To think something was going on here. To cause you to be the subject of gossip.'

The words were right, but they came out forced. Fake. Like Josie didn't believe what she was saying. Like she was saying what had to be said, to what? Keep the barriers up? Keep things professional?

'The only way they could get the wrong end of any stick was if they sensed there was nothing going on between us.' Callan held his breath as Josie's lips parted, then closed.

Her eyes shut as she raised herself up on tiptoes.

This was it. They were going to kiss. His heart rate picked up. His fingers and toes tingled. Nerves sparked in his stomach.

He dipped his head lower. Pressed his lips together softly, puckered them just a little. Closed his eyes. And . . .

Jumped. He nearly leaped out of his skin, as a crack of lightning and rumble of thunder ripped through the sky, before torrential rain bucketed down, soaking through his coat in seconds.

Callan went to tell Josie to run for the bakery, but she was already five steps ahead of him. He followed her path, his hand searching his pocket for the keys, so they could get inside as quickly as possible.

A wild laugh caught him by surprise, and he realised it came from Josie who'd reached the front door and had her head tipped to the sky, that lit up a white-blue with frightening regularity.

He unlocked the door, pushed it open, took her by the hand and pulled her inside before she got struck by an errant bolt and got badly hurt, or worse.

The force of his touch saw her crash into him. Heat emanated from her, despite the frigidity of the night, the chill of the rain. Her eyes were alight, her smile wide and welcoming. Her cheekbones raised high in amusement and exhilaration.

Callan fingered a wet strand of hair that was plastered across her forehead and tucked it behind her ear. He traced the length of her face, from her forehead down, skirting the soft spot by her ear, before trailing the length of her jaw.

'Please don't play in thunderstorms, Josie.' The depth of emotion in his voice, caught even himself by surprise.

He waited for her to push his hand away, to pull away. She remained in his arms, her gaze turning more serious by the second.

'It's just lightning and a bit of thunder, Callan.' Her hand left his and snaked around his waist. 'I was fine.'

'But you might not have been. I didn't want to risk losing you.'

Josie's lips quirked. 'Because the bakery needs a baker. You'd be lost without me.' She made to roll her eyes, but they paused halfway, her attention drawn to the ceiling.

He tipped his head to see what she was seeing.

The mistletoe. Of course. Of all nights, tonight would see them caught underneath it. He wasn't mad about it.

Her gaze met his. The quirk in her lips smoothed out.

'Well, I guess rules are rules.' Josie half-shrugged as her head angled a touch to the side.

'And who are we to break them?' Callan's breath caught in his throat as his heartbeat picked up in anticipation.

Josie's hand slipped under his coat and splayed across his lower back as it pulled him closer still. He imagined he could feel her heart thumping against his chest. As fast as his. Were her nerves stretched as taut? Was she worried it would be awkward like last time? That the spark between them would fizzle as fast as the storm outside, if the quietening of rumbles was anything to go by.

'Stop thinking,' Josie instructed. 'I can almost hear your thoughts.'

Callan smiled as Josie's lips touched his. Soft. Tentative. The simple brushing of lip on lip, skin on skin, sent an electrical storm far greater than the one that had raced over the village, through Callan's veins.

He weaved his fingers through Josie's hair, lightly so she had space to pull away should she want to, should she change her mind.

Josie's lips pressed against his. Deeper. Hungrier. He parted his lips, wanting more, offering her entry. And she took it. Their tongues touched, tantalised. She tasted rich, dark, tangy, and oh so sweet.

Josie's hand clutched his neck possessively as she moaned against him. The vibration heightened his need.

And another vibration, coming from his trouser pocket, doused it.

He stroked her cheek with his thumb as he reluctantly pulled away. 'That'll be Lauren's mum wondering where I am. She probably heard the door shut.'

Josie's eyes were heavy-lidded and happy as she cupped his cheeks, then trailed her fingers down to his chest, where she flattened her palms over his heart.

'I can feel it.' She gazed up at him, her soft lips lifting. 'Strong and steady. Just like you.'

'Could you make me sound any more boring?' Callan placed his hand over hers, not wanting to let her go. Not just yet.

'I like it. I like you.' Josie placed her free hand in front of her mouth. 'I can't believe I just said that. How to get a man to run a million miles. Declare you like them. Good one, Josie.' She closed her eyes and shook her head.

He brought her hand away from her mouth and kissed her. Light and quick. 'I'm not running anywhere.'

Her eyes opened, all hints of self-reproach gone. 'What a night. I never expected our trip up the hill to watch a sunset to turn out like this. Free drinks. A kiss. Well, many kisses all rolled into one long, delicious kiss.' She flipped her hand away from his heart and tangled her fingers in his. 'And I can't wait to see what comes next.' A yawn escaped, and she pulled away. The tips of her fingers lingering on his like she didn't want to go. 'But it really is time for bed. For me.'

146

Callan pushed away the temptation to pull her back, to kiss her again, to ask her to stay. He suspected she'd say yes, but he didn't want to push, to hurry either of them. He wanted to take his time, to explore this new . . . whatever it was going on between them.

He wasn't going anywhere.

And, despite her history of moving on, he couldn't help but think – but hope – Josie wasn't either.

Chapter 15

Josie pulled two cake tins out of the oven, placed another two in, shut the door, whipped her oven mitts off and tossed them on the bench.

'What was I thinking? I'm a madwoman. "A four-tier cake", she said. "Representing four elements of Christmas", she said. *She* needs to have her head read.' Josie leaned over and surveyed the list of things she had to do if she was going to make her entry into the Christmas Cake-off a success. Or, at the very least, not entirely a mess. 'Spun sugar snowballs dusted in edible silver glitter. I mean, really? I must've been on another planet when I decided to add that.'

Another planet was an almost accurate assessment. Her head had been well and truly in the clouds, along with her heart, since she and Callan had kissed under the mistletoe two days ago.

Then kissed right here, in the kitchen, the next day. On her sofa when he'd left Mia with Margo and popped round for a cup of tea, AKA a snog session.

It was like being a teenager again. Snatching moments wherever possible, as they'd both agreed to not confuse Mia with public shows of affection. Adding to the illusion of youthful romance, Callan had yet to try and take things further.

It was the most gentle, delectable courtship.

No hands fumbling their way towards her lady lumps. Or down to other, more private areas. Just kisses. Quick and careless. Long and lingering. Slow and sensual.

Not that she'd have swatted his hand away had he tried. A single Callan kiss made every nerve ending in her body thrum to the hypnotic chant of 'more, more, more'. The sweet nothings he'd whispered in her ear – 'you look wonderful', 'your smile makes me happy', 'those jeans are great', which she took to mean 'your bum looks fab in those jeans' – saw her soul swell with a happiness and warmth she couldn't recall feeling before.

Not that she'd ever given herself the chance to let someone that close. Which was why, in between all the beautiful moments they shared, she had to fight her inner voice who railed against the familiarity, the settling, the potential for commitment.

It was the fear in that voice that had spurred the inspiration for the competition. All the layers, all the elements, all the fiddly handcrafted edible figurines ensured she was kept too busy baking and creating to get in her own way. Because the moment she stopped moving, the moment she took a breath, the voice sprung forth, reminding her of what happened when you trusted another person with your heart.

They'd leave. They'd check out. They'd break your heart, one way or the other.

The second she heard the whispers unfurling, curling through her mind, trying to take root, she pushed back. Powered forward.

Which was how it came to be that she was now preparing to create the biggest, most extravagant cake of her career.

One layer a winter wonderland, with icing snowflakes embedded around the sides, and miniature handmade figurines holding a snowball fight on top.

The next layer would depict Santa's workshop. Little elves creating teddy bears and toy trains, with a giant pile of ribboned boxes stacked around the edges. The third layer would feature a chorus of singers, dressed in red, green and gold, surrounded by fondant musical notes.

149

As for the fourth layer? That's where her giant plan had come a tad unstuck. She wanted it to represent family. Love. Community. Connection. But all she had was a blank cake.

How could she create a family-inspired layer when her own Christmas for nearly a decade and a half had been anything but a family-filled affair?

And that's why what you're doing with Callan is wrong. You don't know how to be part of a family.

She closed her eyes, gritted her teeth and mentally told the voice to take a running jump.

'Josie? Are you okay?'

A warm hand was gently placed upon her forehead, and she leaned into it. Appreciated its warmth, the caring that saw it placed upon her.

This was what she wanted. This was what she'd secretly yearned for, dreamed of. She wasn't letting the Voice of Sabotage destroy her chance at happiness. Of a good life. Not this time.

She took Callan's hand and brought it down, didn't let it go. Allowed its strength to infuse her.

'I'm fine. Just giving myself a mental bashing for deciding to go all out in baking this cake for the competition. I should've started small. Eased my way in. It's not like there won't be other Christmas Cake-offs to compete in.' *Not if things continue as they are. Not if I embrace this new way of life.*

Callan brought her hand up to his lips and kissed the back of it. 'It'll be amazing. At least I can only assume so, because you've not told me a thing about it, which considering it's being cooked in my kitchen, I'm a touch miffed about.' His lower lip dropped into a pout that morphed quickly into a grin. 'So, do I get a clue?'

Josie directed her gaze to the ceiling in thought. 'Well . . . I can tell you it's Christmassy. And it involves cakes.'

'Cakes multiple? Like these two.' He pointed to the tins on the bench.

'Those two, and the two in the oven. And there's four more to come if each cake's going to be a double-layer.'

'Four tiers. Impressive. Not many people have attempted that before.'

A shadow crossed Callan's face, then disappeared as quickly as it came, like a cloud scuttling past the sun.

Was he thinking of Abigail? Of the cakes she'd made? Did he feel that Josie was trying to compete with her? Trying to outdo her?

And if she was successful and placed, or won, would some part of him resent her for it?

'Callan . . .' She searched for the right way to ask the question that had played on her mind the last few days. 'Is it wrong for me to enter this competition? This was Abigail's thing, and I don't want to be seen as treading on her turf. In more ways than one.' She looked down at her shoes as her cheeks flamed hot. She hadn't meant to say the last sentence. It had tumbled out before she could stop it. Yet, she worried about that too.

Coming here. Taking over the baking. Falling for the owner's husband. Would people see her as being an imposter?

Worse, did Callan secretly see her as a convenient fill-in? Would he be with her until someone better came along? Someone more worthy of love? Someone worth going through the thick and the thin for?

And there went the Voice of Sabotage. Finding her insecurities and twisting them, illuminating them.

Callan dropped her hand. She waited for him to step away, to admit his misgivings about the cake, about them. She didn't expect for his arms to encircle her, to bring her close, to hold her tight. His chin upon her head. His hand stroking, soothing, comforting, as it caressed the length of her back.

'If I could go back in time and give that mother and father of yours a good talking-to, I would. I can see you waiting for me to tell you this is a mistake. To push you away.' He looked her square in the eyes. 'You've barely stood still the last couple of days. It's like you're ready to make a move the moment I give you reason to. And I get it, I do. It's not easy being left without notice, without reason, Josie. No one knows that more than me. I'm scared too. But I'm not letting that fear stop me trying. Not when it took everything I had in me to come out of my self-imposed cave, to let myself get close to you.'

The air that had built and caught in Josie's chest, leaving her unable to speak, unsure what to say, whooshed out. How could Callan be so brave? So sure? After all he'd lost. It wasn't that long ago, in the grand scheme of things, that his wife had passed. Whereas she'd had fourteen years to learn to be as brave as he was, yet she had nowhere near that level of courage. Even if she pretended to herself that she did, hoping that if she faked it, she'd eventually make it.

'And don't for a second think that you can't enter the competition, that you're treading on toes, or that people will raise an eyebrow at you throwing your hat in the ring. They won't. You work here, you're talented, it's expected. Besides, the villagers adore you. I can see it in the way they talk to you. The way they keep coming back.'

Josie noticed he didn't mention their burgeoning relationship. That it wasn't in the mix. Callan may talk about being brave, but he wasn't yet brave enough to acknowledge that one day the villagers, and Mia, would have to know about them.

Because he didn't want to admit to it? Didn't want to be seen as betraying his wife? Didn't want to be judged? Or maybe, despite his words, he didn't see them going beyond a fling . . .

Josie forced a smile and told herself she was being ridiculous. It was early days. Callan was doing the rational thing. What she'd have done if she were in his position. He had as much, perhaps even more, to lose than she did if they didn't work out.

'So, I'll keep going on with the cake.'

Callan nodded. 'You must. I insist.'

'Does that also mean you won't mind me rattling around down here tonight? It could be late. In fact, I guarantee it will be late, but I promise to keep quiet. Wouldn't want to wake you or Mia.'

'The kitchen's yours. And don't worry about waking us up. The world could be falling down around us and Mia would sleep through it. As for me, I just hope you don't hear me snoring. Abigail once said I was so loud she could feel the foundations shaking. Although' – he tapped his chin in thought – 'if I'm really that bad it might put you off me. Maybe I need to rescind the use of the kitchen overnight?'

Josie went to object but stopped as a thunder of footsteps on stairs and a plaintive 'Daaaaaadd-eeeee, is it time to go shopping yeeeet?' met their ears.

Callan's arms shot away from her, and he took a giant step back.

Josie crossed her arms and tried to ignore the part of her that felt hurt at the way he'd dropped her as if she were a hot tin straight from the oven. She understood why he wanted to keep their tentative relationship away from Mia, but that didn't stop the little girl who spent years feeling rejected from reliving that feeling.

Josie picked up a knife and turned her attention to the cooling cakes. She ran the knife around the perimeter of the one closest, then unlocked the cake tin.

How had her life come to this? From spending her life avoiding connection, ties, community, to now wanting all of it. Sooner rather than later. She kept a careful eye on the cake as it peeled away from the edge, making sure no chunks tore away. What she needed to do was slow her flow and let things progress naturally. At a speed that wouldn't see their situation implode. Or fall apart.

She took a calming breath as the last part of the cake gave, leaving a perfect circle.

She looked up to see Mia, dressed in the frothiest, pinkest, tulle dress she'd ever seen, being bear-hugged by Callan.

'Nice dress.' Josie grinned as Mia escaped Callan's cuddle and twirled round and round in the middle of the kitchen, sending her skirts flying, until she collapsed in giggles on the ground.

Josie crossed the kitchen and, once Mia had caught her breath and stopped looking like the inside of her head was whirling, pulled her into a standing position. 'You're going shopping? Where are you off to?'

'Can't tell. It's a surprise.' Mia began jumping up and down, trying to retrieve her coat from the hook.

'Here, let me help.' Josie passed Mia her coat and helped her get into it, then lined up her soft pink cowgirl-style boots.

Mia balanced on Josie's arm as she pushed her feet into them. 'Daddy said we can't tell people what presents we're buying them, even though I would want to be told if I were getting—'

Before she could spill the beans, Callan placed a softly cupped hand over Mia's mouth.

'Mia, darling, were you about to accidentally ruin the surprise?' He removed his hand and Mia tipped her head up to his, shaking her head fervently.

'Sorry, Daddy, I forgot.' She shrugged by way of apology.

'And we should get going before she forgets again.' Callan took his keys off their hook next to the coats and jiggled them in his hand. 'You'll be okay for a couple of hours?'

His eyes were as warm as his smile, and any misgivings, concerns, worries and doubts Josie harboured melted away.

Callan wasn't like the people she'd cared about in the past. People she'd given her trust to. He wouldn't pick up and leave like her mother. Wouldn't grow distant like her father.

He was here. Present. He didn't scuttle away, he dug in.

The proof of that was currently tugging his hand with impatience.

'I'll be fine. I always am.'

And for the first time in more years than she could count, she believed the words coming out of her mouth.

She was fine.

More than fine.

She was home.

154

Chapter 16

Rain lashed against the village hall's windows, the weather oblivious to the moans and groans of cake makers from around the district as they raced in from outside, arms full, noses dripping, clothing soaked.

'It's ruined.' A woman one table over from Josie crumpled to the ground, her howl muffled as she buried her head in her arms. 'Ruined.'

Josie eyed the mountain of white and yellow sludge, on which a fondant Santa – his hat now attached to his feet rather than his head – appeared to be skiing down in a haphazard way. She went to console the woman, to tell her the mushed mess could be saved, but couldn't force the white lie past her lips.

The woman uncurled herself, picked up the destroyed mountain, dumped it unceremoniously in the nearest bin and stalked out of the hall.

'I don't think that'll be the last cake to end up there.'

Josie twisted round to see Callan shaking his head and thanked her lucky stars that he'd saved her from the same fate. On seeing the rain bucketing down that morning he'd pulled together a makeshift portable stage, complete with a post on each of its four corners, over which he'd draped a tarpaulin, placed it securely in a wheelbarrow he'd borrowed from Will, and presented it to Josie with a proud flourish and a 'for you, my lady'.

'Poor woman. My heart goes out to her. She must've spent hours making that cake, only for the ski field to have an avalanche.' A ripple of nerves danced through Josie, and she peeked under the tarpaulin to make sure her cake hadn't gone the way of her neighbour's, but it was perfect. Standing straight. Every decoration in place. Not a bump, ripple or wave in the icing.

Josie covered her mouth as the millionth yawn of the day escaped. She'd been up until three that morning perfecting the last tier, inspiration having finally struck in the midnight hour as she'd pondered the meaning of family. Of community. And how it tied into Christmas.

Her heart bubbled with hope. She didn't expect to win, not when she was so new to the area, but she believed her creation would spark interest, maybe even happiness, and once the judging was done and the cakes could be shared with the community, she believed her work would bring more business to the bakery. That Abigail's would be renowned once more.

'Still perfect?' Callan's fingertips briefly touched her hip, letting her know he was still there. That he hadn't left.

Josie ducked out from under the tarpaulin and turned to face him. Even under the unforgiving fluorescent lighting of the hall, Callan looked divine. His eyes shone like freshly stirred melted chocolate. His cheeks were raised high in good humour, his lips as lush as ever. It took everything she had not to reach up, to cup his face, to bring those beautiful lips down to hers.

She closed her eyes so temptation wasn't staring her in the face, crossed her arms and tucked her hands flat against her ribcage. There. Safe. Unable to reach, unable to touch, unable to cross any boundaries in front of the villagers that might lead to unwanted speculation.

She was sticking to the unspoken, but oh so obvious, rules.

Take things slow.

156

Keep it easy.

Keep it on the down low.

The squeal of a loud-hailer pierced the air, forcing her to put her fears aside and focus on what was important right now.

The judging.

'Best of luck.' Callan nodded encouragingly, then left the hall to join those who'd gathered outside to sing carols and get in the Christmas spirit, before it was time to gorge themselves on cake.

Josie took a deep breath, wiped her sweaty palms on her jeans and surveyed the competition. She'd entered the three-plus tier category, which had limited the number of those who'd entered, but those who had were talented and their creations had her dealing with tingling tastebuds and a storm of snowflakes blustering about in her belly.

The judges wasted no time admiring and tasting. Lip-smacking appreciation came from across the hall where the single-tier cakes were being judged, punctuated by moments of ominous silence.

Waves of tension, nerves and hope rose and fell as they moved from cake to cake, leaving relieved shoulders in their wake. Entrants knew their work was done, judgement had been made, and there was nothing more they could do than sit back and watch the spectacle of those who were as jittery as they'd been.

An interminable amount of time, probably only fifteen minutes, passed before the judges reached Josie. She managed a smile and a nod. No smile or nod was returned, instead they stared at her. Kept staring. Paid no attention to the cake.

Her hands twisted around each other as she became convinced she'd done something wrong and was about to be ejected from the competition in a cloud of shame.

'Description? Inspiration?' The head judge. A stout woman in a forest-green buttoned-down cardigan that gave way to beige pants nodded. Her tone even, her eyes encouraging.

'Oh, yes.' Josie mentally face-palmed herself. Of course they'd want to know what they were eating and the inspiration behind her creation. She took a deep breath, centred herself and began.

'The first layer is a fruitcake. So chosen because Christmas is a time of tradition, and fruitcake was always served at our dinner table as part of dessert growing up. I've iced it in snow-white fondant and covered it in icing snowflakes and spun sugar snowballs covered in edible glitter, as – even though it doesn't always happen – a white Christmas is the ultimate Christmas gift.'

She sliced into the back of the cake, keeping the front unblemished so the villagers could visually enjoy it before digging in, and passed pieces to the judges.

Their expressions were inscrutable as they chewed and swallowed, though she swore she caught a tiny nod of approval from the second judge. A dapper gent in a three-piece suit, his iron-grey hair swept up on either side of his head to form a small mohawk.

'The next layer is chocolate mud cake, representing the indulgence of Christmas. The one time where we can enjoy all the things we love without guilt. As a nod to that I've created icing figures of elves hard at work in Santa's workshop, making toys for the children to open on Christmas morning.' She indicated the pile of icing presents, each hand-painted a different colour complete with contrasting icing ribbons.

Her heart swelled with pride as an unsolicited 'ooooh' of approval came from the third judge. A blonde woman of about her age, wearing a cherry-red Fifties-style vintage dress, covered in sprigs of mistletoe.

She sliced more pieces and passed them round. Her nerves dissipated a little as lips smacked together, and she knew her rich, dark mud cake was spot on in flavour and texture.

'The third tier is my homage to Sunnycombe. Again, the figurines are handmade, as are the musical notes. I must admit that when I arrived here I wasn't the biggest fan of Christmas, but the spirit of the village and its people have caused me to rethink my attitude, and I do believe that next year the choir might have an extra member . . . That's if they don't mind taking on someone who's tone deaf.'

The judges laughed as she passed them the cake. Their laughter subsided as the simple but delicious vanilla cake with snow-white Italian meringue touched their tastebuds.

'The final tier is a red velvet cake with a cream cheese frosting embedded with teardrop hearts.' Josie closed her eyes as her throat tightened, like one of the three hearts she'd created and entwined together, then arranged on the top, had become lodged in there.

Except she knew the heart in her throat was not from the cake, but rather a culmination of the happiness she'd experienced in the last few weeks. 'I made the cake toppers – the ring of hearts, with the three hearts entwined in the centre – to represent what I love most about Sunnycombe. The kindness of the people who live here. The generosity of the people who live here. And the love I see between those who live here. I've never felt so accepted, so much a part of a village, so quickly. It's a special place.' Josie forced her eyes open, to see the gentleman judge wiping away a tear.

'And now for a taste?' reminded the elder woman judge, or Ms Cardigan as Josie had come to think of her.

'Of course. Sorry. I did go on a bit, didn't I?' Josie picked up a clean knife and sliced the final slivers of cake for each of the judges.

The silence that followed as they leaned closer to view her detail-work then noted down their scores, was as overwhelming as it was satisfying.

Her work was done. There was nothing more she could do. And if the softening of their appearance tier by tier was anything to go by, she could give herself a pat on the back for a job well done.

Was it enough to win?

She'd find out soon enough, but either way she was proud of herself and believed she'd represented Abigail's well. More than anything she hoped she'd done well by the woman the bakery was named after.

A lowering of the temperature in the hall announced the

arrival of the masses as the main door was opened and they began to spill in.

Josie searched Callan out and found him within seconds as he had a bouncing, excitable Mia sitting atop his shoulders.

He waved to her and made a beeline for the table, ignoring the rest of the entries, then stopped short a metre away.

Her chest tightened with anticipation. Callan's opinion mattered more than the judges. She couldn't say it to the judges, hadn't wanted to lay that much of herself out for random strangers to see, but the three hearts entwined were representative of the two people who'd brought her the most joy, the most happiness she'd experienced in years.

They'd given her the chance of a life she'd long ago given up on and, eventually, refused to even consider.

Until now.

Callan's mouth opened. Shut. Opened again. Clamped down once more.

Her case of the nerves became more unbearable with every second that slipped by. Her hands were gripped at her chest. Her jaw was so tight it could have been wired shut. The unspoken words 'what do you think?' begged to be set free.

'It's fabliss.' Mia reached out to touch it, and Callan ducked back a step, even though they were nowhere near it.

'Fabulous,' Callan repeated.

'Fabliss.' Mia tried again. 'That's what I said.'

'She's right.' Callan looked past the cake to Josie. 'It is fabliss. I mean fabulous. Best cake here.'

'You haven't looked at the rest,' Josie pointed out.

Callan lifted Mia down from his shoulders, then shrugged. 'I don't need to. I've been to enough of these to know when I see the best. And it is. It's perfect. Too beautiful to eat.'

His eyes held a mixture of awe, appreciation, and something she couldn't quite get a handle on. A strain, that was matched by the set of his jaw. The tension around his eyes.

Josie went to ask him if he was all right, but the loud-hailer squealed into action once more.

'Ladies and gentlemen. Thank you for coming to the Great Christmas Cake-off. We are ready to announce the winners.'

A hush fell over the crowd. Anticipation rose, so thick you could almost taste it.

'First we'll start with the single-tier category . . .'

The coming moments were filled with cries of joy and cheers of success, as the winners and place-getters came to the front of the hall to collect their golden cups, rosettes and certificates.

Somewhere, at some point, Callan had slipped around to Josie's side of the table.

'You've got this,' he whispered.

'I've got all that matters.'

Josie glanced up to see the delicious creases around his eyes had deepened, his lips turned up into a smile.

If a heart could burst from happiness, Josie was sure hers was on the verge.

'And the winner of the multi-tiered cake category, and the overall Great Christmas Cake-off champion, goes to . . .'

Josie, unable to keep her cool one second longer, buried her face into Callan's arm, not caring that she was touching him in public. That people might see it as a sign of affection between them.

'Josie Donnelly of Abigail's Bakery.'

The crowd burst into applause that echoed off the walls and quickly became a roar of approval.

Josie squealed and giggled as she found herself being swept off her feet then whirled round in circles.

'I can't believe it.' She grabbed hold of Callan's arms to steady herself once he set her down.

'Believe it. Now go get your prize.' He took hold of her shoulders, spun her towards the front of the room and sent her on her way.

Kind words in her ears and hands clapped her on the back

and propelled her forward. The judges' huge smiles became increasingly blurry as tears filled her eyes. Josie was torn between jumping up and down or running away and finding a quiet spot to process what was happening to her.

It was a heady mixture of too much and not enough all at once. She wanted to be here, claiming the prize, but more than anything she wanted Callan and Mia at her side, because this was as much about them as it was her.

'Thank you.' She wiped away the tears, then took the two golden trophies that were thrust in her direction – one small and featuring a golden slice of cake, the other large and featuring a baker holding a cake, a proud smile on their golden face.

'These are for you too.' The vintage-dress judge thrust a bouquet of Christmas lilies into her spare arm. 'Congratulations. The competition was fierce, but yours was head and shoulders above the rest.' She lightly touched Josie's waist and turned her to face the audience. 'Speech time.'

Josie took a deep breath and tried to piece together her thoughts, but all she could come up with was 'don't make an idiot of yourself', which was as good a starting place as any.

'I'll keep this short. I don't want to make an idiot of myself. I'm a baker not a speechmaker.'

The crowd tittered at her off-the-cuff attempt at humour, and she felt herself relax. Her heartbeat dropped from thunderous rib-cracking thumps to a steady pit-pat. She pushed her shoulders down. Lifted her chin. Found Callan and Mia, and knew by the pride on their faces that even if she jibber-jabbered her way through the speech she'd still have done right by them.

'Thank you, first of all, to the judges. When I saw the quality of the entries I honestly didn't expect to get anywhere. So all of this . . .' She hefted the trophies and flowers. 'Well, it's floored me. And bravo to my fellow bakers. You really are amazing, and I can't wait to enjoy the fruits of your work.' Josie turned her attention to Callan and Mia. 'I said I'd keep this short, so I just need to say one more thank you. And that's to Callan and Mia Stewart. I couldn't have done this without your support, your kindness . . . and your kitchen.'

The crowd laughed again, and Josie joined them when Callan rolled his eyes, which earned him a telling off from Mia, complete with wagging finger.

'Now, go forth . . . and enjoy.'

The crowd didn't need to be told twice and quickly dispersed as they beelined for the cakes that caught their attention.

Josie's heart sank when she noticed her table was empty. Had the cheering been of the polite variety? Had she misread the situation?

She sidled up to Callan, her spirits deflated.

'You okay?' Lines of concern bracketed his mouth. 'You're meant to be looking happy right now, you know that? Meant to be as proud of yourself as I am of you?'

'But no one's eating the cake. It's like they're actively avoiding the area. Or maybe there's a forcefield around the table keeping them away.'

Callan's hand clamped the top of her head like a claw and gently turned her head to the left. 'Your answer.'

A photographer was standing off to the side, camera in hand. 'Are you done with the private congratulations? Because I'd love to get a picture of you with the cake. It'll be on the newspaper's website tonight, and the story will be in Monday's paper.'

Josie looked back at Callan. 'I'm an idiot.'

'No, you're wonderful. Talented. And if anyone had dared touch a smidge of icing before the photo was taken, the event coordinator would have dragged them to the village square by their ear, put them in stocks and thrown leftover cake at them.'

'Vicious.' Josie grinned, then turned back to the photographer. 'I'm ready when you are. Actually . . .' Josie hooked her arm through Callan's before he could step away. 'This one here will have to be in the picture too, if it's okay? He's the owner

163

of the bakery where I whipped this up. Couldn't have done it without him.'

'Or me.' Mia interjected with an indignant shake of Josie's free hand. 'I was a good girl and left Josie alone like Daddy told me to,' she informed the photographer with serious eyes.

Callan unhooked himself from Josie and swooped Mia up onto his hip. 'Are you sure? I wouldn't want to steal your glory?'

Josie rolled her eyes. 'Steal my glory. You're part of it. You both are.' She reached out and mussed Mia's hair, then smoothed it down again for the photo. 'On the count of three?'

'And we have to say cheese.' Mia nodded. 'That's the rules.'

'In that case . . . can I get you all closer?' The photographer waved at Josie to snuggle in next to Callan, then gave her the thumbs-up when she was close enough. 'In three . . . two . . . one . . .'

The three sang 'cheese' in unison. Then said it four more times as each picture wasn't quite right according to the photographer.

'There we go . . .' He flicked the viewfinder round for them to check his handiwork. 'You all look smashing.'

The image misted in front of Josie as fresh tears sprung from nowhere. The photographer was wrong, they didn't look smashing. They looked like a family.

One she'd never asked for. One she'd never expected.

One she hoped they might become one day, once they'd had enough time to get used to each other's rhythms, once Callan was ready, once he could be sure there was no chance of Mia being hurt. Or himself, Josie suspected.

Which there wasn't.

She knew that in her heart.

She'd spent her life avoiding this. Ensuring there was no chance of forming bonds with anyone, anywhere. Not wanting to deal with goodbyes, or abandonment. Not risking the chance of a broken heart.

Until now.

164

Now, if she were allowed to, she would give her heart to Callan. To Mia. Because they'd stolen it anyway. It belonged to them. She couldn't imagine a day without hearing Mia's curious tones or the patter of her busy feet. To never see Callan's thoughtful face as he considered a question or posed one. To not feel his hand in hers, his arm around her waist, his lips upon her lips.

An icy shiver raced through her at the mere thought of it.

She'd always been the one to leave. To keep those who might wish to get to know her at arm's length.

No more.

This was it for her.

It might not be the simplest of circumstances. Falling for a man whose wife had passed away. Treading lightly into a relationship, slowing discovering love, where others had the opportunity to rush headlong into less complicated situations. But this suited her. It suited *them*. And she would do everything in her power to keep the three shining, happy faces staring at her from the viewfinder together.

Forever.

Chapter 17

Callan pulled his reading glasses off, placed them on the desk in his small home office, closed his eyes and pinched the bridge of his nose. He'd been up since well before the crack of dawn working on a client's accounts, after a late night finishing off another client's accounts.

Since it had been made known through word of mouth that he was open for business once more, his old clientele had slowly but surely enquired about his taking over their accounts again.

It had turned out that the first client to approach him wasn't the only person to have been financially stagnating the past year. Many of his clients had ignored filing their taxes, and simply decided to wait for him to deal with his grief. To move on from his own stagnation.

Which he was. Slowly, but surely. While his love for Abigail had all the nerves and exhilaration of doing a running jump into a cold pool, his affection for Josie was of the getting into a cold pool inch-by-inch kind. Testing the water. Getting used to it. Eventually, going all in.

At least, that was the plan, if things kept going as well as they were.

His ears pricked up at the shuffling and rustling from the kitchen below. The sounds so familiar, yet so different. Abigail had been a clatterer, a banger, her morning routine serving as an alarm for himself and even Mia, whether they wanted to wake or not. Josie was quieter, more deliberate. Had he been asleep, he'd have stayed that way, and in the weeks that he'd entrusted the running of the kitchen to her, Mia had not once stirred.

Guilt eddied low in Callan's gut, and he automatically reached for the gold wedding band on his ring finger. It wasn't right to compare the two, and he didn't mean to. Not in a way that pitched Abigail and Josie against each other. But it was hard not to notice the things that separated them, that made them both special.

Abigail had been vivacious, out there, embracing of all in a way that had spun his head at times. Josie was warm, kind, reserved, but not in a way that was standoffish.

Abigail was who he needed then.

Josie was who he wanted now.

But was it right for him to expect her to be okay with his snail's-pace approach to their relationship? He hadn't been able to progress beyond handholding, kissing and hugging. Not that his thoughts hadn't strayed to other, more intimate, moments, but when they had he'd become aware of the ring on his finger. Of the place Abigail still held in his heart, and always would do.

Broaching the topic with Margo was a possibility, but she was busy finally discovering the love she deserved and he didn't want to interfere, or to bring up anything that might see her pull away from Brendon, who was the happiest he'd seen him in years.

'Daddy?' Mia's slight figure appeared at the door, her hair a mussed-up halo around her head. Her bunched hands rubbed the sleep from her eyes. 'Cuddle?'

'Always.' He opened his arms for Mia and she ran to him, settling on his lap, curling her legs around, and snuggling into him like a warm, little kitten. 'Did you have sweet dreams?'

Mia pressed her head against his chest and nodded. 'Mummy and I made a cake. Josie was there too. I was allowed to lick the bowl and the spoon.'

Callan stroked her hair, unsure of what to say. What to make of it. Was this Mia's mind's way of accepting Josie into her life? Did she see her as much a part of it as she had Abigail?

'You like Josie, don't you, Daddy?'

'I do.'

'Me too. I hope she never leaves.'

Callan went to echo Mia's answer. To say 'me too'. But Mia's answer stirred the last part of uncertainty he'd been trying to contain. Josie had been known to leave. To move. She'd admitted that to him, and he'd heard her. Understood why. And while he never intended to give her a reason to leave them, that didn't mean she wouldn't, if their relationship hit a rough patch, as they tended to do, even in the best, most concrete relationships.

Was this a relationship worth risking his and Mia's happiness for? Should he? When he was younger he would have, in a heartbeat. But now he had his daughter to consider. And himself. His heart had been ripped apart once. He didn't know that he could handle it happening again.

* * *

The knife she'd been using to ice the sides of a carrot cake clattered to the floor. Josie silently cursed as she picked it up and dumped it in the sink. She'd been a complete butterfingers all morning.

Not all morning, she amended, only since Callan had come down to help her out and had behaved . . . oddly.

No small touches. No hugs. Not even a peck on the cheek by way of hello.

She'd tried to tell herself that it was because Mia was buzzing about, happily offering to mix icing and carry ingredients back and forth, all the while feeding ginger loaf offcuts to the dolls she'd set up in a corner.

The excuse didn't sit right with her. Even though Callan had never been outright affectionate in front of Mia, he'd still been warm. This morning Callan had been as cold as the butter she needed to make the day's shortbread.

He's changed his mind. He's going to reject you like everyone you've ever cared about.

And if he had changed his mind? Josie knew better than anyone that once a person changed their mind, that was that. It was done. The future wasn't only written, but set in stone.

She picked up the display stand the cake was set on and carried it through to the store, placing it beside the Christmas tree-shaped gingerbread biscuits.

The door opened and an elderly couple entered arm in arm and made their way up to the counter. Their eyes scanned the contents that Josie had been refilling all day.

The publicity from the Cake-off's online article alone had seen them run off their feet with people grabbing last-minute cakes, slices and biscuits to fill their tins or to have on hand in case people dropped by in and around Christmas Day, which was all of two days away.

'Welcome to Abigail's. What can we get for you?' Callan's words sounded as wooden as his actions. Like her presence caused him to seize up.

'One of everything from the award-winning bakery, please.' The elderly gent pointed to the lemon drizzle loaf. 'And maybe all of that.'

His wife batted his arm. 'Gerald, leave something for those who come after us. Sorry about him . . . He eats with his eyes and forgets he can't put that much food away anymore.'

'I was thinking of the grandkids, pet. You know what they're like. Bundles of energy. They eat us out of house and home on a good day. What with them coming tonight, along with their parents, for a whole week? We need as much food in the house as possible.'

Mia sneaked in between Josie and Callan and eyed the customers with interest. 'How many people are coming to your house?'

'Eight.' The woman held up eight fingers. 'Both our sons, with their wives, and they each have two children. What about you? Are you having a big family Christmas?'

'Just us.' Mia answered. 'I invited Santa, but Daddy said he would be too tired after all the present dropping off to come.'

'Well, I'm sure you three will have a lovely Christmas together. Far more peaceful than ours. Such a beautiful family you are, too. Your wee one's the perfect mix of you both. Absolutely adorable.'

Josie's tongue tangled, caught between embarrassment and wanting to correct the customer in a way that wouldn't be awkward for anyone.

'Oh, no, Josie's not my daughter's mother. She just works here in the bakery.'

Callan's words, so matter of fact, so emotionless, set Josie's world into slow motion. The phrase 'she just works here' rolled through her head on repeat. Just. Works. Here.

Just.

No recognition of their closeness. That they were more than employer and employee.

Not even a small touch of the elbow, a smile in her direction, to let Josie know that Callan was just keeping things simple, professional, for the customer's sake.

'Mummy died last year.' Mia added. 'Josie is my friend. Daddy's friend too. They sometimes kiss. They don't know that I know, but I do.'

Callan's ears burned bright red as his gaze zeroed in on the countertop. 'It's erm, new. Er, nothing serious.'

The air, caught in Josie's lungs, rushed out with Callan's admission that she didn't mean anything. That what had gone on between them hadn't been serious. In his mind anyway.

Self-preservation took over and she went into action mode. 'Mia? Can you check on your dolls? I'm sure I can hear one of them asking for a cup of water?'

'Dolls don't talk, Josie. It's just make-believe.' Mia side-eyed

170

her like she was dealing with a madwoman, then skipped back into the kitchen.

'What else can we get for you?' Josie picked up a paper bag and a pair of tongs. The sooner she served them, the sooner they'd leave, and the sooner she could hang up her apron, hurry home and lick her wounds. Figure out her next step. Find a new place on the map to call home.

No. Not home. She didn't do home.

Her time in Sunnycombe had made her forget that, and now she was facing the harsh reality of letting her guard down.

'All the slices of lemon loaf you have. A dozen of the Christmas tree gingerbread biscuits. Half a dozen pieces of the peppermint swirl chocolate brownie. And half a dozen of the red velvet cupcakes. How pretty are those icing hearts?'

'Very.' Josie ignored the pain that ripped through her heart at the innocuous compliment. She wished she'd never made miniature versions of the cake that had represented everything she felt about Sunnycombe, the people, the lives, the loves. She turned to ask Callan to help, but he'd disappeared.

Of course he had. He'd put his foot in his mouth, revealed his true feelings and had gone into hiding.

Good. She didn't want to see him right now. Didn't want to see him ever again.

She packed the rest of the order, placed it carefully in a box, took the customers' money and sent them off with the cheeriest 'bye bye' she could manage.

As soon as the door had shut, she swivelled around, marched into the kitchen, took off the apron and tried to pretend she didn't see Mia looking up at her, concern creating the tiniest crease between her brows.

'Where are you going, Josie?' Mia set the doll down that she'd been playing with. 'Did I make you mad because I talked back? I'm sorry. I won't do it again.'

Josie sucked in a breath and begged the tears that built to stay put. The last thing she wanted was for Mia to think any of this was her fault, not when the fault was entirely at Josie's feet. She could've turned the job down when she saw it was a small family business. Could've kept herself to herself. Could've decided it wasn't up to her to help Callan move on from his deep-seated grief in an attempt to do for him what she could not do for her own father.

She crouched down and hugged Mia. Kept the contact short. Didn't want to breathe in her pear-shampoo scent, to feel the tickle of her silky hair against the underside of her chin, to relax into the cuddle as Mia did, the comfort of being embraced melding their bodies together.

'It's not you, Mia. Truly. You're a star. I'm just not feeling all that well and I have to go home. Wouldn't want you getting sick.' The white lie fell off her tongue easily – as any white lie did when it meant keeping a child happy, secure.

Josie went to tell Mia she'd see her when she felt better. But that was a promise she couldn't make. Christmas was nearly here. The village would go into slow mode. The bakery was set to close over Christmas and New Year. And after that? Callan could manage on his own.

He'd have to.

She couldn't stay. Couldn't spend hours working with him knowing he didn't feel the way about her that she did him.

Mia patted her hand, her eyes wide with worry. 'Go to bed. Have some orange juice. Get some sleep. That's what Mummy used to tell me when I was feeling yucky.' She leaned over and kissed Josie on the cheek, then turned back to her toys.

Josie grabbed her coat and ran for the door, the tears she'd held back unable to stay put one second longer.

Yanking the door open, she rushed out, not noticing the steady rain. Or the way her hair and clothing became saturated. Or that by the time she reached the cottage door her teeth were chattering and she had no idea where the tears ended and the raindrops began.

She dumped her coat and hat on the floor, squished herself

172

into the sofa, pulled her knees up to her chest, arranged the throw over her body, buried her head into its softness and drew in a long shuddering breath, followed by a slow exhale.

Get it together, she ordered herself. This was not her. She didn't lose her head over a man. Didn't lose control. She'd learned after her teenage rebellion that channelling her feelings into extremes – whether it be acting out or becoming overly emotional – did nothing to fix any situation.

And this wasn't a situation she could fix, so there was no point in weeping all over the place.

Yet the tears continued to run down her cheeks, turning the soft 'fur' of the throw wet and matted.

Three polite taps came from her front door.

'Josie? Are you there? Mia said you were sick.'

Callan. Of course it was the last person she wanted to see, especially in the state she was in.

Josie pulled the throw over her head and huddled down in case he thought to look through the window.

The squeak of unoiled hinges met her ears, and she cursed herself for not locking the door.

She held her breath, forced her shaking shoulders to still, hoped that her teeth wouldn't begin chattering again. She willed Callan to not see her hunched form on the sofa, or if he did to think it was just a bunch of cushions covered by a throw.

Despite her eyes being squeezed shut she knew she'd been discovered. The light from the outside, once Callan removed the throw, made the darkness behind her closed eyes less so. Though it did nothing to brighten the darkness within.

'Josie, my God, are you okay? You're soaked. What happened? Why didn't you put your raincoat on? Or grab one of our umbrellas? Why are you still wearing wet clothing? Mia said you were sick. You'll only make things worse if you don't change into something dry and get the fire going. The sooner the better. Josie? Are you listening? Do I need to call someone?'

The only thing stopping her from screaming 'get out, leave me alone' was her heart in her throat. How could he care so much yet not be able to acknowledge her, who she was to him, to strangers or the villagers or his own daughter?

'I'm calling the doctor. I'll make you an appointment. Or see if he can make a house call. He doesn't usually, but if you can't move or talk . . .'

'Stop.' The word came out a croak, but it was enough to break the paralysis that had kept her glued to the sofa, that had kept her eyes shut and her thoughts stuck in her head unable to be verbalised. 'Callan, stop. Everything.' She opened her eyes, tossed the throw aside and pushed herself up.

If the only way to get rid of him was to pretend she was fine, then she'd just have to fake it.

'So you're not sick? You're okay? But why are you wet? And your eyes? They're all red and puffy.' He took a step closer, reached out, made to touch her forearm.

Josie ducked back, all too aware she was a world-class ugly crier, and not wanting to be comforted by the person who'd caused the tears.

'You've been crying.' Callan didn't attempt to touch her again, but he didn't look like he was going anywhere either.

Josie shrugged and aimed for nonchalance, like a bit of a cry was no big deal. 'It happens.'

'Not to you. Except maybe it does to you.' Callan ran his hand through his hair, gripped a hunk of it and tugged. 'I don't know. I mean, we've only known each other a few weeks.'

'Exactly.' Josie registered the surprise in Callan's eyes at the bluntness of her tone. The hurt. Her heart threatened to soften, to apologise, but she wouldn't. She couldn't.

If she weakened, if she relented, if she allowed herself to feel a sliver of hope, she'd be tempted to stick around. And then what? She'd spend day after day mooning around after a man she could never have.

No. Better to hold herself tight. To keep it together, just long enough for Callan to realise there was nothing more to be said, then go.

'Is this about what happened at the bakery? What I said in front of those people?' He released his hunk of hair and sat on the edge of the sofa.

Josie stifled an annoyed huff. So much for Callan going sooner rather than later.

'Because, if it is, I'm sorry.'

Josie's rising ire paused. He was sorry? No one she'd cared about had ever said sorry to her before. Not her mother in the note she left. Not her father for distancing himself.

She didn't know what to do with the apology. Wasn't sure that it changed the fact that his words back at the bakery had spelled out the simple truth that she didn't mean to him what he had come to mean to her.

She folded her arms across her chest, ordered her shoulders to relax. 'What part of what happened back there are you sorry for?'

'All of it?' Callan's hands were raised, palms upturned. 'For how badly I handled it. I made you sound like nothing but an employee. Then I didn't explain it properly when Mia talked about our . . . you know.'

He couldn't even say the words. Couldn't admit to their shared intimacies. Like they embarrassed him. Or had meant nothing.

'Yeah well. You said what you said and I know where I stand now. So that's good.' Josie focused on the ashes in the fireplace and fought the bubble of hysterical laughter that rose. How apt. The fireplace was the perfect representation of her life. It had gone up in flames once more. Now it was time to sweep her own personal hearth and start again.

'Callan, while you're here I may as well tender my resignation. I'm sure, considering the circumstances, that you won't mind that I'd like it to take effect immediately.'

Callan sprung up from the seat and began pacing the room.

'Resignation? What? I don't understand. I know I handled the situation back there badly. Terribly, in fact. But to leave because of it? Because my foot was firmly in my mouth and I didn't say that you were . . .' A long silence followed.

Unsurprising, considering Callan had no idea what she was to him.

And if Josie were honest, she had no idea either. 'Girlfriend' felt too . . . cheap. Their connection – or so she'd thought – was too deep for such a simple term. 'Partner' went the other way. It was what you called someone who you'd been with forever. Not known for a few weeks. Either way, if he couldn't name it and neither could she, maybe it was because there was nothing there to name.

Josie wiped her palms over her damp cheeks. 'Callan, I can't keep doing what we're doing, and after what happened back at the bakery, I don't know that I want to anymore. You can't describe what we are to each other. Neither can I. It's too hard. Too . . . vague. And while I'm happy to take things slowly, to not rush into a relationship, I can't do that *and* hide my feelings. Or be okay with it when you hide yours in front of others. The secrecy hits me right in here.' She touched the spot between her breastbone. 'It leaves me feeling like I'm not good enough to be your girlfriend, or partner, or whatever it is that I am. I'm afraid it means you'll leave me at any second like I never meant anything to you, and that all that'll be left between us is distance. And I can't do that again. Not with someone I've given my heart to.'

Josie forced her gaze up. Hoped to see understanding in Callan's eyes. That he got what she was saying.

Prayed that he would tell her she was wrong.

Her heart seized when she saw anger darkening his eyes.

'I can't give what's going on between us a name because I don't understand it myself. It's more than a fling. It's too new to be called long term. But I do know it was serious. That I was serious about you.' His hands curled into fists as he tucked his

176

arms across his chest. 'Yes, I was taking things slowly. I didn't want to hurt you because I know how badly you'd been hurt by those you've loved in the past. I also didn't want to hurt Mia. Or myself.' Callan's shoulders deflated like the fight had gone out of him. 'I just can't believe you'd think I would treat you like you were nothing if things didn't work out between us. I never could. I never would. Not when you pulled me out of my sadness. Showed me I could live again. That I could feel again. That I could maybe even love again.'

With each point made Josie inched back, until she hit the wall behind her. Callan had liked her. He'd wanted to do the right thing. Because he didn't want to hurt her. Because he had cared. And perhaps could have done more than cared, had she given him more of a chance.

'I'm sorry.' The words came out so small, so quiet, she had to say them again. Had to make sure he heard. 'I'm sorry, Callan. I shouldn't have jumped to conclusions. I shouldn't have taken off like that.'

Callan shook his head. 'No, you shouldn't have. But by jumping to conclusions and leaving without a word, you did me a favour, so I should be thanking you.'

'Why would you thank me?' Josie knew the answer. Could've predicted what Callan would say word for word, but she had to hear it. Had to punish herself for creating a self-fulfilling prophecy.

'Because you're leaving now, before we – Mia and I – could fall for you more. Before you could cause more damage. More pain. More anger. Because I am angry, but not at you. I'm angry at myself. I shouldn't have let you under my skin. Shouldn't have let you close. Not when I'm still grieving. Not after I discovered how badly your parents' behaviour had scarred you. The thing is . . .' Callan pressed his lips together like he'd said too much. Or as if what he was going to say wouldn't make an iota of difference anyway.

'The thing is . . . what?' Josie asked, holding on to a thread of hope that they could talk this out. That she could make things right.

'The thing is, I can't change my situation, any more than you can change your past and the way you act whenever things get tough. I can't rush in. I can't give my all. Not immediately. Maybe not even ever. Not that it matters anymore. Not now that you're leaving.'

Josie waited for . . . she wasn't sure what. A nicety. Absolution. Maybe even a throwaway 'Merry Christmas'. She'd heard it so often that day as customers came into the store and left loaded with treats, she'd come to expect it. 'Twas the season and all that. But no twee season's greetings came.

Not another word was said.

Not as Callan shoved his hands deep into his coat pockets.

Not as he broke eye contact.

Not as he spun on his heel.

Not as he made his way out into the cloudy day, that was crying once more.

Along with the woman, who'd sunk down into a ball, and was realising that if something didn't change she'd never have a Merry Christmas.

Not now.

Not ever.

Not at all.

Chapter 18

Callan thanked his customer, then went to the door and flipped the sign from 'open' to 'closed' before another person could enter.

It was only midday, but the morning had been punishing, and he'd promised himself the moment the last of Josie's baking had sold he'd shut up shop and . . . well . . . he didn't know what he was going to do.

Stare at something he couldn't see in the far distance?

Count the hairs on Mia's head?

Purposefully ignore the kitchen, because every time he paid it any attention he became all too aware of how empty it was. How Josie-less.

'Daddy, I'm hungry.' Mia slipped her hand into his and gave his hand a tug. 'Can I have sweets for lunch?'

'Sure . . . whatever you want.' Callan blinked, then caught himself. 'But not sweets. Shall we go to the pub for a treat?'

The last thing he wanted was to go out, to see people, to force smiles and conversation, but anything had to be better than feeling stuck at home, where the walls closed in around him, whispering words of remorse. Telling him he should have stayed longer, talked things out, given Josie another chance.

179

'Can I have fish and chips, and a fizzy?' Mia jumped up and down, her face radiating excitement.

Callan silently congratulated himself on hiding his feelings from her. The last thing he wanted was for Mia to feel his pain, his disconnection. He'd not expected to need all the skills he'd learned around mindfulness and being present after Abigail's passing again so soon, but he was glad he had the tools to be there for Mia, to keep his own worries and sadness at bay so as not to taint her world view.

'Maybe you should have fizzy and fish and chips too, Daddy. Maybe that will make you smile in your eyes.'

So much for hiding his feelings.

Callan dropped down to Mia's level and wrapped her in a hug. 'Maybe it will. Sorry, my little love, I haven't meant to be sad.'

Mia pulled away and turned her big eyes on him, so full of love and trust and caring. 'Is it because Josie's not here? I hope she gets better soon. Will she be here tomorrow? She should be, because we love her, hey? And Mummy always said that Christmas was when you should spend time with the people you love.'

Callan ran his thumb over the back of Mia's hand. So soft. So tender. Like his little girl. He hoped she kept those traits. That no matter what life threw at her she retained the sweetness that seemed so innate. 'Do you remember a lot of what your mummy used to say?'

Mia nodded. 'I try and keep it on the hook in my head. And I keep her love in my heart.'

Callan nodded and tapped his chest. 'Me too.'

A tiny frown line appeared between Mia's brows as her lips pursed in thought. 'Do hearts grow bigger, Daddy? To fit more love in?'

'I know for a fact they do.' Callan cupped Mia's cheeks. 'When I met your mum I loved her so much, I couldn't imagine loving anyone more. Then we had you, and just like that my heart expanded to fit more love in. And I couldn't imagine loving anyone more than you and your mummy.'

'Then Josie came along and our hearts 'spanded more.' Mia's frown disappeared and was replaced by a concise nod. 'Right, Daddy?'

Callan's throat closed up. He didn't have the heart to tell Mia that Josie was never coming back. Not with Christmas one day away. He'd planned for the day to be filled with happiness, excitement and joy, and he was darn well going to make it happen, even if every fibre of his being wanted to curl up and hide until enough time had passed that his feelings for Josie had dimmed. Or – if the universe chose to be kind to him, even though he didn't believe he deserved such kindness after the offhanded way he'd treated her – spluttered out completely.

'That's right, Mia.' He ruffled her hair then pushed himself up and went through the motions of getting them ready to head outside for the short walk to the pub.

A layer of cloud hung low and grey and, despite his many layers, Callan felt the winter chill soak into his body. Either that, or the numbness was a protective mechanism to keep himself from falling apart.

They trod down the lane in silence. Mia unusually quiet, her hand tightening around his periodically, like she was sending him comforting vibes.

He shouldn't have been so surprised at her awareness. She'd grown so much in the last year. Gone was the little tot who thought the world revolved entirely around her. He was dealing with a little girl now, one who was sensitive to those around her. Fake smiles and overly bright vocal tones weren't going to cut it anymore. Honesty would have to be the order of the day, which meant as soon as Christmas was done he was going to tell her that Josie had left. Even if it would break his heart all over again to do so.

Golden light glowed through the pub's windows, its warmth matching the ambience as they walked in and made their way to the bar.

Callan lifted Mia onto a seat, then searched out Brendon,

181

who was back in his new favourite spot. At the end of the bar chatting to Margo.

He waved to the two, and before he knew it he had Margo sitting at his side, and Brendon across from him, passing a glass of lemonade to Mia.

'No Josie?' Margo asked. 'Is she at the shop?'

Callan ignored Margo's question and turned to Mia. 'Mia? How do you feel about being in charge of that table by the fireplace?'

Mia's eyes went to Margo, then Callan. 'Okay, Daddy.' She turned over onto her tummy and inched her way to the ground, took her lemonade in both hands and made her way to the table.

'She's getting to be so grown up,' Margo observed.

Callan sighed. 'I know. I can't hide things from her the way I used to.'

'Like Josie leaving?'

Surprise inflated Callan's chest. 'You know?'

'Of course I do. Although I do wish she'd change her mind. I wish there was a good enough reason to keep her here. Brendon, sweets, can you get Callan a beer?'

Brendon grabbed a pint glass, poured the beer and placed it in front of Callan. 'I can't believe I'm saying this again, but it's on the house.' He paused, his lips twitched like he wanted to say something, but also didn't. 'You know, I had my bet on your being bestowed with the sunset's luck. I'm guessing I was wrong. And I'm sorry that I was.'

Before Callan could respond, Brendon swivelled round and went to serve another customer.

'I think we all thought it was you. Or Josie.' Margo picked up a coaster and circled it round. 'I'm sad that it's not.'

Callan sipped his beer and set it down. 'Me too.'

Margo fixed him with a shrewd eye. 'Then why are you sitting here feeling sorry for yourself? Why aren't you stopping that girl from packing her life up into her little car and leaving town?' Her shoulders rose and fell as she expelled an exasperated huff. 'Did my story not teach you anything? I could've been as happy as I am now years ago. Instead I let my fears get in my way.'

Callan's stomach knotted up with indignation. Margo was putting the blame for this at his doorstep. 'I'm not the one running, Margo.'

'You're not the one fighting either.'

'It's not just about me. It's about Mia, too. I can't entrust her heart with someone who might leave at any given second.'

'The way Abigail did? Lightning rarely strikes in the same place twice, Callan.' Margo reached out and touched his forearm. 'I've seen the way Josie looks at you. Like you're her everything. You and Mia both. If she's running, it's because you didn't give her any other option.'

Callan closed his eyes and wished he could as easily close his ears.

'The way I see it you two have some talking to do. Real talking. Not just talking at each other, but *with* each other, if you've any hope of experiencing the kind of love so many dream of.'

God, there was that word again. Love. First Mia, now Margo. 'Why must it go straight to love? Why can't you say that it's like? That we liked each other. Because we did like each other.'

'If it were just "like" you wouldn't be walking around with the pallor of a man who's just received the worst news ever.'

'I've already received the worst news ever, remember? And you said lightning doesn't strike twice.' Callan glanced over his shoulder to make sure Mia was still in her seat. She waved, then blew into her straw, causing a small bubble volcano to rise in her glass.

'Don't be facetious, Callan.' Margo's stern demeanour softened. 'And don't let that mind of yours get in the way of your heart. Promise me?'

'Do I have any other option?' Callan slid off his stool. 'I promise that whatever I end up deciding, it will be the best for me and Mia. Is that a good enough answer?'

'I guess it'll have to be.'

'Excellent.' Callan picked up two menus and pretended not to see the sympathy in Margo's eyes.

He'd had enough sympathy to last a lifetime. What he wanted was to get on with things. To get through Christmas. To move on.

But could he do it without the woman who'd breathed life back into his world?

* * *

The cottage's door whooshed open, cold air blasted through the living room.

Josie ran to slam the door shut, and stopped short as she realised the only thing she'd be slamming, or slamming into, was Brendon.

'Brendon? What are you doing here? Are you okay? Is it Margo? Is she okay?' Josie skirted round him and shut the door.

He turned to face her. 'We'll get to that.'

The growl in his voice didn't match the kindness in his eyes.

A shiver rippled over Josie. Why did she feel like she was about to be given the kind of talking-to that a father might give his headstrong daughter?

'Can we sit? Have a cuppa? A bit of a chat?' He made his way through to the kitchen, without waiting for a yes.

'Sure.' Josie didn't know what else to say. Not when it appeared this conversation, whatever it was, was happening whether she liked it or not.

Josie deposited the duster she'd been cleaning the skirting boards with on the kitchen table and made her way to the kitchen sink, where her lunch dishes were soaking, ready to be washed, dried and put away before she left. For good.

Josie filled the kettle, set it down on the bench and flicked it on. 'So, what's brought you out here?'

'Out here? You make it sound like I traipsed for miles to visit you. I know for a fact that this place takes eight minutes to walk to from the pub. I walked it enough times to know. I was fond of this cottage. Those that resided in it.'

Realisation dawned on Josie. Margo must've told him she was leaving, which meant Brendon was either here to talk sense into her, to get her to stay, or he was worried Josie wouldn't pay the rent money she owed Margo as per their agreement and was about to give her the hard word.

She grabbed two cups from the cupboard and dropped a teabag in each, then poured the hot water. 'If you're worried that I won't pay the next four weeks' rent to Margo, then you can stop worrying now. I may be leaving early, but I'm still going to pay. I wouldn't do wrong by her, not when she's been so good to me.'

'And what about Callan and Mia? They've been good to you too, have they not?'

So he was here for a good old-fashioned guilt trip. Well, he could lay it on as thick as he liked. It would only be the icing on the cake to the layers of guilt she already felt.

'Milk, Brendon? Sugar?'

'Spoonful of sugar and a dash of milk. Not too weak. I'm not fond of weak things.'

Josie caught what Brendon was laying down, and she didn't care much for it. He thought she was weak? She'd spent her life being strong.

She picked up the mugs and set them down on the kitchen table with enough force that a wave of tea licked up the inside and threatened to spill.

'Didn't much like that wee dig, did you?' Brendon wrapped his large hand around the mug and brought it towards him. 'Touched a sore spot, did I?'

Josie folded her arms and tilted her chin in defiance. 'I'm not sore. I'm just not fond of people making a judgement call about me when they don't know half of what's going on. Of what's gone on.'

Brendon's head tipped back and laughter filled the room.

It wasn't a cruel sound. Not meant to hurt. It was the kind of laugh that bubbled up when a child said something that was too cute, but also very wrong.

After fanning himself for half a minute, Brendon calmed down. Got his breath back. 'Oh, Josie. You don't run a pub for as long as I have without getting a handle on people. I had you pegged the moment you stepped into The Squeaky Wheel.'

'Oh really? Enlighten me about myself.' Josie sat back in her chair and turned her attention to the corner of the room, where she'd swept a pile of dirt, dust and debris.

'You drove down into the village in that tiny car of yours and rented a fully furnished home. No moving truck ever followed. That tells me that you carry enough with you that you can leave the moment you feel you have to. The moment things get tough, because no one ever leaves when things are good.'

Her heart flinched. No one ever left because things were good? She knew that better than anyone. Her mother's inability to stick around was proof of that.

But did that make her like her mother? Was she just as bad?

No. She pushed the idea away. She wasn't. She didn't have a family waiting at home for her. A loving husband and an adoring daughter. She wasn't leaving without explanation, without even saying goodbye, to the two people who had been the centre of her world.

Except she was doing exactly that.

Josie reached out and gripped the warm mug as icy cold realisation rippled through her. She could lie to herself all she wanted. Tell herself she was nothing like her mother, but her heart knew the truth.

She might not be married. She might have only been in Sunnycombe for just shy of a month, but that didn't mean that two people hadn't become the centre of her world. She couldn't speak for Callan, and she wouldn't blame him if he never wanted to speak to her again. But Mia deserved more than having another person she cared for disappear.

Mia's mother hadn't had the chance to hold her daughter one last time. To whisper sweet words of love, but Josie did.

'As always, I decided to withhold judgement, because people change.' Brendon reached out and touched her hand.

Could he feel her shaking? Did he know he was getting through to her? Josie couldn't meet his eyes. She was afraid if she did she'd break down completely.

'But I saw how you first treated Lauren.'

'Lauren?' Josie shook her head. What was Brendon on about? She'd been nothing but friendly to Lauren from the first time they'd met. Had liked her immediately. 'I don't understand what you're saying? That night I met her when Callan and I came to the pub? I was nice. I let her in, became her friend, which is something I never do. How is that treating her badly?'

'And that right there shows how insular you were when you first arrived. She sidled up to you the first night you were here. You were at the bar, nursing a wine. She came up to get her and Will's usual. She said hi, you stonewalled her. Luckily for you, Lauren isn't one to hold a grudge. She believes in second chances. Probably took your inability to muster much more than a half-smile as shyness.'

Nausea tumbled and turned in Josie's gut as the vague recollection of a warm 'hello' and a smiling face that she'd turned away from ignited in the back of her mind.

'I didn't know. Didn't realise,' she whispered. 'I was trying to keep myself to myself. To avoid exactly all of this happening.' Josie squeezed her eyes shut and tried to figure out what step she should take, how best to fix things. Lauren believed in second chances. But did Callan? And did she deserve one? After everything she'd done, everything she'd said, could she even bring herself to ask for his forgiveness? To face further rejection?

And if she didn't, would that not be running away metaphorically, as well as physically?

187

She gripped the mug tighter, forced herself to open her eyes and meet Brendon's gaze. 'Brendon, why did you come here? Why have this chat with me? What's in it for you if not making sure that Margo gets the rent money?'

'Honestly?' Brendon pushed the mug away and looked out the kitchen window where the stark branches of the rose bush tapped against the glass. 'It's about seeing an old friend continue to thrive.'

It all made sense. Brendon had mentioned to Josie the day she moved out of her room above the pub that he wanted to see Callan down at the pub again. And she'd made that happen. With Margo's help. Brendon didn't want to see Callan go backwards. Retreat into himself.

And if he did, Brendon would put the blame squarely at her feet.

Where it belonged.

Unless she found the wherewithal to break the habit of a lifetime.

'I'm sure Callan's not going to go back to being the way he was before I came along. He's got his business up and running again. He's back to playing darts once a week, and he was talking about joining the pub team again. He can hire another baker and keep Abigail's running. My leaving needn't change any of that.'

Brendon's broad shoulders lifted and fell in a shrug. His bushy brows knitted together in disbelief. 'You didn't see the man I saw earlier. He looked lost. Like he didn't want to be at the pub, but he didn't want to go home either. He barely touched his lunch, and I could see what an effort it was for him to interact with that wee poppet of his.'

Fear clutched at Josie's heart. All her hard work. Everything she'd done to bring him out of his shell, to stop Callan from becoming like her father, it was falling apart. More than that, the situation had worsened. When she'd met Callan he'd still had a thread to hang onto. Mia.

Now? If what Brendon said was true, that thread was tenuous. In danger of breaking.

All because of her.

Not on her watch.

'Ah, I see a straightening of shoulders. That morose look on your moosh has disappeared. Have you finally gotten through to yourself?' Brendon pushed the chair back and got up. 'Because I really hope you have. When two people meet and there's a spark of magic between them, they owe it to themselves to not let that spark go out. I should know. I kept my spark for Margo burning for years.'

'Was it worth it? Waiting that long?'

'Love always is, my dear. You'll see.'

Brendon tipped Josie a wink, and before she could collect her thoughts, he'd seen himself out.

Josie shook her head in amazement. Who'd have thought hope would come in the form of a gruff publican with a heart of gold?

The big question now, though, was one she didn't have a clue how to answer . . .

After hurting someone so badly, after showing them the worst side of who you were, how did you convince the person you were falling in love with that you were worth falling in love with too?

Chapter 19

The bed bounced and shook, and through the pillow pulled over his head Callan could hear Mia repeating at high speed, 'Santa's been! Santa's been! Santa's been!'

Her small hand found his under the pillow and began to pull. Each tug more impatient that the last. If he didn't force himself out of his fug and get up soon, he was in danger of losing his hand, if not his whole arm.

'I'm coming. I'm coming.' He tossed the pillow aside and pulled himself up onto his elbow and gave his sleep-deprived eyes a rub.

'It's so pretty, Daddy. It's magical.'

Mia whirled round and round and Callan wished he could feel even an ounce of her excitement. How he was going to survive today, when all he felt like doing was crawling back under the covers, he didn't know.

'Come on, Daddy. You have to see.'

Mia had his hand in hers once again, and before he knew it he was out of bed and being dragged into the lounge where the tree's gold fairy lights were twinkling away, and the stack of presents he'd bought for Mia were deposited under the tree. The wrapping was a touch haphazard, more so the higher the pile got.

Unsurprising, since he'd bribed himself with more whiskey than necessary in order to get through wrapping them.

He went to sit down in front of the tree so he could hand the presents to Mia, one by one, rather than have her rip into them without having time to appreciate what was in each.

'What are you doing, Daddy?' Mia's face was a picture of confusion. 'Santa said to go downstairs.'

Downstairs? Santa said? Callan curled his fingers so his nails dug into his palm. He was awake, right? This wasn't a stress dream brought on by the emotional upheaval of the last two days combined with wanting to make this Christmas as special for Mia as her mother had made previous ones.

'What do you mean Santa said we had to go downstairs?'

Mia held out a piece of paper. 'Here. He left this in my stocking with the oranges and chocolates. Look.' She reached into the pocket sewn onto the chest of her pink unicorn-patterned flannelette pyjamas and pulled out a folded piece of paper. 'I can't believe Santa got me a stocking.' Mia hugged herself and twisted back and forth. 'I've always wanted one.'

What was all this about a stocking? He'd not bought one because they'd never done so before. It wasn't one of their family traditions.

'One second, Mia?' Ignoring the piece of paper, he held up his index finger, then twisted round and strode to her bedroom.

Sure enough, on her bed was a bright red stocking with a white faux-fur trim. Surrounding it were oranges and chocolates.

He was going barmy. It was the only explanation. That or he was stuck in the most realistic dream he'd ever had.

He returned to Mia, who'd crossed her arms and was tapping one toe with impatience.

'Mia? Can you pass me the note?'

He unfolded it and took in the rough sketch of a kitchen bench with a present sitting on top of it. 'Well, I guess if Santa wants us to go to the kitchen, that's what we should do.' He glanced

191

back at the piles of presents he'd spent hours wrapping. 'What about those?'

'Will they still be there when we get back?'

'Of course. Santa doesn't take back his gifts.'

'Then we'll open those after. Treasure hunt first.' Mia curled her finger and indicated for him to follow her.

Treasure hunt. It rang a bell. Reminded him of . . . His heart upped its pace. Surely not? He was just being . . . crazy. Or hopeful. Though hopeful was a daft feeling to have. One that would only make his feelings worse when his hopes were dashed. Better to stick with crazy.

He snatched up his mobile phone as he passed the little table by the door and grabbed his keys, too. If this was a true treasure hunt, who knew where it would take them?

Flicking on the stairwell's light, they trooped down the stairs and into the kitchen.

A circle of battery-powered tealight candles illuminated not one but two gifts on the kitchen bench.

'Santa can't count.' Mia rolled her eyes.

'Or maybe he didn't have time to draw two pictures. He's a very busy man, you know.'

Mia ran to the bench and picked up the present wrapped in cartoon reindeer. 'M. I. A. This one's mine!' She went on tiptoes to get a closer look at the gift wrapped in navy blue with silver stars. 'C. A. L. L. A. N. It doesn't say Daddy. Daddy starts with D.'

'This is true, but it spells my name.'

'Callan.' Mia grinned. 'You can't tell me I can't say it because Santa wrote it and it's Christmas.'

'This is true. Now pass it here. I want to know what Santa brought me.'

They opened their gifts in silence, Mia ripping into hers, Callan peeling back the tape and unwrapping his gift with care.

'Look!' Mia held up a pink woollen beanie, complete with

white furry pompom on top in one hand and matching mittens and scarf in the other.

Callan reached into his present and pulled out a basic blue beanie. One that would cover his ears and not cause people to look at him like he'd lost his marbles when he walked into the pub.

'And there's another clue!' Mia showed him a drawing of a hilltop scattered with stick figures watching the sun go down.

'It looks like Santa wants us to go for an early-morning tramp, Mia.'

'He wants us to go in our pyjamas?'

Callan laughed at the outrage in Mia's voice.

'I suppose we could get dressed, but where's the fun in that? Best we put our coats and wellies on and—' Callan went to tell Mia to put on her new presents but she already had the hat on her head and was winding the scarf around her neck.

'I wonder what else Santa has for us!' She clapped her hands together, her gaze softening as she entered a gift-filled daydream.

Callan stepped into his gumboots and jammed his hands into his gloves. What else did Santa have in store for them?

That was the big question. One his heart couldn't wait to find out.

* * *

The bobbing of a mobile phone's torch darting about the ground told Josie that Callan and Mia were on their way. That, and the incessant chattering from one excited little girl, no doubt fuelled by the little bags of sweets and chocolates with notes saying 'eat me' that she'd dotted along the path she'd expected them to take.

It wasn't quite as elaborate as the treasure hunts her father had created for her when she was a young girl, but time hadn't been on her side, and the shops had been closing as she'd driven to the closest village with a clothing store. She'd counted her lucky stars when the owner had allowed her an extra five minutes to shop, despite their closing the door as she ran towards it.

She smoothed out the picnic blanket and opened the cooler bag that was serving today as a warmer bag. It was lined with foil to keep the heat in, and contained a breakfast fit for a king and his little princess.

She straightened up as the torch touched her feet, then travelled up her body, stopping shy of her face.

'Daddy! Santa brought us Josie for Christmas!'

Mia threw herself at Josie. Her little arms wound their way around her hips and held on tight.

'Daddy said you were busy this Christmas. Too busy to see us. But Daddy was wrong.' Mia turned an accusing glare on her father that lasted all of a second before she turned back to Josie. 'Look! I got gloves and a scarf! And we got hats! And there's a million presents under the tree. And I got a stocking – I've never had a stocking. It had chocolates! And oranges.' She stuck her tongue out in disgust.

Josie planted her hands on her hips and shook her head. 'What was Santa thinking putting oranges in your stocking? That's far too healthy for Christmas Day.'

'I think Santa rectified his mistake by leading us down a sweet-filled trail.'

Callan's words were measured, his tone without censure.

Josie attempted to interpret how he was feeling, what he was thinking, but hit a blank wall. Whatever he thought about this expedition, about her leading them up the hill, she had no idea.

Which meant if she were going to find out, she'd have to plough on with her plans.

'What's Christmas without a breakfast feast? Mia, take a seat. Callan, you too . . . please.'

Callan hesitated. Fear clutched at Josie's chest. Was he going to take Mia and leave? Not even give her a chance to explain? To try?

A whisper of self-defeat curled up from deep within. Tried to tell her she wasn't worth Callan's time. That he deserved better. She stamped it out as quick as it rose. It was that inner voice that had seen her keep people at a distance for years. She wasn't listening to it. Wasn't giving it the time of day. Especially not when her future, her happiness, was on the line.

With a look of resignation, Callan settled onto the blanket and pulled Mia into his lap.

A barrier, Josie noted. A way to ensure things didn't get tense, to ensure no one spoke out of turn.

She couldn't blame him for taking that possibility into consideration, but she had no intention of getting angry, of saying the wrong things, or of hurting anyone. She wanted the opposite. She wanted – needed – to say the right things, to explain to the two people sitting in front of her how much they'd come to mean to her. It might have been far too early in their relationship to say the 'l' word, but it was never too early to show it.

'Great. Right. Well. For breakfast this morning we have . . .' She opened the bag and began arranging the food before them. 'Bacon and scrambled eggs. Croissants. Breakfast sausages.' She opened another container. 'Er, slightly cold cooked mushrooms. And tea.' She lifted the thermos she'd bought with her. 'And milk for the little lady.'

'No pancakes?' Mia leaned forward and looked in the cooler bag.

'Sorry. No pancakes. Next time.' Josie crossed her fingers behind her back and wished for a next time.

'Why breakfast? Why all the effort?'

Callan's questions took Josie by surprise. She didn't think he'd be so blunt in front of Mia. She'd hoped he'd go with the flow and see where things led.

Which of course he wouldn't. And nor should he. He had no reason to think she had their best interests at heart. She'd have acted the same. Would've done anything and everything to protect her child's heart, her own heart too, were she in his position. Including keeping the person who was trying their best to say sorry, to make up for what they'd done, at arm's length until she knew she could trust them again.

Josie set spoons and miniature tongs into the containers, then straightened up, gripped her knees for support, and hoped her tongue wouldn't tangle, wouldn't mash the words she'd worked on half the night.

'We didn't do the traditional Christmas lunch in our family. Mum's parents lived in Penzance and preferred to spend Christmas at my uncle's house with his family as they lived down the road. My dad's parents had retired to New Zealand and weren't big on travelling. So because it was just us, my mother decided we didn't have to follow tradition, that we could create our own, so we did breakfast instead. A huge spread. Followed by all the traditional Christmassy desserts. It was a feast that had us holding our bellies groaning for hours afterwards. Then once we could move, my dad would take me on a treasure hunt to work up an appetite for dinner, which would be homemade burgers and chips, or a curry, or whatever Mum felt inspired to whip up, followed by Christmas cake.' Josie glanced out over the valley, not seeing much as the sun had yet to rise. 'In hindsight I should've realised my mother was never one for doing the "done" thing. That being a mother and wife, stuck in an estate where the homes all looked the same, living a life of routine, was never going to stick.'

'You were a kid. You couldn't have known.'

'I don't know about that. Just because you're young doesn't mean you don't see things for what they are.'

Callan's eyebrows drew together, his gaze turned distant. 'I suppose you're right.'

Josie loaded up Mia's plate and passed it to her. 'Anyway, it's taken me far too long to come to this conclusion, but I've decided that instead of spending the rest of my life ruminating on the bad bits of my past, I should celebrate the good bits. The Christmas breakfasts. The treasure hunts that led Dad and I all over the neighbourhood. The times when Mum slipped into my bed in the middle of the night for a cuddle, fell asleep, and we'd wake up all hot and sweaty and entwined, and so utterly happy.' Josie sat back on her haunches and settled her hands on her knees. 'I spent so many years wondering why she didn't love me, but I've come to realise her leaving wasn't about me, or her lack of love for me. Because she did love me, and she showed it in so many ways. I think, if anything, it was herself she didn't love – or she didn't love the way she wasn't satisfied with life, that she wanted more, and felt guilty for it – and that's why she left. Because Mum was afraid if we discovered she didn't love herself, we might stop loving her. Even though that would have never happened, but how was she to know that? It's like how I've always thought that if people found out I was unlovable, because one of my parents left and the other pushed me away, they'd think I wasn't worth loving, which is why I pushed people away. I never let them get close. Something I know now is a silly belief to have.' Josie shook her head at her own ridiculousness. 'Part of me wishes I'd figured that out years ago. I would've made life much easier on myself. A bigger part of me is glad I've figured it out right here, right now, in a village where I've fallen for the people. And I hope, someday, some of them might even feel the same way about me.'

And just like that, something broke deep within Josie. The chains that had shackled her, kept her from finding freedom, disappeared. She wasn't her mother. She didn't need to leave. To run. She wasn't her father. She didn't have to push people away to protect her heart. She was her own person. And the kindness that Callan saw within her was there because that's who she was, and kind people didn't go out of their way to hurt people or let them down.

'So here we are. Now that the food, and all my feelings, are out on the table, welcome to a Donnelly Christmas tradition. As brought to you by Santa.'

She waited for clapping or cheering or even a grunt of acknowledgement. Anything other than the ominous silence that emanated from Callan. Even Mia was uncharacteristically silent. Josie's heart sank further with every passing second. Had this been a mistake? Had she pushed Callan so far away there was no going back?

'Well then, if it's a tradition, who are we to get in the way of it. Mia, tuck in. I think I'll be trying these bacon and eggs.' Callan began piling up the plastic picnic plate that Josie had laid out for him. 'What was the strangest Christmas dinner your mother ever made?'

Josie tucked her legs under her and began to fill her own plate. 'Weetabix with melted marshmallows on top, surrounded by a sea of jelly.'

Callan's nose wrinkled. 'Sounds disgusting.'

'Oh, it was. Although if you separated the Weetabix and marshmallow out from the jelly, it wasn't the worst. The worst was tripe.'

'Then why didn't you say tripe?'

'You said strangest, not most repulsive.'

'Now I know why you really hate Christmas.'

Through the dusky morning haze and the barely-there torchlight coming from their mobiles, Josie saw what she'd longed for. A smile. Coming from the direction of Callan.

'Josie hates Christmas?' Mia spluttered, sending half-eaten bits of eggs everywhere. 'Whoops. Sorry.'

She grinned, and Josie noticed a gap where a baby tooth had been two days ago.

'Your tooth. It's come out! Did the tooth fairy come?'

Mia nodded. 'She did. And she brought money. And I'm going to use it to buy some sweets so my teeth rot and fall out faster so I can have more money.'

Over Mia's head, Callan grimaced, then shook his head. Josie pressed her lips together so as not to laugh, or smile, or give any indication to Mia that what she'd said was probably not the best idea.

'Well, that's some sound logic you've got going there, Mia. Although I've heard that the tooth fairy gives *more* money for teeth that are in good condition. So maybe you're better off looking after those teeth of yours, and then putting any money you make towards buying a new toy or dress-up costume?'

'More money?' Mia's eyes lit up.

'More money.' Josie nodded.

'I'm going to brush my teeth a hundred million times a day.' Josie set the smile she'd held back free. 'Sounds perfect.'

Quiet settled over the trio as they ate their breakfast. Not the most comfortable kind, but nor was it uneasy. Just a touch awkward. Made all the more so thanks to Callan looking at her every five seconds, screwing his face up, and letting out a little huff before forking more food into his mouth.

Far too quickly the last of the food was eaten, and the nerves jittering in Josie's stomach, that had only just begun to settle, ramped up once more.

'That was lovely, thank you.' Callan handed her the empty plates and cutlery, then tapped Mia on the shoulder. 'Up you get. Time for presents at home.'

Josie's heart thumped in her chest as she saw Callan begin to rise. It was too early. They weren't meant to go yet. She had a plan, and their leaving wasn't part of it. She had one more present up her sleeve. One she'd planned to give Mia if things didn't work out, but if it meant keeping them up on the hill a little longer, then there was no time like the present.

'I've one more gift for Mia, if you don't mind me giving it to her?' She rifled in her bag and brought out a glittery red gift box.

'Go ahead.' Callan's gaze followed the box as Josie passed it to an excitable Mia.

Mia ripped the top off, pulled out the gift and hugged it to her chest. 'I love it. Thank you, Josie.' She pulled it away for a closer look. 'It looks old.' Her little face crumpled in confusion. 'Did you drop it in a puddle?'

Josie reached out and tweaked Mia's nose. 'No. It was mine. My mummy gave it to me. An angel to watch over me, she said. And I thought maybe you'd like an angel to watch over you, too.' *An angel to replace me if I end up having to go.*

She held her breath and made a Christmas wish. *Please don't let me go.*

Mia pressed it to her chest once more and dropped a kiss on its head. 'Can I call her Belle?'

'You can call her whatever you want.'

'Good.' Mia nodded. 'I love you, Belle.'

Josie sucked in a deep breath. She had to talk to Callan. It was now or never. And 'never' wasn't an option. 'Callan, can we have a quick word? In private?'

His hand was on his chin, stroking the bristles covering it. His eyes hooded over, not letting Josie in on what he was thinking. How he was feeling.

'Mia?' Callan picked up his mobile. 'Are you okay to play with Belle while Josie and I have a chat?'

Mia nodded without looking up from finger-combing Belle's snarled hair.

'Shall we?' Callan jerked his head to a spot a few metres away.

'We shall.' Josie tightened her scarf as goose pimples crawled down her neck, then followed Callan's lead until they were within eyeshot of Mia, but not earshot.

Callan stood next to her, shoulders squared, jaw tense, head held high. Like he was doing her a favour by hearing her out, but once she'd finished talking he would be done with her.

Even if that were the case, at least she'd have said her piece. Come forth and been open instead of shutting down and scarpering.

Josie shifted from foot to foot. The words she'd carefully crafted nowhere to be found. 'So, er, thanks for hearing me out. And thanks for coming. For following the clues.'

'We didn't have much choice, did we? Setting up a treasure hunt and making it look like Santa did it? Honestly, Josie, I'm torn between being furious that you'd come into our home without permission and skulk around in the middle of the night, and thanking you for giving Mia a Christmas surprise that she'll never forget.' A white plume of air whooshed from Callan's mouth as he squeezed his eyes shut and massaged his temples. 'Even if I am a little thankful, I'm still beyond annoyed that you entered my home without asking.'

'Would it help you be less grumpy if you knew that it wasn't me who did it?'

Callan stopped massaging and stared at her like she'd just suggested the craziest thing ever. 'If you're going to try and tell me that Santa really did put that stocking in Mia's room and set up the presents in the kitchen, then I'm going to have to ask you to give me some credit. I'm long past believing in Santa.'

'What about Santa's elves? Because he has one called Margo who, with quite a lot of persuading and the promise of a lifetime supply of banana date loaf, agreed to use my keys' – Josie dug into her jeans pocket, pulled out the shop keys and dropped them into Callan's outstretched hand – 'to help me with my plan.'

Callan's chest puffed out. 'I'm going to have to have a talk with her about respecting boundaries.'

'That's a talk you should've had with her months ago. You know that. She'll do anything to make you happy.' And lucky for Josie, that extended to a little not so much breaking but definitely entering. Something Margo had seen as romantic as opposed to illegal.

Josie peered out over the horizon. Was it her imagination or was the cloud, that hung so low she was surprised it wasn't brushing their heads, lifting? Was the weather going to play along with her plan?

A snowflake drifted down in front of her.

So much for the cloud lifting. Or the weather working with her. She took a deep breath. If she was going to say what had to be said, now was the time. Bugger hoping for the clouds to break so they could witness a sunrise together. She had no more control over the weather than she did over Callan's heart. She only had control over her words, her actions, her feelings. And it was time they were laid out on the table. Or on the hillside, as it were.

'Callan, do you think either of us really gave each other a chance?'

'It was early days,' Callan shot back. 'Committing to someone after knowing them for a few weeks is madness.'

'And how long did you know Abigail before you decided to commit to her?'

Callan stilled. 'That was different.'

'I don't see how. Love is love.' Josie turned to face Callan. 'Look, I don't know what it's like to fall in love again. For the second time. I've only ever fallen in love once, and it wasn't in the traditional way. You expect dizzying heights of lust. Grand gestures. Sleepless nights where you're pining to see the person again. Wanting to breathe the air they breathe, to see the world the way they see it. To feel physical agony with a goodly dose of paranoia when they don't call or text.' Josie sucked in a breath. Slowed her heartrate. Told herself baring her soul would be worth it. Even if her most desired outcome did not happen, doing this would lead to growth within herself, which was the most important thing of all. 'Instead love sneaked up on me. It started with sweet smiles and a slow-building trust. Then came the shared dislike of the festive season. Then the mutual adoration of a little girl. And the desire to see a very special business, named after a very special woman, succeed.'

Did she see a softening in Callan's demeanour? Had his chin dipped, just a little? The little vein pulsing at his temple looked to have abated. Was she getting through to him? Or was she seeing what she wanted to see? What she needed to see?

'It started with the world's most awkward, painful kiss. One that was remedied by the loveliest, most tender kiss. And hand-holding. So much handholding. Little touches. Lingering looks. No rush. No hurry. How could I not have fallen in love?' Josie bit her lip. Had she overdone it? Gone too far?

She waited for Callan to reply. To say something. But no words came. Not even the slightest acknowledgement that she'd put her heart out there, ready for him to trample on.

Or to pick up, hold tight and treasure forever.

The silence was so deafening her ears began to throb.

'You know, that wasn't what I planned to say. At all. Not even remotely. The plan was for me to bring you here. For the clouds to magically part. For us to watch the sunrise together and, as it illuminated Sunnycombe, for me to talk about how being here has illuminated my life. Shone some hard truths on myself. Truths that needed to be rectified. I was going to tell you how you've shown me what home feels like. That Sunnycombe has, too. The people have treated me like one of their own right from the start. Heck, even after I told Margo I planned to leave she was still willing to help me when I decided to give this whole situation one more shot. I wouldn't have blamed her if she'd told me to stuff off and never come back.' Josie was aware she was rambling. Hugely. But if she stopped, the silence would return.

Or she'd have an answer.

And she was terrified it would be the one she didn't want to hear.

'Anyway, it seems the sunrise isn't happening. I mean, it is happening. But it's hidden behind the clouds.' Another snowflake fluttered in front of her. She held her hand out as another settled then slowly melted. 'Snow. On Christmas. How often does it snow? Did you wish for it? I've been convinced since we watched the sunset that it was you who was granted the three wishes. That it was your hopes and dreams that would come true. Especially the last part. The love part. Wishful thinking on my behalf, I guess.' She looked out over the village, which was slowly waking up. Golden lights dotted the landscape, and spirals of smoke swirled up from chimneys. 'I'm going to miss this place. And Mia. And you.'

'But you're not going anywhere, are you? At least that's what I've taken from this whole conversation.' Callan's gloved hand reached out to hers. Their fingers slowly entwined as he moved to stand in front of her and reached for her other hand. 'So you won't have to miss anyone.'

Josie's heart bloomed with hope. Was that the most reassuring and assured sentence ever uttered?

'I'm sorry, Josie. I shouldn't have minimised our relationship in front of our customers that day. And I shouldn't have been so quick to throw what we have away because I was scared.'

Our. We. Have. The words warmed Josie's body. Chased away the chill that had settled soul deep.

'I was petrified. I had come to believe that I could never feel for someone the way I did for Abigail. I'd convinced myself that it would be a betrayal of everything we shared. So when confronted with the reality . . . that my feelings for you were far greater than I'd allowed myself to believe, so great Mia could see how important you were to me without me having to tell her . . . well, I went into full-blown denial. And I used your planning to leave after the abhorrent way I treated you at the bakery in front of those people as a way to further push you away. As a way to convince myself that I'd been imagining my feelings, that I couldn't possibly love you. Even though I did.'

Callan closed his eyes and let out an exasperated sigh. 'Wrong choice of words. What I meant to say is . . . even though I *do* love you.'

'Really? Truly?' Josie wrapped her arms around Callan's waist and brought him closer.

'Really. Truly. For always.' Callan leaned down and pressed his lips to hers.

Feather-light, but full of promise, full of forever.

'Oomph.' Josie grunted as a force hurtled against them, sending them sideways, breaking their kiss.

'Hugs for me, too!'

Callan picked Mia up, placed her on his hip, and the three weaved their arms around each other in a hug that lasted long enough that they missed the ray of rising sun that shone through the clouds for a split-second, illuminating the village, the hills surrounding it, and the three people huddled together who, as long as they were together, had found their home.

Epilogue

'Stop right where you are. Don't move an inch. Either of you.'

Josie grinned as the two customers looked at her like she had gone mad. Then looked at each other in a 'what the heck's going on' way, then, so simultaneously she had to smother a giggle, looked up. Matching grimaces flourished on their faces as they sighted the mistletoe dangling above them.

'Rules are rules.' Josie held her hands up in an 'I don't make the rules, I just have to enforce them' way.

It was the third time that day she'd gone through the routine. The tenth time in two days. And she still wasn't tired of playing the helpless lass who had no choice but to enforce the rules of Sunnycombe's Christmas traditions.

Not when in among the blushes and awkwardness, she'd seen sparks of interest. The beginnings of what could be true love.

The magic of Christmas was in full flight once again, and unlike last year when she'd been forced to take part, this year she was driving it. After everything Sunnycombe had given her, it was the least she could do. So she'd signed up to deliver the mistletoe to the local businesses and put herself in charge of organising the choral group's practices, only stopping short at joining herself, because no one needed to hear a voice like nails on a blackboard among all the mostly perfectly in-tune notes. Lastly, she'd accepted an offer to be a judge at the Christmas Cake-off.

Entering had been an option, but the bakery's business had grown more than she could have hoped for – especially once word had grown of her abilities, and cake commissions had started coming in not just from the locals but from all around the wider district. While the challenge of topping her last creation was intriguing, Josie knew with the way things were growing she had enough on her plate, so she was more than happy to sit back, eat some cake, and let another baker shine.

'Kiss. Kiss. Kiss. Kiss.' The customers at the bakery's tables began to chant. Whooping and hollering when the two trapped under the mistletoe finally puckered up, touched lips, then broke away in a blink of the eye.

They approached the counter, their cheeks as red as the berries on a holly bush.

'I'm so sorry.' Josie placed her hand on her chest and gave her most heartfelt apologetic look. 'It's tradition. Perhaps a little old-fashioned, but without it I probably wouldn't have this on my finger.'

She held up her left hand, on which a dainty gold band circled her ring finger. Next to it a simple diamond solitaire engagement ring.

'You got married after kissing someone under the mistletoe?' The young man's eyes widened. 'Seriously?'

'Seriously. Right in that very spot.'

His face lost its colour, and the girl beside him flushed so deeply Josie began to wonder if she was in danger of becoming permanently purple.

'It was a terrible kiss, to be honest. Took a bit of perfecting.' She picked up her tongs and directed their gaze to the rows of Christmas-inspired cupcakes, loaves, biscuits and slices. 'Now what can I get you?'

'Er, nothing for me. I've lost my appetite.' With a shudder, he turned and scuttled out, shutting the door with a bang that had the locals roaring with laughter.

Josie turned her eyes on the girl. 'You wouldn't want him anyway. Someone who runs at the hint of a relationship? He'd be no good for you.'

An arm curled around her waist, brought her close. 'You'd know that better than anyone.'

Firm lips pressed against her temple and Josie breathed in the clean, musky pine scent, and thanked her lucky stars – as she did every day – that she'd ended up in Sunnycombe.

'I guess I'm living proof that people can change.' She addressed the girl. 'So there's hope yet. The mistletoe could work its magic.'

The girl shuddered. 'Yuck, no. He dated a friend of mine. Ghosted her. Then breadcrumbed her. Then ghosted her again. Such a loser.'

'Terrible. Horrifying.' Josie arranged her features in a sympathetic smile. 'You're definitely better off without him.'

'I know, right? I'd much rather one of your gingerbread men than that pitiful excuse of a man. So gross.'

'A gingerbread man, it is.' Josie picked up two and placed them in the bag. 'One for you. One for your poor ghosted, breadcrumbed friend. On the house. Merry Christmas. Consider it a sorry for having to do the mistletoe kiss.'

'Really? Wow! Thank you!' The girl took the bag then all but skipped out of the shop.

Josie turned to Callan. 'Maybe we need to rethink that kissing under the mistletoe tradition. Poor girl.'

'Not as poor as her haunted and hungry friend. I mean, really. What's the world coming to? And what was she going on about anyway with all that breadcrumbed and ghosted talk?' Callan's brows drew together as he shook his head. 'Maybe we need to tell your dad about those terms, get him to research their meaning. Prepare him for the dating world now that he's signed up to one of those apps. The man spends as much time swiping left, right or whichever way you swipe, as he does scouring the internet for toys to buy Mia. I'm not sure what to fear for more, his heart or his credit card.'

'I think his heart will be fine. And, lucky for Dad, his son-in-law is a whizz of an accountant. So I'm sure if he gets himself into too much toy-buying financial trouble, you can sort him out. Did he say if he was going to pop into the store later on?'

'He did, and he's going to. You know, I wouldn't be surprised if your dad ends up moving here. He seems quite charmed by the place.'

'And by his granddaughter. Mia's got him wrapped around her little finger.' Josie's chest expanded with happiness.

She hadn't been sure how to reconnect with her father. She hadn't wanted to make him uncomfortable, or cause him to retreat further by putting pressure on him to be part of their little family. As it turned out, she'd spent hours worrying her lower lip while figuring out the best way to approach him for nothing.

While she'd been wondering how to revive their relationship, he'd been pondering the same, but years of guilt at holding her at such a distance had stopped him from making any advance, and when she'd invited him to their wedding – a sweet, small affair held on a late summer's day on the hill where Josie and Callan had first admitted their love for each other – he'd accepted.

And returned regularly for visits ever since.

'What are you two grinning about?' Margo walked through the door, followed by Brendon who was holding two dripping umbrellas at arm's length. 'And will we see you up the hill later on? There's a chance the clouds will break, you know.'

The teeming rain told Josie otherwise, but she wasn't about to break Margo's bubble, not when she and Callan were considered to be the most recent recipients of Sunnycombe's magical Christmas sunset wishes.

As romantic as the notion was, Josie had her doubts. The legend said only three wishes could be granted, but every day that she woke up with Callan and Mia in her life, felt like a wish come true.

'I think we'll skip the hill this year.' Callan's arm circled Josie's waist and pulled her close.

She snuggled in, loving how protective he was. How much he cared. How there wasn't a doubt in her mind that he would ever up and leave or push her away. Knowing she wouldn't either.

He was hers as much as she was his.

'Josie can't go up the hill because she'll be sick on it.' Mia's bright, clear voice filled the bakery. 'Because there's a baby in her tummy and she goes . . .' Mia mimed throwing up. 'In the morning. And at night a lot of the time, too.'

'So much for keeping that quiet.' Callan's gaze went to the ceiling as he shook his head. 'And here I was saying she could keep a secret if we explained how big a secret it was.'

Josie beckoned Mia over and picked her up. 'You kept that secret for eight weeks. Good work, you.' She kissed Mia's forehead and set her down again.

Margo's mouth opened and closed. Her smile grew wider by the second. 'Truly? Honestly?' She clapped her hands together, squeezed them tight, then released them and ran around the counter, her arms open wide, and swept Callan and Josie into a hug.

'This is marvellous news. Truly stunning. I'm so happy for you both. A new baby in the village. A new grandchild for me. My little adopted family is growing. Brendon, we're skipping the hill tonight. This is all the good news I need.'

Brendon shifted from foot to foot, his face stricken. 'Er, no. I mean. We really should go. Just in case, you know. Tradition. And wishes. Dreams come true. And all that.'

Margo shook her head. 'No, let's not bother. We've got all the people we need looking after the pub so we should use that time to put our feet up and relax. Spend some one-on-one time together.'

'But Margo . . .' Brendon's face had gone strangely pale. His usual high colour had vanished.

'I need to start knitting booties. And a cardigan.' Margo's

steepled fingers tapped against each other as she spoke. Her gaze was not in the here and now, but in a baby-filled future. 'Maybe even pull out my sewing machine and start fashioning some toddler clothes.'

Josie clapped her hand over her mouth as Brendon rifled through his coat pocket and pulled out a black, velvet box, sunk down on one knee and held it up to Margo. His hands shaking as sweat beaded at his temples.

'I knew you were going to make this hard, woman. Lord knows you've never made us all that easy. But if I don't get to do this on the hill, where you have no choice but to say yes in front of all those people, then I'm going to say it here. Margo, my love, my everything. You've been the woman for me for nearly a decade. My heart is yours, and will be for all eternity, if you want it that is. Will you marry me?' Brendon paused, his chest rising in anticipation.

'Say. Yes. Say. Yes. Say. Yes.'

The demand from the customers started quietly, tentatively, then in seconds became loud enough that Mia clapped her hands over her ears, and Josie was tempted to do the same.

'Oh, you silly bugger.' Margo took Brendon by the hand and pulled him up to a standing position. 'You didn't need an audience for me to say yes. You didn't even need a ring.'

Brendon opened the jewellery box to reveal a radiant-cut emerald surrounded by diamonds on a gold band.

'Can I take that last bit back?' Margo splayed her left hand out. 'You definitely needed a ring. And this ring is perfect. I adore it.'

'So that's a yes?' Brendon slipped the ring on, then brought Margo to him.

'It's more than a yes. It's a promise.' Margo pulled Brendon two steps backwards so they were under the mistletoe. 'Now kiss me already.'

The hoots and hollers that followed were said to be heard up and down the lane, but Josie couldn't speak to that as her heart was too full to hear the whoops of approval or the following words from those around her congratulating her and Callan on the impending arrival, and Margo and Brendon on their engagement.

She snuggled into Callan, her hand finding its way to the tiny mound on her stomach, and wondered for the millionth time how she'd got so lucky.

How in one year she'd made real friends, like Lauren, who she saw most days, even if only for ten minutes over a quick cup of tea.

How she'd created an extended family in Margo and Brendon, and repaired her relationship with her father.

How she'd found the love of a wonderful man and got to share in the joy of raising an amazing little girl who she loved with everything she had.

Josie didn't know if it was luck, or village legend, or simply fate. But she did know one thing . . .

Two things, in fact.

Hopes and dreams could come true.

And Christmas wasn't so bad after all.

Acknowledgements

The Little Bakery of Hopes and Dreams is dedicated to my daughter, but no dedication is large enough to express my feelings for her. Neither is an 'acknowledgement', to be honest. Nothing prepared me for the depth of feeling I'd have for my wee girl. The absolute adoration and, at times, the utter frustration. From very early on she surprised me with her empathy, her ability to see through the flotsam and jetsam in order to get to the truth. Without her I don't know that I could've written this book, because I wouldn't have been able to imagine what it would be like to have someone you loved so truly, so purely - despite the emotional ups and downs that such a relationship brings - ripped from your life. She is my everything. My little love. My greatest love. Daisy, I'm thankful for every second, every minute, every hour, every day – yes, even the ones where we're grumpy at each other – that you're in my life. Never let me go.

Of course, it would be remiss, and possibly divorcable, to not thank the man who not only helped me with said daughter's creation, but who has supported my authorly endeavours right from day dot. Thank you, Aaron. I'm so grateful to the great Cupid in the sky for bringing us together. I love growing old with you. Never let me go.

Writing is a solitary thing – well, if you're not counting the people living in your head – and it helps to have amazing author friends who support, champion, and are there for you. Jaimie Admans, Sarah Bennett, Victoria Cooke, Susan Edmunds, Susie Frame, Clementine Fraser, Lucy Knott, Steph Matuku, Belinda Missen, Ian Wilfred – you're all amazing. I so appreciate the kind words, the 'you've got this' gifs, the retweets, shares, and all you do to support me and my books. I'm lucky to share this writing world with you.

Lastly, what's a girl without her champion? The person who goes into bat for her. Who pulls the best out of her? A huge thank you to my amazing editor, Charlotte Mursell. You're not just a star, you're a shooting star – and I can't wait to see how high you fly!

If you loved *The Little Bakery of Hopes and Dreams*, then turn the page for an exclusive extract from *The Little Bookshop at Herring Cove* . . .

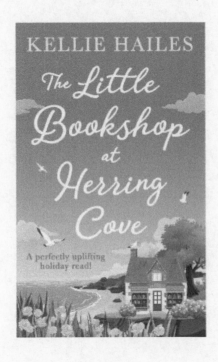

If you loved *The Little Bakery of Hopes and Dreams*, then turn the page for an exclusive extract from *The Little Bookshop at Herring Cove*.

Chapter 1

She just had to survive for a few more months. Six months, to be exact. Then the Christmas rush would see enough money in her bookshop's bank account to scrape through for another year. Maybe. Hopefully.

Sophie sucked in her lower lip as she tightened her grip on the hammer's wooden handle, slowly practising lowering the head to the nail before raising it again.

She forced herself to put aside all mental images of the spreadsheet she'd been looking at earlier that morning. It told a terrible story. Of loss. Lacklustre book sales. And looming financial disaster. She could tell herself things would get better but the numbers didn't lie. Sales were getting worse. Year on year, even during the festive season, she'd seen a fall in profit. People weren't buying books the way they used to, at least they weren't buying them from her little bookshop.

She held her breath as she raised the hammer a little before bringing it down on the display case she was trying to fix.

'Ow!'

The pained word filled the room as she pressed her lips together, dropped the hammer onto the ground, doubled over, and gripped her thumb and forefinger, hoping the pressure on

219

them would ease the throbbing that was building second by second.

'Are you okay there? Should I call an ambulance? Perhaps a funeral parlour?'

Sophie forced her eyes open, ready to give the owner of the bemused voice the kind of glare that would make him think twice before being cheeky to a woman in distress.

Except no glare came forth.

And her racing heart, which had only just begun to slow down to a canter, picked up once more.

Cripes. The smart-arse was a babe. Dark brown hair, shorn short at the sides with a touch more length on top, made way for a face that no doubt spelled trouble. Green eyes, dancing with good humour, twinkled down at her. Lips that were all hard-edged on the outside and plump in the middle twitched to one side. Cheekbones, sharp enough a model would be envious, were raised high.

He was laughing? At her? Well, he could take his babealiciousness and bugger off.

Taking a step back, Sophie folded her arms over her chest, lifted her chin and adopted her most professional tone. 'I'm fine, thank you. Just a little mishap between my finger and a hammer. Now, what can I do for you? Are you after a book?'

The smirk straightened out as his eyes ceased twinkling. 'Actually, I'm looking for Sophie Jones. Is she about?'

Sophie Jones. Her name rolled off his tongue. Smooth, sweet. With a hint of seduction. And the way he was staring at her. Penetrating. Lingering. Like he could see past her red A-line knee-length skirt and simple white T-shirt all the way into her soul, where worry and loneliness huddled together as uncomfortable bedmates.

'That would be me. And you are?' She raised an eyebrow and tightened her grip on herself. There was no way he knew who she was, not really. She was crazy to even consider it.

'Alexander Fletcher.' He offered her his hand to shake.

Manicured nails. He had manicured nails. She shouldn't have been surprised. It matched his outfit: a tailored, form-fitting navy suit, which gave way to a lighter blue shirt, accented with a tie the same shade of the suit with a white geometric pattern running through it.

An outfit that was completely at odds with the fashion of Herring Cove, where the dress code was strictly T-shirt and shorts in summer and jeans and chunky sweaters in winter. Even the village clerk avoided suits – said they didn't suit the blink-and-you'll-miss-it Cornish fishing village's laid-back image.

And what was it about his name that was ringing a bell? And not the tinkly, light ding-once-for-service ring that told her when she was out back that a customer was ready to be attended to, but a clanging alarm-that-gave-you-a-migraine kind of bell.

She glanced out the window at a poster that had been taped to a pole. 'Stand up for Herring Cove' was emblazoned on top of a picture of a fancy hotel with a big X struck across it.

'Fletcher. As in the resort builders.' The words escaped before she could stop them. Before she could pretend she had no idea who he was in order to find out what exactly he wanted when she'd already made her position to the Fletcher Group crystal-clear.

'Well now that you know who I am, then this will make the visit that much quicker.' He flashed her a boyish grin, then picked up her abandoned hammer, squatted down beside the display stand and gave it an experimental shake that saw it wobble back and forth, in danger of complete collapse. 'She's seen better days.'

Sophie didn't answer. Didn't give him anything. She knew why he was here. What he wanted. And he wasn't going to get it, no matter how polite he was, how nice he seemed . . . or how much money he was offering.

An unwanted image arose of emails with 'Urgent – payment due' in the subject line, and old-fashioned paper bills stamped with 'Overdue'. The most terrifying of the lot was the council tax. If she didn't pay that, and soon, they could force her to sell.

Not going to happen. She gritted her teeth and shoved the image into the darkest corner of her mind where it held less power. Where it couldn't freeze her with fear, unable to make solid decisions.

She just had to figure out a way to boost sales. To change the downward trend that had come with the shrinking of Herring Cove's population. That's all. No big deal.

Except it was. A huge deal. Massive. The bookshop was her livelihood and the flat above was her home. The place she'd been born and raised. The living memory of her parents who'd passed away when she was five. She wouldn't let that go. Couldn't.

Alexander picked up the nail that had fallen to the floor, repositioned it, then with one quick movement knocked it into place. 'Got another? We don't want it falling apart in two seconds, do we?'

Sophie shook her head. 'No, there's not another.' She felt a slight blush at the fib. 'Besides, I didn't ask you to help, and I don't have the time for small talk. I'm busy.'

Alexander's gaze roamed over the empty shop. Bare of customers. And, if Sophie were honest, a touch too bare of books.

'Busy? Doing what? Trying to break your fingers?'

His tone was gentle, teasing, which only set Sophie further on edge.

'I have to ready the shop for the Herring Cove Book Appreciators' Club.' Which consisted of two people: Natalie and Ginny. Also known as her two best friends. And, if the truth were told, not exactly massive book appreciators. So much so that they'd cancelled the meeting for that week, both citing family obligations. But Alexander didn't need to know that. 'The kettle needs to go on. Biscuits need to be arranged. I can't let my customers down.'

'Well then, I'll help. Where's the kettle? Out the back?' Alexander took a step towards the doorway that led to the small storeroom and office.

Sophie shot an arm out, blocking him. 'It is out the back but you're not to go there. Staff only.'

222

'Well I'm not leaving until we've had a proper chat. I understand that you declined our offer.'

Sophie widened her stance, squared her shoulders and crossed her arms over her chest, hoping it would perform a dual purpose: as a blockade should Alexander try and head out back again and to show him that she meant business when she said no.

'You understand right. I did decline your offer. I have no desire to sell this place.'

'Can I ask why?' Alexander's head tipped to the side, a small furrow appearing between his brows as they drew together.

If she didn't know better, if she hadn't figured out he was one of *the* Fletchers – a family whose fortune was built on taking small villages and transforming them into tourist hotspots – she'd have thought he might genuinely care. Except she knew better. He was here for one reason and one reason only: to get her to sell.

'You can ask, but I'm not going to tell you. It's none of your business.' Sophie inwardly cringed at the curtness of her tone. It wasn't like her to be so sharp, but then again it wasn't every day that a big business tried to buy your land and that surrounding you in order to build a towering monstrosity that could only be a blight to the quaint charm of the little village she called home.

'Well if you're not going to tell me why, then could you at least hear me out? Let me explain our vision for Herring Cove? Maybe we could take a seat over there?' Alexander indicated to the vintage bobbled-fabric turquoise sofa.

Bathed in the summer sun, it was the perfect spot to curl up with a book. Something Sophie did regularly. A way to pass the time when the shop was quiet. Which was a lot of the time.

She breathed out low and slow. The irritation that had her shoulders hitched up towards her ears disappeared with the whoosh of expelled air. 'If I listen, will you leave me alone? Never talk to me again?'

Alexander shrugged, the too-hot-for-its-own-good smile was

223

back. 'Can't promise that. I have a few more people to see and it's a small village. There's always a chance we'll bump into each other.'

He had a point. Although if he hoped bumping into her would see her change her mind, he was mistaken. There was no number of pennies pretty enough to make her sell. And the pennies the Fletcher Group initially offered had been exceptionally pretty. More than the place was worth. But not enough for her to see her home, her place in the world, reduced to rubble.

'Fine. You can talk.' Sophie flicked her hand, hustling him towards the sofa and the two armchairs that flanked it. 'You go first.'

'No, you go. Ladies first.' Alexander stood his ground.

'I never said I was a lady.' Sophie brought her hands to her hips.

'Only calling it like I see it. Besides, if I don't let you go first my mother will be disappointed in me. She worked hard on my manners. It's a point of great pride for her.'

Sophie's lips twitched to the side. *Do not smile.* Too late.

Seeing a man in a suit worrying about his manners because he didn't want to disappoint his mother was . . . well . . . adorable. Even if said adorability was coming from a man she was sure was a wolf in sheep's clothing.

'Fine. I wouldn't want to be responsible for undoing all her good work.' She crossed the room and settled into the burnt-orange armchair and indicated for Alexander to sit on the sofa. 'So, talk.'

'I know you've got the book club coming so I'll keep it quick.' Alexander leaned forward, his forearms flat upon his thighs, his hands clasped loosely together. His voice calm, collected.

Like what he was wanting to do was no big deal. Like he made visits to people who weren't playing ball regularly. Which, maybe he did.

'The thing is, we think Herring Cove has so much potential. Potential that's not being realised. If we built one of our resorts here, created a proper path down the cliffs to the beach, then the local economy would be revitalised. There'd be more jobs. More people. More money.'

And a whole lot less soul. Sophie kept her thought to herself, there was no point in trying to change Alexander's mind. It would be like trying to change her mind about selling the shop. A waste of time.

'The reason I came here is that I wanted to talk to you in person about what it is you're missing out on by not saying yes.'

Sophie's spine stiffened. This was what he was here for? To give her the hard sell? To guilt her into selling? Good luck with that. She'd long ago learned that listening to men with silken tongues was a bad idea. 'Fool me once' and all that. She wasn't about to be fooled twice.

'I'm not missing out on anything. I have everything I want right here. I don't need anything else.' *Or anyone else.*

'Here. This is for you.' He reached into the concealed pocket of his suit jacket, pulled out a folded square of crisp cream-coloured note paper and slipped it across the teak Scandinavian coffee table. 'We've upped our offer.'

Sophie let it sit there. 'Not interested. I said it to your lackey over the email, then again over the phone, and I shall say it now – my home is not for sale.'

Alexander sat back in the chair, his expression unchanged, unperturbed. 'And why not? In my experience, everything is for sale . . . as long as the price is right. And, trust me, the price is right.'

Sophie eyed the small square. How much was in there? Crazy money? Her fingers itched to pick it up, unfold it, and see what was on offer.

No. She mustn't. Besides, whatever number was written down wouldn't make her budge. 'All Booked Up' was the last thread of her family. All she had left. It was her home and she loved it. Nothing could make her move.

What if you go broke? Because that could happen. What if you

225

can't afford to pay the rates on the place? You won't be moved out, you'll be chucked out.

Not going to happen. She'd survived all these years – even after her horrid ex, Phillip, had stolen the money she'd saved for lean times, then disappeared to who knows where. She'd find a way to make things work. She'd save 'All Booked Up'. Bring it back from the brink. She just had to figure out how.

'You're not even going to look at the offer?' Alexander's head tipped to one side, as corrugated lines wrinkled his forehead.

'I don't need to. I'm not going to sell. Now if you don't mind, I have work to do.' Sophie stood, strode as purposefully as she knew how to the counter, then opened up her laptop and pretended to be engrossed with what she saw on the screen.

Footfalls on the wooden floor told her Alexander was up and, hopefully, leaving. A shadow fell over the counter.

Wishful thinking, then.

'That piece of paper contains enough money for you to do anything you want in the world. To go anywhere. To start fresh.'

Sophie fixed her most unimpressed look on her face, then looked up. 'But what I want is to stay here in Herring Cove and run the bookshop. I don't want to do any old thing. Go any old where. Or start fresh.'

Despite his tan Alexander's face paled, the hint of colour on his cheeks gone.

She'd rattled him? Interesting. But not interesting enough for her to waste any more time on a man who wanted to take her life away from her.

'Well, I've heard what you've had to say. You can go now.' Beside the laptop, her mobile buzzed and lit up as an email notification came through.

Sophie closed her eyes as she noted another reminder notice. This time for the power. Could she go without power? Could she run the bookshop without it? What did she really need power for? She ran through the list: no till, no cash machine, no kettle

226

for cups of tea, no light to read books by late into the night. Conclusion? Allowing the power to be cut off was not an option.

She glanced up at Alexander to remind him it was time to move on, but his eyes were on her phone, his hand on his chin, fingers stroking its smooth, freshly shaved skin.

Had he seen the bill? Was he going to use it against her?

His eyes met hers and he gave no indication that he'd seen evidence of her finances being in dire straits. Instead he pulled a wallet from the back pocket of his trousers, opened it and produced a nail.

'Before I go, allow me. Please.'

Before she could answer he knelt down, picked up the hammer and hit the nail square into the display shelf. He gave it a nudge and nodded. 'That'll hold.'

'You didn't have to do that.' Sophie shut her laptop and made her way to the door, opened it. A sure sign to Alexander that it was time for him to leave.

'I didn't have to, but I wanted to.' He gave the display shelf a pat that Sophie could almost describe as loving, then made his way to the door. 'Well, thanks for hearing me out.'

'No problem.' Sophie waited for him to leave.

And waited.

Alexander showed no sign of leaving as his gaze flitted around the shop.

'Waiting for me to bow?'

'No, just thinking how great this place would look if the books were displayed in bookshelves like you find at a library. Though you'd need a few more bookshelves knocked up to make that happen.'

Sophie followed his gaze. Saw what he saw. Row after row of bookshelves, the titles in order, neatly shelved, with popular books displayed throughout. One simple change could transform the store, without changing its rustic essence.

One problem. Shelving cost money. And she didn't have that.

'Well, thanks for the advice.' She inclined her head toward the street.

'Anytime. See you around, Sophie.'

'Ah, no you won't. The deal is done, remember? You spoke. I listened.'

A gleam of sparkling white teeth appeared as Alexander smiled, the lines of worry on his forehead disappearing. 'I know that's what I said, but here's the thing. I don't believe in the word "no". I believe "no" is the first step of a business negotiation. It's the first word on the way to a "yes".'

Sophie gripped the door knob, hoping it would hide her hand, which had begun to shake with anger. 'If that's the case, you're about to discover what it feels like to hear a solid, firm, absolute "no" for the first time. I'm not selling All Booked Up. Not now. Not ever.'

Sophie turned away from the door – Alexander could see himself out. Her outrage deepened as she caught his grin broadening. She curled her fingers into her palms, dug the nails in, let the pain focus her as she marched back to the counter.

He had no idea who he was dealing with. Sophie had spent her life treasuring what was left of her family. The bookshop meant everything to her. And she wasn't going to sell it or lose it without a fight.

Alexander wouldn't take no for an answer? He'd have to.

Because Alexander Fletcher had met his match.

Dear Reader,

Thank you so much for taking the time to read this book – we hope you enjoyed it! If you did, we'd be so appreciative if you left a review.

Here at HQ Digital we are dedicated to publishing fiction that will keep you turning the pages into the early hours. We publish a variety of genres, from heartwarming romance, to thrilling crime and sweeping historical fiction.

To find out more about our books, enter competitions and discover exclusive content, please join our community of readers by following us at:

🐦 *@HQDigitalUK*

f *facebook.com/HQDigitalUK*

Are you a budding writer?
We're also looking for authors to join the HQ Digital family!
Please submit your manuscript to:

HQDigital@harpercollins.co.uk.

Hope to hear from you soon!

DIGITAL HQ

If you enjoyed *The Little Bakery of Hopes and Dreams*, then why not try another delightfully uplifting festive romance from HQ Digital?